THE SHADOW OF NATURE

THE SHADOW OF NATURE

JADE MUSTO

For everyone who understands that love and connection are what makes us strong.

The Blessings

Sun – Nurture
The power of the Sun blessed rests in the forehead and is the blessing of growth
Many Sun blessed gravitate towards professions such as farming and child rearing

Water – Serenity
The power of the Water blessed rests in the throat and is the blessing of temperance
Many Water blessed gravitate towards professions such as teaching and the sciences

Moon – Healing
The power of the Moon blessed rests in the heart and is the blessing of health
Many Moon blessed gravitate towards professions such as physicians and therapists

Fire – Passion
The power of the Fire blessed rests in the stomach and is the blessing of strong will
Many Fire blessed gravitate towards professions such as soldiers and politicians

Earth – Strength
The power of the Earth blessed rests in the soles of the feet and is
the blessing of stability
Many Earth blessed gravitate towards professions such as builders
and law keepers

Nature – Balance
The power of Nature is found throughout the whole body and is the
blessing of balance
Only one Nature blessed is currently known

1

Chapter 1

The catacombs were as dark as they had always been. They were the only part of the palace that hadn't been filled with the eternally burning candles and torches that Queen Lila had invented. This was partially out of respect for the dead that dwelled within the many stone tombs, and partially an attempt to stop people from wandering down there without permission, especially curious children.

"Blossom, could we have a little light please?" Emma whispered from somewhere to his left.

"Are you sure? It'll bring them right to us."

"I don't think anyone else is down here yet; we lost them in the hallways," Emma replied, although she didn't sound all that sure of herself.

Blossom nodded even though he knew no one could see him doing so and spread a small amount of Sun's blessing over his skin, glowing faintly in the darkness. Next, he concentrated a larger amount into his palm until a tiny replica of the sun floated above it. Emma and Asher's faces came into view, Emma looking around at the plaques lining the walls and Asher staring mutely into space, still in too much shock to say anything. Blossom reached out with his free hand and slipped it into

Asher's, a small smile passing fleetingly over his face when he felt the prince squeeze his fingers.

"This way," Emma gestured down one of the branching corridors, "it's not far."

"What's not far? Emma, what's happening?" Blossom asked, their brief break from running had allowed his thoughts to settle somewhat and now he wanted answers.

"Once we're safe I'll explain everything," Emma responded, still scanning each plaque they passed; every bronze marker holding the name of the ruler or member of the royal family that was entombed behind it. They stopped in front of a familiar marker, the plaque still shining, even after all the years that it had been there.

Blossom pulled Asher closer as the prince let out a sob upon reading the name emblazoned on the metal. They were stood in front of Queen Lila's tomb.

"Emma what are you..."

Emma shushed him with a finger to her lips as she reached out and pressed gently on the plaque. Blossom watched, dumbfounded, as first the plaque sunk into the wall and then the whole tomb itself seemed to sink away into darkness.

Emma gestured for them to follow her again as she stepped into the newly revealed tunnel. Blossom was just about to ask another question or refuse to move until Emma explained what in the blessings was happening, when a distant shout caused him to reconsider. He ushered Asher into the tunnel, the blank tomb wall closing behind them soon after as Emma pressed another hidden button.

"You can dim the lights now," Emma said, far too cheerfully for the situation in Blossom's opinion.

"Surely it'll be even darker in here," Blossom replied but let Sun's blessing dissipate anyway, plunging them into a momentary darkness.

The darkness didn't last long as burning lights began to flicker to life overhead, revealing a seemingly unending tunnel that continued to slope down away from them.

"Follow me," Emma said again and began down the tunnel, stopping when she realised that neither of the boys were following her. She turned back to them as Blossom crossed his arms stubbornly.

"We're not moving another step until you explain what just happened, what this place is, and why you seemed to know that our wedding was going to end the way it did."

Emma sighed and returned to them, "we're still not safe yet Petal, please just wait until we are." Blossom didn't move, staring her down until she sighed again. "I didn't know exactly how the wedding was going to go, but I knew that there was a possibility that it would go badly. The king never wanted you two to be wed so something had to have changed. Ever since the announcement we've been preparing for a quick exit, and then I saw Evelyn with the other Blossomites and knew this was going to be even worse than we'd thought."

Blossom was about to ask who else Emma had been referring to when the fact that she'd said his mother's name drove all other thoughts out of his head. "Wait, how do you know who she is?" he asked as Emma continued to try and usher them down the hallway.

"Evelyn is my sister," Emma said quietly, like she hadn't just turned Blossom's world upside down for possibly the 5th time that day.

"You're my aunt?" he shouted.

Emma shushed him urgently, pressing a hand over his mouth when he refused to quiet down. Just as he was about to push her away and resume his shouting Blossom heard the muffled sounds of voices, still indistinct but overlapping as though there were many speaking at once.

"Not here," Emma hissed, "when we're safe, I'll explain everything. Now follow me." She stepped back slowly, as though unsure as to whether or not she would have to silence him again.

Blossom huffed and glared at her until he felt a warm hand in his. He looked over to Asher who was gazing back at him sadly. "Come on, Flower, let's just follow her for now," he said, his voice barely above a whisper.

Blossom's shoulders slumped; he had never seen Asher look so defeated before. He nodded silently and they continued down the corridor, the sounds of the people in the catacombs growing quieter as they went. They walked in silence for about 20 minutes if Blossom's internal clock was correct, and during the walk Blossom stared hard at Emma's back. This woman had raised him for the past 12 years and he suddenly felt like he knew nothing about her.

Why had she never told him that she was his aunt?

Why hide that from him?

And why had he never seen her in the cottage before he'd been taken?

Surely, she and Edwin would have visited at some point. Wouldn't they?

Asher was stroking his thumb over the back of his hand as they walked, and Blossom wasn't sure if it was to calm him or if it was a way of Asher reassuring himself, probably a mixture of both. He was thankful for the small gesture anyway and attempted to send calming energy through their bond in response.

The tunnel was silent except for the sound of their footsteps and breathing until Emma whispered, "we're here." They had stopped in front of what appeared to be a dead end, just a flat wall of earth, no different from the rest of the tunnel they had walked down.

"Emma what...?" Blossom's question died on his lips as Emma pressed another hidden button and a click resounded through the tunnel. The wall ahead of them shifted and a heavy stone door swung inwards on silent hinges to reveal a large and oddly familiar cavern. Blossom didn't have time to contemplate his feeling of déjà vu as Edwin came hurrying towards them, Kara following at a much more sedate pace.

"You made it, we were beginning to worry that they'd caught you," Edwin said as he reached them, hands clasped in front of him in relief.

"Both of you were in on this?" Blossom asked with a sigh. All his previous adrenaline had left him on the walk, and he was too exhausted to be surprised any longer.

"You make it sound like we planned this. We simply set up a contingency plan in case Silas did something stupid," Kara responded, and Blossom felt Asher squeeze his hand at the mention of his father's name. "How are you holding up, Your Majesty?" Kara asked, clapping Asher on the shoulder, seemingly oblivious to the impact her previous statement had had on him.

"Well, my father's dead because of me, so about as well as could be expected," Asher responded sourly, and Blossom felt another surge of grief through his chest.

He took a step closer to the prince, in effect distancing them both from the rest of the group. "Emma told us some of the story, but you still have a lot of explaining to do, all of you."

"I believe that I can help with that."

Edwin and Kara stepped aside wordlessly to reveal another occupant of the chamber. As she rolled towards them in a very familiar wheeled chair, Blossom felt Asher go rigid.

"Mother?" the prince gasped, his grip on Blossom's hand now tight enough to bruise.

"You've been through a lot today, my darling boy, but I'm afraid this is only the beginning," Queen Lila said, her eyes wet with unshed tears.

Blossom barely had time to register the sudden emptiness in his own chest before Asher collapsed to the ground.

Chapter 2

"Asher!" Blossom shouted, dropping to his knees next to the unconscious man.

"He must have gotten overwhelmed; I'm not surprised after the day he's had. Kara take him to his room," Lila ordered, turning her chair in a tight circle, and wheeling over to the curved wall of the chamber.

Blossom wanted to argue, he didn't want any of these people near Asher, not right now. Not until they explained themselves. Before he could protest beyond pulling Asher's head into his lap Kara had already scooped the unconscious prince up, and was carrying him over to the queen as easily as she would carry a baby. Queen Lila brushed the back of her hand over Asher's cheek before pressing a button on the wall, causing yet another stone door to slid open.

Blossom hurried after Kara into what appeared to be a bedroom, with an opulent four poster bed made up with dark sheets. He froze in the doorway, this wasn't just a bedroom, this was his bedroom. Or more precisely a perfect blend of his and Asher's bedrooms. He stumbled further into the room as Kara placed Asher on the bed, turning his shocked gaze towards Emma who was loitering in the doorway.

"It was you?" he asked, hurt and disbelief clear in his voice.

Emma nodded silently, "Edwin and I have been preparing for weeks. I started moving your things as soon as the king announced your wedding date."

Blossom gaped at her, stuttering in anger as yet another betrayal stabbed his heart. He knew that in the grand scheme of everything happening this was a relatively small betrayal, but it was the final straw.

"Get out," he snapped.

Emma blinked in shock.

"Blossom," Kara said calmly, reaching towards him.

"All of you out!" he shouted, advancing on the small crowd in the doorway.

"Blossom, remember who you are talking to," Kara said, gesturing towards the queen.

"I don't care, out!" Blossom screamed, his eyes blazing with the orange light of Fire's blessing. The group stepped backwards as Blossom slapped the button on the wall and the heavy stone door slid shut again, leaving him alone with Asher.

Blossom stared at the closed door in silence as he wrestled to get his breathing under control, fighting to stop the warmth that had built up behind his eyes from turning into actual tears. With a final cry, he kicked angrily at the closed door before turning on his heel and striding towards the bed. Kara had placed Asher atop the sheets and Blossom couldn't help but notice how pale the prince looked against the dark bedding.

At least he looked peaceful now.

He reached down to brush some stray hair from the prince's forehead and a movement, out of the corner of his eye, caught his attention. The mirror that had once stood in his bathing room was now hanging on the wall across from him. Blossom found his eyes travelling the length of his own body, taking in the sight of himself in Asher's betrothal cloak, and felt his chest constrict painfully. Of all the ways that he had imagined his wedding day playing out it had never been like this. He reached up and plucked the circlet from his hair. Turning it in his hands he inspected each precious jewel, a different gem representing each of the Blessers.

He sank down onto the bed, his head resting lightly on Asher's stomach, still staring at the circlet as he sighed, "what's happening Ash?" He sat up again and turned back to face the prince, his eyes landing on his neck, the creamy white skin now unmarked. "How has everything changed so quickly?"

Scooting further onto the bed Blossom placed his hand on the spot where Asher's death mark had been. He'd felt Asher's anguish and confusion as his curse had erupted from him, but he had also felt its power. The dark force that had bucked against his attempts at blessings for all these months coming to the forefront in all its power. He replayed Silas' last words over in his head as he stroked his thumb back and forth over Asher's neck.

"See what you've done."

Had Silas known?

Is that why he had forbidden them from bonding?

How had he known that the curse would be released like that and not destroyed?

There was a lot that didn't sit right with him, and the more Blossom thought about it the more questions he had. Why had the curse only released when Asher had tried to protect him? Surely it should have been instantaneous.

Following a hunch, he pushed a little bit of blessing into Asher the way he always had, closing his eyes to focus its power into the tips of his fingers. He snatched his hand back suddenly just as Asher's eyes opened.

"Blossom?" Asher asked, voice still thick with sleep, as Blossom stared at him in shock.

"Y-yeah?" he breathed out in reply.

"What was that?"

Blossom didn't need their connection to know what Asher was referring to; he'd felt it just as keenly as the prince had. "It's still there," Blossom said finally, still cradling his hand. The dark force that had always lurked somewhere beneath Asher's skin, the power that had pushed back against Blossom's blessing, the curse that had killed Silas.

It was still there.

Asher placed a hand over his own neck. "You mean it's come back?"

Blossom shook his head. "The mark is gone but the curse is still there, although..." he trailed off, his brows knitting in confusion.

"What?" Asher asked warily, pushing himself into a sitting position.

"I don't know, it doesn't feel right."

A wan smile spread over Asher's face. "It's a curse Blossom, of course it doesn't feel right."

"No that's not what I mean. It almost feels...I don't know how to explain it." Blossom trailed off again with a defeated shrug. "Anyway, we have more pressing things to think about right now," he said after a pause.

Asher looked around the room at his words. "So, I didn't dream it then," he said quietly, looking down until Blossom placed a gentle hand on his cheek.

"No, my love, you didn't dream it."

Asher's gaze dropped again as he curled a hand in the cloak still settled on Blossom's shoulders. Blossom allowed Asher to tug him forward into a kiss, the prince pulling away a moment later. "I'm not sure I can face her yet," he whispered, resting their foreheads together.

"Then don't," Blossom replied, the words ghosting out of him. Asher looked back at him, and he shrugged. "You don't have to leave this room until you want to. As far as they're concerned, you're still unconscious."

"You don't think that we should try and find out what's going on?" Asher asked, lying back against the covers even as he spoke.

Blossom shrugged again before lying down next to him, he threaded the fingers of his right hand with Asher's left and rested them atop the prince's chest. "Probably, but to be honest, I don't want to speak to or even look at any of them right now."

Asher huffed out a humorless laugh and the room settled into a silence that was broken only by the quiet sound of their breathing.

3

Chapter 3

Blossom wasn't sure how much time had passed since they had escaped from the palace. With no windows in the room it was hard to track the passing of the day, but he was somehow certain it was now night. Asher had fallen back to sleep quite soon after their conversation and was breathing deeply and calmly next to him. Pushing himself off the bed as gently as possible so as not to wake his sleeping husband, Blossom made his way back to the stone door separating him from the people whom earlier today, he would have considered the most trustworthy in his life. With a sigh he opened the door and stepped into the main chamber.

"How is he doing?" Lila asked as soon as she noticed Blossom.

"About as well as could be expected. At least he's sleeping now," Blossom replied, scrubbing a hand over his face. He walked over to where Lila sat and sank to the ground next to her. "How are you alive?" he asked quietly.

Queen Lila smiled down at him, her expression just as open and loving as he remembered. "It's complicated, my darling boy."

"Don't do that," Blossom said. Seeing his own evasion tactics being used against him he was suddenly aware of how infuriating they were. How had Asher put up with it for so long?

Lila sighed, fiddling with something unfamiliar on the table next to her. It looked like a small circle of glass, but it was reflecting the light in an odd way, turning the wood that Blossom could see through it a slightly pink colour. "When I discovered what Silas was doing, what he had planned, I began doing everything in my power to stop it. He found out, and well, my presence became more harmful to you and Asher than it helped. The only choice I had left was to fake my death and continue trying to protect you from the shadows. With Emma and Edwin's help I did the best I could."

Blossom stared up at her; her speech hadn't really answered any of his questions. If anything, he now had more than ever. "What do you mean what Silas was doing? How did your leaving help? As soon as you 'died' he started torturing me even more."

Lila opened her mouth to reply but closed it again as a noise came from the other end of the chamber. Emma walked over to them, casting a nervous smile Blossom's way, one that he didn't reciprocate.

"I think it would be best if we start from the beginning, Your Majesty."

"You're probably right, although if that's the case we should wait for my son to wake up."

Blossom wanted to argue but he saw the sense in what they were saying, and he would have let it drop if Asher hadn't stumbled into the room in a blind panic at that very moment.

"Ash," Blossom cried, standing up as Asher looked around wildly, seemingly still half asleep and completely disorientated. The prince's gaze landed on Lila, and he froze. "Ash," Blossom said again, more gently this time, taking a tentative step towards Asher. Thankfully the prince seemed more than happy to close the distance between them and clasped his hand. "Okay, no more excuses. Explain," Blossom said firmly, his gaze flicking between Emma and Lila.

The two women looked at each other, communicating something silently until Emma nodded. "I think it best if I start." Blossom sat back down, pulling the prince with him. Emma waited until the two were settled before speaking again, "I'm afraid there have been many things that we have had to hide from the two of you over the years."

"Clearly," Blossom responded sourly. Asher squeezed his hand, and he once again fell silent.

Emma ignored the jab and continued talking. "It may be hard to believe right now, but it really was in an attempt to protect the two of you." Emma took a deep breath just as Edwin and Kara entered the main chamber. "We are part of a group called the Balance, and we have existed for centuries," Emma explained, gesturing to Edwin and Kara.

"Or at least the Balance has," clarified Kara, causing Emma to shoot her a look.

"The Balance has members in every kingdom and our job was to maintain the balance of nature and the blessings."

"What do you mean was?" Asher asked.

Emma sighed and perched against the edge of the table. "Twenty-five years ago, Silas started a crusade to expand Vaten into the neighboring kingdoms. The Balance didn't act initially, we've seen wars before. Kingdoms come and go, it's just the way of things."

Blossom frowned, surprised that Emma would take such a blasé attitude towards something that would cause so much death.

"What we didn't realise, at least until it was too late, was the real reason for Silas' crusade."

"The real reason?" Blossom and Asher looked at each other in confusion.

"Silas was looking for something. Something that would make him the most powerful person in the world. If he found it, he would have been able to conquer any kingdom he desired."

"What could possibly give him so much power?" Blossom asked, slightly breathless as he got lost in the story.

"The very thing the Balance was created to protect... the source of the Blessers' power."

The two men stared at Emma in silence, trying to comprehend what she was saying.

"The what?" Blossom finally whispered. "What do you mean the source of the Blessers' powers? Aren't they the source of their own powers?"

"I guess it would be more accurate to say it is the center of their power on earth, as opposed to the source," Lila chimed in.

Blossom was still trying to wrap his head around the idea of a well of blessing power, especially one that no one knew about, when Asher spoke up.

"But how did my father know about it? I'm assuming that part of protecting it would involve concealing its existence. Whatever this thing is."

"Well..." Emma started haltingly, glancing at the queen who was staring down at her lap, her face grave.

Lila was quiet for a moment longer before shaking her head. "It was my fault," she answered finally, her voice barely audible.

"What do you mean your fault? How would you even know about it...unless." Blossom felt Asher's grip on his hand tighten just as another flash of betrayal swept through him, but this time he knew it hadn't originated from his own emotions.

Lila finally looked over at both of them, her face carefully neutral. "It has been a long-standing practice for the Balance to place its members among the powerful, especially the ruling families. I admit that when I married Silas it was because it was my duty and had very little to do with love. The Balance tried to keep the kingdoms in check by steering them from within. But I was young, he was charming, and before I knew it, I was besotted with him." Lila's smile was wistful, and also a little sad as she spoke. "It blinded me to what he truly was, and I broke my oath to the Balance. I thought I could bring him into the fold," she looked away again, "I told him everything."

An uncomfortable silence filled the chamber for a moment until Asher spoke. "What happened then? After you told him?"

Lila shrugged.

"What do you think happened? He went in search of it."

Blossom jumped at the sound of Kara's voice, he'd almost forgotten she was there, and she'd spoken with a venom he hadn't heard before. A venom which only grew in intensity the longer she spoke, until she was practically spitting her words.

"The only thing Silas has ever truly desired is power. More power at whatever cost. It also happens to be the thing he was most afraid of. That's why he tried so hard to suppress your powers Blossom, he knew you were stronger than he was, and it petrified him. So, he broke you down so that you'd never think to use it against him."

Blossom could feel Asher's anger and indignation boiling in his gut, but he also knew that what Kara said was true; Asher himself had even said as much. "I just thought he hated me because of where I came from," he said in response.

"I won't deny that was probably part of it," Emma responded, "but again, before the raids Castilla had power, and it had been growing." She sighed, changing the subject back to what they had originally been talking about. "Luckily Lila didn't know the location of the island, so Silas never found it, but he came close."

"Is that where the Blessers' power resides, on some kind of island?" Asher asked and Blossom had a sudden flash of recollection. The island he'd been seeing in his dreams.

"An island forever cloaked in shadow," he said, more to himself than anyone else but Emma heard him anyway.

"I'm surprised you remember it Petal, you were so young when Evelyn took you away."

Blossom's brows furrowed in confusion. "What do you mean?"

"It's where you were born."

The hall fell silent once again before a quiet 'what?' came from Blossom, no louder than a whisper.

Emma came and sat on the other side of him, keeping a respectful distance as she spoke, her hands hovering over his knee like she desperately wanted to touch him. "We found you on the shore during one of our patrols, you were barely a day old. The person who birthed you was nowhere to be found. We thought that maybe your proximity to the Blessers at the moment of your birth might explain why you received all of their blessings, but Evelyn was convinced that you had been born of the Blessers themselves."

Blossom and Asher shared a glance; it was the same reasoning the Blossomites used, and then the rest of what Emma said sunk in. "You mean my mother wasn't the one who gave birth to me?"

Emma shook her head. "No, we still don't know who gave birth to you, we never found them."

Blossom stared at his knees, deep in thought as he tried to parse out the new information he was being bombarded with.

"What did you mean when you said that Evelyn took him away?" Asher asked, as though he sensed that Blossom was done speaking for the time being.

"When we found you, the Balance decided we would raise you as one of our own. It wasn't an unusual thing; we often took in foundlings. Because of your power, I believe it was decided that you would be raised to become the next leader of the Balance. Evelyn, Edwin and I were to be your main caretakers, but finding you changed something in my sister. She became obsessed with you, with what your existence meant, what you could become. One morning, we woke up and you were simply gone."

Blossom found himself reaching for Emma's hand. He didn't know what to feel about any of this, the mixture of Asher's emotions with his own was beginning to muddle things. What he did know was that he was far too tired to be angry about any of it, in fact he could feel himself beginning to tune out as everyone continued to speak around him.

"We tried our hardest to find you, but she hid you so well. Then you turned up in the palace, so the Balance sent us to watch over you."

He felt Asher's arm around his shoulder, and leant against him, suddenly very weary, right down to his very core.

"I think we should let them rest now, Em, it's been a trying day," Edwin piped up from somewhere to his left, but Blossom didn't know exactly where. His eyes had closed as soon as his head touched the prince's shoulder.

"But I still have questions," he murmured.

"I know you do Petal, I'm sure you both do, but Edwin is right. It's time to rest now. We have a lot of planning to do, and in the meantime, it's still your wedding day."

Asher and Kara helped him to stand up, he had no idea why he suddenly felt so weak, but he found that he couldn't quite walk by himself. He leant heavily against Asher as they led him back to what he guessed was now his bedroom. Their bedroom.

Chapter 4

Asher turned back to Kara as Blossom wobbled over to the bed and promptly fell face first onto the sheets. "He's not taking this well," he said quietly. The swarm of emotions that had been flowing from the blesser during their earlier conversation had almost been enough to make him dizzy, but they had dimmed now as Blossom's exhaustion overtook him.

"Are you?" Kara asked, "you've been oddly quiet during this whole thing."

Asher shrugged, "I finally get to marry the love of my life but in the process, I kill my father and find out that my mother is alive, and what's worse, she abandoned both me and Blossom to hide away in this fucking dungeon. How exactly am I supposed to handle that?"

Kara placed a strong hand on his shoulder, giving it a firm squeeze before jutting her chin behind him to where Blossom was laying. "Just focus on the first part, enjoy tonight like none of the other shit happened. Tomorrow we'll figure out the rest." She stepped back without another word and the stone door slid silently closed in front of her.

Asher sighed and turned his back on the door, focusing his attention on Blossom. His husband. He realised this with a sudden flair of joy that made the blesser look over at him and raise his eyebrows in a silent question. "My husband," he said quietly, surprising himself at just how much that simple phrase made his chest ache with happiness.

"Yeah?" Blossom responded, like Asher had asked him a question, pushing himself into a sitting position and wrapping the shining, black, betrothal cloak still draped over his shoulders tighter around him.

With a conscious effort Asher decided to block out any thoughts that did not center on the man currently in front of him, and practically dove onto the bed, causing Blossom to squeak in surprise. Asher clasped his face between his hands and kissed him firmly. "My husband," he said again when he pulled away.

Blossom giggled, placing his own hands atop Asher's. "Yeah," he whispered.

∞

Later, with their clothes scattered about the room, they lay together beneath the sheets in a light doze, neither of them willing to fall asleep just yet.

"You know, I've just realised something," Asher whispered, running his hand up and down Blossom's bare arm as he spoke.

"Hmm?" Blossom responded sleepily.

"For all of the talking they did earlier they didn't really answer any of our questions."

"What do you mean?" Blossom shifted closer to the prince, tangling their legs together.

"You know, like how is my mother alive? How is your mother alive? What do the Blossomites want? What in curses name did I do earlier and how?"

"Maybe they don't know," Blossom responded, placing his hand on Asher's neck against the spot where the death mark had been. "My biggest question is what are we going to do now?"

Asher shrugged in response, "go to sleep and hope that tomorrow makes a bit more sense?"

Blossom smiled back at him sadly but nodded, tucking his head beneath Asher's chin as he wound his arms tighter about Asher's waist. Asher gazed up at the dark ceiling, sure that his thoughts would keep him awake, but he soon fell asleep to the sound of Blossom's gentle breathing.

∞

Blossom woke before Asher; he had no idea what time it was, but he was fairly certain it was morning. He realised vaguely that this was the first morning where he had awoken naturally and not due to Emma bustling around the room. As he watched the prince's sleeping face, he wondered if this was how it would be from now on. He'd always figured that Asher would be the first of them to wake in the mornings, but it had been years since they'd shared a bed properly.

Asher was lying on his side facing him, his left hand resting on the pillow. Blossom reached out and gently placed his own hand atop the prince's, giving it a squeeze when Asher sighed in his sleep. Their bond had quietened during the night. It was still there, but Blossom figured that their emotions must grow less intense during sleep. He knew that it would take some getting used to, feeling Asher's emotions alongside his own, but it had surprised him just how well the prince could control his own feelings.

There had been a point during Emma's explanation last night where it had felt like Asher had simply shut his emotions off, and again when they'd returned to their room. It seemed like a useful coping mechanism and Blossom knew he did something very similar when he felt himself getting overwhelmed, but it couldn't be healthy. The more he thought about it the more he realised that Asher had never really spoken about his feelings. He was very good at stating his intentions and what he wanted but not how he felt at any given moment.

As he was pondering this, the prince's eyes flickered open, and a slow smile spread over his face. "Morning Flower," he whispered, his voice rough and deep after a night of sleep.

Blossom felt his cheeks warming, because when Asher wasn't actively masking his emotions, the outpouring of love he could feel through their bond was almost overwhelming. He tried to reciprocate, thinking of everything he loved about the other man and pushing it though their connection. He smiled when Asher blinked, and his pale face turned red.

"Good morning, my love," he whispered back, placing his hand on Asher's cheek and brushing his thumb over the prominent bone there. "Are you ready to face them again?" he asked, inclining his head towards the door, frowning when he felt a sudden emptiness as Asher's emotions retreated.

The prince took a deep breath before nodding and pushing himself into a sitting position. "I guess we can't put it off forever."

"Why do you do that?" Blossom asked, sitting up and touching him lightly on the shoulder.

"Do what?"

"Close off your feelings like that."

Asher looked back at him in confusion for a moment before realisation dawned. "Oh, you can feel that?" he asked, leaning back and pressing a kiss to Blossom's lips when the blesser nodded. "It helps me think clearly, emotions have no place when it comes to ruling a kingdom. My father always said that you must lead through logic, not through feelings."

Blossom felt the briefest spark of grief from the prince before it was tamped down again. "I don't agree," Blossom said, his brows knitting in concern as Asher stood and stretched.

Asher turned his back on the wardrobe he'd begun rummaging through, mirroring Blossom's look of confusion. "What?"

"How can you rule effectively if you don't care about your subjects?"

Asher sighed and closed the closet, climbing back onto the bed. "Of course I care about my people, but to do what's best for them I need to be objective. And besides..." He gripped Blossom's chin, tilting it upward and leaning forward as though to kiss him. "... It's not like you're any better."

Blossom stared at him; his mouth slightly open as he tried to think of a response. "What do you mean?" he asked instead.

"I've watched you check out when things are too stressful. You shrink into yourself, like if you can make yourself smaller then maybe the bad things won't find you."

Blossom pulled his face free of Asher's grip but didn't argue, the prince was right after all. Asher smiled smugly at him. causing Blossom to huff. "Fine," he conceded, "that doesn't mean what you do is healthy though."

Asher held up his hands in surrender, but the smile didn't drop. "Fair enough," he said, "now, shall we get dressed and venture out there?"

Blossom followed Asher back to the wardrobe, his eyes widening as he pulled out one of his winter robes, tracing a finger down the black stitching that now accompanied the previous silver. He looked over at Asher who had pulled out a soft black dress shirt, the silken collar now laced with silver ribbons and silver stitching down the sleeves. "How long do you think they've had these," he asked, "to have already added our wedding colours?"

Asher seemed to ponder the question as he stepped into a pair of plain black breeches. "That day after the summer solstice, you couldn't find your riding trousers," he reminisced, straightening and placing his hands on his hips, "but my father hadn't announced our wedding then."

Blossom absently ran his thumb back and forth over the stitching on the breast of his robe. "I'm not sure how much stock I put into their words. Emma said she started moving our belonging after Silas made his announcement, but I think whatever plans have been put in place started much earlier."

Asher nodded gravely, holding out his hand for Blossom to take. "Let's see what truth we can pull from them today."

When they emerged from their bedroom, they found Queen Lila, Emma, Kara and Edwin all huddled around one of the tables at the back of the main chamber, or what could serve as the back in a completely circular room. It was that thought and the reminder of the déjà vu he'd felt the day before that caused Blossom to look around suddenly. He strode into the middle of the room, ignoring Asher's questioning call of his name as he spun slowly, counting the hidden doorways and noting their familiar spread.

"It's the blessing school," he breathed.

"What?" Asher asked, joining Blossom in the center, watching him with a worried expression.

"This place has the exact same layout as the blessing school. The door we came in yesterday is the same as the entrance, our bedroom is where the Moon blessed classroom is." Blossom pointed to each doorway in turn before looking over to the queen. "I'm right, aren't I?" he asked.

Lila nodded at him, "you are my darling. This place is directly below your school. There is a harmony to the blessing school that feels natural. Sacred and healing in a way that I can't describe. When I instructed the architects to build your design above ground, I had this place secretly made as a mirror."

Blossom opened his mouth, but whatever response he had been about to say vanished as he realised what the queen had said. "My design?" he asked, "but you designed the blessing school."

Lila shook her head, wheeling herself over to him and taking hold of his hand. "I may have drawn up the official designs, but they were all based on the drawings you did as a child." She smiled at him, her face lighting up with a familiar kindness that made it almost impossible to distrust her. "Here, come with me," she ordered gently, before taking him over to another desk and rifling through one of the many drawers in it. She produced a yellowed sheet of paper and handed it to him. "You were always drawing things like this during your early lessons, don't you remember? It used to drive the tutors to distraction."

Blossom looked down at the image on the paper, frowning as it tugged at some half-forgotten memory. It was crude in the way all children's drawing are, but he could see where the inspiration for the blessing school had come from. One large circle with 6 smaller circles spaced evenly around its edge, each small circle bled slightly into the larger one and each was shaded with a deity's distinct colour. Blue, silver, orange, green, yellow and black. He traced the black circle that represented Emma's classroom, feeling a familiar itch in the back of his mind, like he was trying to remember a dream. There were straight lines emanating from each circle, again in the deities colours, meeting in the middle where a small dot of pink lay.

"I don't remember this," he said quietly.

"I do." Asher's voice was closer than he'd expected, and Blossom jumped, his shoulder making contact with the prince's chin. "Whoa," Asher chuckled, stepping back to give him room.

"You remember this?" Blossom asked, holding up the paper.

Asher smiled, "yeah, you gave me a couple of them. I remember because it was back when we had our lessons together." He shrugged and Blossom felt a subtle tightening in his gut like Asher was nervous. "Master Kayla was always at her wits end because you spent your time drawing these instead of your letters and I spent my time watching you instead of her."

Blossom flushed and turned back to Lila. "Can I keep this?" he asked.

"It's yours darling boy, you can do whatever you like with it." She gestured for him to take it.

Blossom folded the paper and put it into one of his deep pockets. He felt like he was missing something when he looked at it, something important. But there were more pressing matters to deal with right now. "Thank you, now I believe there are more questions you haven't answered yet," he stated, looking around at the gathered group to ensure they knew he was including all of them in that statement.

"You should eat something first, Petal," Emma said gently, gesturing to a table set with various cold breakfast foods that he had somehow missed.

"I'm not..." His dismissal was cut off as Asher laced their hands together and tugged him towards the food.

"Explanations can happen whilst we eat," the prince said, pulling out a chair and gripping Blossom by the shoulders before pressing him down into it. "So, we've established that Evelyn ran away with Blossom, and you don't know what happened to him until he turned up at the palace. What I want to know is who brought him to the palace? It couldn't have been Evelyn," Asher said, piling two plates with cut fruit and a few slices of toasted bread. He placed one in front of Blossom and didn't touch the second until the blesser had taken his first bite.

"Silas did," Lila said simply and both boys stared at her.

"What?" Asher asked around a mouthful of bread.

"Silas had been heading one of the raids into Castilla; he had never given up hope of finding the island, and with you so unwell his obsession had only increased. He returned with Blossom one night and brought him to your room. I very rarely left your side in those days my darling, so he would have known that I was there. I'm not sure why he was so convinced Blossom could help you, but the second you saw each other it was like a new life had sparked within you." Lila leant over the table and squeezed Asher's hand. "You already seemed to be getting stronger, and then Blossom kissed you and you were healed."

"Well, partly," Kara added as Asher touched the spot on his neck where the death mark had been.

Blossom chewed silently on a piece of orange. Why couldn't he remember returning to the palace with the king? His memories had always been of a faceless soldier, and what little he remembered of the journey back to the palace had been rough, sleeping outdoors or in stables, nothing he imagined Silas would ever willingly put himself through.

"Did you never question why he kidnapped a child? Why Blossom was bought to us without his parents?" Asher asked and Lila looked over to Emma briefly.

"I was so relieved that you were okay Asher, and by the time I thought to question it Emma and Edwin had arrived. They informed me of who Blossom was and where he had come from. By that point the Balance had restricted my information, so I had not yet heard about your miraculous appearance. My own fault, I know." She directed the last sentence towards Emma, raising her hands in surrender. "And it was decided that for the time being it was safer to keep Blossom in the palace." The queen paused, looking intently at her son for a moment before seeming to come to a decision. "Also, it wasn't the first time that Silas had returned from war carrying a child."

5

Chapter 5

Asher froze as the words sunk in; the feeling of Blossom's shock serving to amplify his own. "What are you saying?" He asked quietly, unsure he even wanted to hear the answer.

Queen Lila took a deep breath, looking down at where her hands rested on the tabletop. "We tried for a long time to have a child; we'd been married for 7 years when we finally accepted that it wasn't going to happen. The physician said that due to my poor health it was probably for the best that I never conceived, but that didn't stop me from wanting a child." She reached across the table, brushing the tips of her fingers over her son's. Asher tensed but didn't move his hand away, relaxing again slightly when Blossom took hold of his other hand under the table. "And one day Silas brought me you."

Asher could feel tears pricking at the backs of his eyes. "Why did you never tell me?" he asked, "it's not like it would make you any less of a mother to me."

Lila smiled at him; relief clear on her face. The relief was short lived as she returned to her previous seriousness. "It was Silas' command. He hadn't told anyone about you. When he appeared in the middle of the night with you in his arms, he told me that I had to pretend that you had come from my body. I had been bedridden for much of that winter already, so the story was easy to fabricate. He never told me why, and then you became ill, and it didn't seem so important anymore."

Asher pulled his hand free of Blossom's grasp, rubbing it over his face as he tried to come to terms with the news.

"Asher," Blossom said quietly, resting his hand on the prince's arm, but it was the feeling of worry and pity from the blesser that caused him to stand.

"I have to..." He trailed off, not sure what he was trying to say. "Sorry, this is too much." With that, he turned and marched back over to their bedchamber, the stone door sliding closed behind him seconds later.

∞

Blossom watched Asher's retreat with a mixture of emotions; it was already getting harder to determine which were his and which were Asher's, but he knew for certain the disappointment wasn't his.

"Maybe you should go after him, Petal," Emma pushed gently but Blossom shook his head.

"No, he doesn't want me with him right now. It will be best if we give him space to think by himself for a bit," he explained as he turned back towards the gathered people. "And I still have questions for you."

Emma nodded at him; her eyebrows drawn in what seemed to be confusion. Confusion over what Blossom wasn't sure.

"Firstly, I want to know why you knew what was going to happen at the wedding. Don't try and placate me with that wishy washy 'we just knew something was going to happen' crap. You were way too prepared for it to have been a hunch. And as Asher pointed out, my things started going missing before Silas even announced our wedding date."

"We are telling you the truth when we say we didn't know exactly what was going to happen," Kara said, "we had no idea that Asher's curse would react like that."

Emma put a hand on her wife's shoulder, causing her to fall silent. "We knew that something was in the works when Silas disappeared on his months long journey. The last time that happened was when he returned with you, then I spotted Evelyn in the market and knew this was even bigger than we had thought."

Blossom blinked. "She's been around this whole time?" he asked, and Emma nodded.

"The Blossomites have been growing stronger and more outspoken for a few years now, ever since you and Asher came of age," Edwin piped up. He seemed more at ease in this cavern than Blossom had ever seen him before, and it made him wonder if the man's timidity had also been a lie. "Silas has always had an...intense interest in them. Which was odd considering his feelings towards you."

"Yes, thank you Ed," Emma said in exasperation, "we knew that Silas' absence and Evelyn's appearance had to have been connected but we didn't know how. We simply prepared for the worst outcome. We had to ensure that you and Asher would be safe. The wedding threw us off a bit I will admit, but it made Evelyn show her hand. Seems she's just as power hungry as Silas was."

Blossom was silent for a few moments, deliberating whether or not to accept that this was all he was going to get. "I think Silas knew that Asher was going to kill him," he said with a sigh.

"How so?" Emma asked.

"When he slapped me, he said it was to show us why our bonding was a bad thing. Then when the curse, or whatever it was, came out of Asher, he didn't seem surprised."

The rest of the table looked at each other with matching expressions of confusion on their faces.

"Do you not think that it is a curse, dear one?" Lila asked.

Blossom hummed in thought. "I'm not sure; it doesn't feel like one. Although saying that I don't really know what a curse feels like, but it feels almost...familiar in a way. And not just because I've been fighting it all these years."

"You keep using the present tense, Blossom. I thought your last blessing had destroyed it, or at least released it so that it was no longer tied to the prince."

Blossom looked Kara in the eye as he spoke. "It's still there," he said, "the mark is gone but I can still feel it in Ash, like it's hiding just under his skin."

Blossom returned to their bedchamber a little later, exhausted and strung out. He felt like he'd gotten all he could out of the others and had finally accepted that they genuinely didn't know more than they were letting on. However, when talk turned to what they were going to do next, how to deal with Evelyn and the Blossomites, the fact that Asher was both king and not, he demanded they halt until the prince was present.

"How are you, my love?" Blossom asked quietly. The room was dim, and Asher was curled up on the bed, staring blankly at the wall.

"Why ask when you know how I'm feeling already?" he responded, looking over at him with a frown as Blossom felt a stab of pain at the question. "Isn't this what you wanted?" the prince asked, sitting up properly as Blossom made his way over to him, "for us to be connected this way."

Blossom sat on the edge of the bed, feeling the now familiar heat burning the backs of his eyes. "It is. That doesn't mean we don't need to talk to each other. Me knowing how you feel doesn't stop me from wanting to hear about it, how else will I know how to help you?" Asher looked away and Blossom rubbed a hand over his eyes, wiping away a few stray tears. "I thought that you also wanted this. I thought you wanted us to be bonded."

"I do, but that doesn't mean it's easy to feel your pity. Or your sadness," he looked back as Blossom scooted further onto the bed, grasping his hand.

"It's not pity Ash, it's empathy. I've always been sad when you're hurting. I don't think it's something I can stop."

Asher pulled his hand free of Blossom's grasp, but before the blesser could feel hurt by the gesture the prince was pulling him onto his lap, wrapping his arms around his waist and resting his head against his chest. "I don't know what to do, and that terrifies me," he said quietly.

Blossom remained silent, not wanting to risk interrupting whatever Asher might say next.

"I'm supposed to be a ruler, but I can't even begin to think about what that means now, about what we need to do next."

"You don't have to do it alone, my love," Blossom whispered soothingly, petting Asher's dark hair. "You have me, and everyone else in that chamber. You don't have to do it alone."

Asher didn't respond, just tightened his hold on the other man. They sat that way for a while, Blossom was still unsure of the passage of time in the windowless space, but it had to have been a few hours.

"I think it's time you had a bath," he said, running his fingers over the stubble that had started to darken the prince's cheeks over the past day or so. "It will make you feel better," he added when Asher made no attempt to move, instead pulling Blossom even tighter against him.

"I'm too tired," Asher murmured against his chest before heaving a heavy sigh.

Blossom didn't respond for another few moments, letting Asher hold him in the quiet dark of their room. "I'll wash you," he said finally, "you won't have to do anything other than walk there. I'll do everything else."

Asher pulled back to look at him. "You're set on this happening, aren't you?"

"No offense, my love," Blossom placed a quick kiss on his lips, "but after everything that happened yesterday, you are beginning to smell. So yes, this is happening."

Asher released what may have been a laugh but was really no more than a quick exhalation of air. "Fine," he said, letting go of Blossom's waist so that he could climb out of his lap.

Blossom helped the prince to his feet and guided him back into the main chamber. It was empty of other occupants this time, so he took a guess and pressed the button for the door that corresponded with the Water blessed classroom. They entered a small cavern lined with burning torches and hollowed out recesses which served as shelves. Blossom spied a stone partition behind which he assumed must be the toilet, but his main focus was the large pool of clear water that took up most of the room. It appeared to be fed by a small waterfall that sprang from the wall and a dark tunnel in one corner served as drainage.

"That water looks really cold, Flower," Asher muttered, wrapping his arms around himself.

"It won't be for long, now come on, up." Blossom gestured with his hands for the prince to raise his arms as he began to help him out of his clothes. Once the prince was naked, shivering in the slight chill of the room, Blossom placed a hand in the water, pulsing enough of Fire's blessing into the pool for the water to begin steaming. "In you get," he said cheerfully, smiling at the blissed-out sigh that emanated from Asher as he sank into the water.

He let Asher sit there for a while, letting the water ease some of the tension from his body as Blossom busied himself with collecting different bathing items. He knelt on the floor behind Asher and began lathering his hair with soap, digging his fingers into the prince's scalp until Asher let out a frankly obscene moan. "Told you it would make you feel better," Blossom said as he filled a jug with warm water. "Okay tilt your head back," he instructed, pouring the water over the prince's hair before repeating the process a few more times.

"Lean forward for me, sweetheart," he said once he was satisfied with the state of Asher's hair. He felt a flutter in his chest as the prince did as instructed and grinned. Leaning over the edge of the bathing pool he pressed a kiss to Asher's shoulder. "I take it you liked that name," he said with a smirk, which bloomed into a full smile when Asher turned his head to look at him, the prince's pale cheeks flushed from more than just the hot water.

A wet hand emerged from the water to grasp the back of his head, pulling him closer until their lips touched in a firm kiss. "I think it's only fair that you warn me before you start using new endearments, my beautiful boy," Asher replied, his breath ghosting over Blossom's cheek.

Blossom cleared his throat in an attempt to distract himself from how much Asher's new pet name was causing his face to heat. "Well played," he muttered, pushing himself upright again as the prince grinned. "Okay lean forward, let me wash your back." He dipped a cloth into the water, sending another pulse of Fire's blessing when he found it cooler than before. Asher hummed appreciatively as the water warmed, pulling his knees up to his chest and resting his chin on them.

Blossom brushed the longer parts of Asher's hair away from his neck, pausing when he noticed a small, round scar at the top of his spine. "When did you get this?" He asked, tracing it with his finger. The skin was mottled in a way that Blossom was familiar with, and he felt his stomach clench as he realised why. It was a burn scar, the kind you only got from Fire's blessing.

Asher shrugged, "it's been there for as long as I can remember. My father told me that it was from a candle that fell on me when I was very young."

Blossom sat back on his heels, his brows furrowed in confusion as Asher turned to him. It was possible that Silas had tried to cure Asher's curse himself with Blessing transference and failed, but healing transference shouldn't leave a scar even if it wasn't successful. His fingers itched with the urge to reach behind him and touch the identical scar that lay between his shoulder blades. He felt memories flooding his mind, painful ones of Silas pressing his fingers to that spot and pouring burning fire into his heart, the main source of his own blessings.

He felt something click into place as he looked from Asher's pitch-black hair to his shining black eyes. The stories were that his death mark had changed the prince's eyes to black, but he had a feeling that was just another embellishment created to hide the truth.

Asher's eyes had always been black.

"It's not a curse," He breathed as realisation crashed over him in a wave.

"What?" Asher asked as Blossom dug frantically in his pocket, pulling out the drawing that Lila had given him earlier that day.

"Your mark, it's not a curse, it never was," Blossom said, tracing his fingers over the black circle on the drawing. A black room that had come to represent the unblessed, a place for the things that couldn't be given by the deities. Because there had only ever been 5 blessings, just as there had never been a person alive who could use more than one of them.

Until Blossom had been born.

He looked back up at the prince. "It's a blessing," he said, turning the paper and tapping the circle, "Asher you're...you're blessed."

6

Chapter 6

"Blossom you're not making any sense," Emma said, watching worriedly as Blossom paced the main chamber.

He'd spent the last 20 or so minutes trying to explain his theory, stopping periodically to look at Asher whenever he felt him getting overwhelmed, trying to soothe him through their bond. He wasn't sure how well it was working though.

"What do you mean I'm not making sense? It all adds up, doesn't it? Why else would Silas use blessing transference to burn him? It wouldn't have done anything if he was unblessed, and it explains why I drew a sixth circle every time I drew...whatever this is." He waved the picture at Emma as he spoke. "I must have felt the existence of another blessing, another deity, and that was the only way I could express it." He stopped pacing and spun to face the queen. "How long did it take for Asher to grow sick? How long after Silas brought him to you?" he asked.

"He was always sick," Emma said but Blossom held up a hand to silence her.

"Earlier you said that Ash became sick after he was brought to the palace, how long after?"

"About 2 years," Lila answered. Emma and Asher looked at her in shock, but Blossom only nodded.

"And was that around the time he got that burn?"

The queen was silent for a moment as she thought back. "I...yes I think it was, it was a few months after but yes."

Blossom scratched at his chin, staring up at the domed ceiling in thought. "Now this is just a theory, but I think Silas knew that Asher was blessed. He probably thought he could harness his power and use it. Being in possession of the only child blessed by whatever deity has chosen Asher would give him some of that power he craved. I'm guessing things didn't go to plan and so he sealed your ability to receive and use blessing inside of you. He did it by burning away your connection to them right at the spot in your body where your power lies," he tapped the back of his neck, "that's why the death mark always started on your neck as well."

"That's a big leap, Petal," Emma said in response, pulling Blossom's gaze away from the prince, who had touched his scar as the blesser was talking, a deep frown on his face.

"Not really," he said, "he tried to do the same to me." Everyone stared at him, a mixture of shock and horror in their expressions, and he shrugged. "I didn't understand it at the time either, but I think he wanted to leave me with just enough power to keep Asher alive. He didn't want me to become strong enough to restore the connection with his deity. I guess, when it didn't work, he just resorted to torture to keep me too scared to even try."

He watched Emma's face harden at the reminder of what Silas had done to him, so similar to how she had always looked when someone hurt him that he couldn't help but smile slightly. He decided to push on with his theory to prevent them from getting sidetracked, but felt some of the betrayal he still carried lessen at the realisation that she did genuinely care for him.

"Think about it," he continued, "the death mark was probably a build-up of the blessing power that Ash couldn't use. And he has the colouration of a blessed as well." He gestured to the prince, well aware that he was talking about him like he wasn't in the room.

"No deity has that colour, Blossom," Kara said, "just because you used black in your drawing doesn't mean that...well that it means anything. You were a child. Maybe you just wanted to include Asher in your picture."

Blossom groaned before walking over to the prince and kneeling between his legs. "Before you found me there had been no blessed with my colouration either. There's nothing to prove that the five Blessers are truly the only ones out there." He cupped Asher's face in his hands, rubbing his thumbs over the thin skin beneath his eyes. "Have you ever seen someone with eyes like these?" He asked, smiling when Asher placed his hands on top of his, "I mean truly black eyes, not just dark, dark brown."

"But that was because of the curse. Asher's eyes were a different colour before, right?" Emma directed her question over to Lila who looked at her in confusion.

"No, his eyes have always been black," she answered.

"Okay, let's say he is blessed. Blessed by what?" Edwin asked and Blossom shrugged, still not breaking eye contact with his husband.

"I'm not sure. Darkness maybe? Shadow? Who knows."

Asher snorted and looked down. "Makes sense that darkness would give the blessing of death," he said quietly, the grief that he'd been suppressing sparking up again.

Blossom frowned, "I don't think that's what it is." He pushed on as Asher opened his mouth to argue, "all blessings have the ability to harm others if that's what the blesser wishes. But all blessings have the ability to do good too. If darkness or shadow has gifted you its power, it isn't for death, my love."

"How do we find out what it is?" Kara asked, and Blossom was glad to see she seemed to have accepted his theory.

"I'm not sure." He rested his elbows on Asher's knees, looking back up at the ceiling in thought. "How do you communicate with a deity when you don't know its name? Or the word to call its power?" He mused aloud.

"How did you find Nature's word, Flower?" Asher asked. He was brightening somewhat, the heavy feeling of confusion and overwhelm dissipating into something like curiosity.

Blossom placed his chin in his hand, looking back up at Asher serenely. This was territory he was familiar with; he may not know much about strategy and military planning, but Blossom could talk about blessings for hours. "It was kind of just there. Something I always knew, like the sound of my own breathing." Asher's shoulders slumped slightly but Blossom pressed on. "When you used your power, what did you feel? What were you thinking about?"

"That I wanted to protect you. That I was angry at my father for ever laying his hands on you."

Blossom hummed in thought. "You didn't hear anything? There wasn't a word that came into your mind?"

Asher shook his head with a slight grin. "No Flower, there wasn't."

The blesser heaved a sigh and stood back up. "Yeah, figured it wouldn't be that easy." He looked around, noting the various dark recesses in the cavern. "At least we're not short of darkness down here. We'll figure it out."

Asher watched him closely for a few more seconds before giving in with a stretch. "I guess we should go back to the other pressing matter then. Namely how do we plan on getting the palace back from the Blossomites, and what are we going to do about the fact that the heir to the throne killed the ruling monarch?"

No one mentioned Asher's use of language, it was evident he was trying to remain objective and not slip back into the miasma of guilt he'd been wallowing in since the wedding.

"Well, you wouldn't be the first successor to gain a throne after removing the person previously sat on it. Once everything Silas did comes to light no one is going to begrudge your claim," Kara said, her tone just as impersonal.

"Our main goal is to get you both out of the palace. I've sent word to the Balance, and they should be sending someone to extract us," Emma said, looking around the group, "all of us."

"What good will that do?" Asher asked.

"It's about time the Balance stops working behind the scenes and starts making an active effort to set things right. We will need both of you to do that. Evelyn was once one of us, it's up to us to bring her to justice."

∞

After the whirlwind of the wedding, the momentous revelation that Lila was still alive and the realisation of Asher's blessed nature, the next few days were oddly subdued. It would take a while for the Balance to get a message back to them so until then Blossom, Asher, and everyone else had very little to do. That didn't dissuade Kara for long however as she quickly devised a training plan similar to the one Asher had undergone when with his knights.

This was how Blossom found himself sitting on one of the stone benches near the perimeter of the main chamber, five days into their exile, watching Asher and Kara sparring with wooden swords.

"Come on now, Your Highness, move your feet," Kara was saying, swinging down violently with her weapon.

Asher spun out of the way, gritting his teeth and swinging up to try and take out the lieutenant's arm. Despite the grimace of concentration on his face Blossom knew he was enjoying himself, and despite being bored out of his mind he was happy for him.

The blesser's eyes wandered over to where Lila was bent over one of her many worktables. His gaze focused in on her wheeled chair and with a determined huff he stood and walked over to her. "Your Majesty," he said quietly, and Lila smiled up at him.

"You've been wearing my son's colours for five days now, darling boy. I think we can move past the formalities," she replied, her expression warm, "and I don't remember you ever calling me that before."

Blossom felt himself flush slightly at the reminder. Silas had always made it clear how much he hated Blossom's irreverence, but Lila had never once berated him for slipping up and using her name. Once upon a time it would have felt odd to call her by her title but now the idea of simply calling her Lila settled uneasily in his gut.

"Sorry," he said, kicking at the floor sheepishly, and Lila waved a hand at him as though to dismiss the apology.

"Never mind, now what's caught your interest?" She asked, gesturing to the table. It was littered with half-finished projects, spools of copper wire, and brass contraptions that Blossom couldn't even begin to guess the use of.

"Um actually, I wanted to ask you how you are," he said, gesturing to her chair, "how long has it been since you last walked?"

He felt a weird stab of guilt in his heart. Before the queen had faked her death Blossom had regularly soothed her various aches and maladies with Moon's blessing. He could never cure her, according to one of the royal physicians her body's propensity towards pain was something she'd been born with. No amount of Moon's blessing could change a person's make up, but he'd been able to help. He'd been able to reduce the number of times her limbs became paralyzed out of the blue.

Lila took hold of his hand and squeezed it. "Do not beat yourself up over this, my dear. You thought I was dead, as I intended. There is no logic in feeling guilt for not being able to help me."

Blossom huffed again and looked away. "How are you still able to read my thoughts?" He asked, causing Lila to laugh.

"Because you wear them on your face, little flower."

Blossom turned back to her at the nickname, he'd almost forgotten that she was the first one to call him flower. "Will you let me heal you?" he asked. "Or I could soothe you instead?"

Lila let go of his hand and wheeled back from the table. "That would be very much appreciated," she said, and Blossom smiled.

He followed her towards her room. Lila had chosen the chamber that mirrored the Earth blessed classroom on the opposite side of the cavern, so they passed by the still sparring knights on their way.

"What are you doing?" Asher asked conversationally, distracted enough that he didn't notice Kara's blow until it was too late. He let out a shout as her wooden sword connected with his shoulder with a loud crack, causing him to drop his own weapon, his arm now hanging uselessly by his side.

It was only due to being surrounded by various blessed for so long that Blossom spotted what was happening, even if it was unlike anything he'd seen before. Instead of glowing the way most blessed did when they called their power it was like Asher was sucking in light, the whole cavern growing darker for a few seconds as a coil of black smoke snaked down his arm and began to stretch towards Kara.

"No!" Blossom screamed, grabbing Asher's uninjured hand and yanking him away.

"Blossom be careful," Kara shouted as the blesser caught hold of the hand producing the smoke.

"Blossom, I don't..." Asher said, his voice strained with panic.

Blossom shushed him absently, closing his eyes and pushing his own mixture of blessing through their bond until he felt the now familiar dark force. Instead of fighting it like he had before Blossom opened himself up to the power, coaxing it towards him and away from Kara. He gasped as the blessing took the invitation and rushed into him, his eyes flying open as it refilled the well of power settled in his heart.

"Blossom, your eyes." Asher breathed - Blossom's eyes had turned black.

Blossom swallowed, trying to get a grip on the flood of blessing energy but unable to stop it without knowing the right word. "Nineshim," he grit out between clenched teeth, hoping that Nature's word might be enough, but it did nothing. He could not command the power pouring from his husband, only stand there as it continued to consume him.

"Asher do something!" Someone screamed.

"I don't know...wait, wait I hear something," Asher said, although his voice sounded far away. After what seemed like an eternity as his body tried to contain the seemingly never-ending flow of blessing power, his muscles burning with the effort of withstanding something so volatile, the prince spoke again. "Keshanil." His voice was low, but it reverberated through Blossom's head like he'd screamed it, and suddenly the power was gone.

Blossom dropped to his knees, tears streaming down his face. "Fuck!" He cried, as yet another realisation slammed into him. Asher knelt beside him, wrapping his arms around his shoulders as he whispered soothing nonsense against his hair, rocking him from side to side the way he had when they were children.

"What was that?" Kara asked, approaching them slowly like she was worried the dark force would erupt again.

"Keshanil," Asher repeated, the word ringing like the name of a long-lost brother through Blossom's mind.

"Shadow's blessing," Blossom said, continuing when the prince didn't, looking first at Asher then at the small group of his family members. "The blessing of protection."

7

Chapter 7

I'm sorry, I'm so sorry, Flower," Asher said as he helped Blossom to his feet, "I didn't mean to hurt you."

Blossom shook his head, wiping at his cheeks to get rid of the tears that were still falling. "No Asher, you didn't hurt me, I invited the blessing in, it wasn't your fault. That's not why I'm crying. I'm so sorry my love."

Asher looked at him in confusion.

"It's my fault," Blossom continued, hiccupping another sob.

"What are you talking about?" Asher asked, his voice quiet and coaxing as Blossom pressed the back of his hand to his mouth. He was shaking all over, tears still streaming down his face.

"I didn't know that *that* was what I was doing, I'm so, so sorry," Blossom said instead of answering him.

"Doing what? I don't understand what you're saying."

"Blessing transference," Blossom replied, staring pleadingly into the prince's eyes, "I thought I was using blessing transference to heal you but instead...I was using it to suppress your power. Just like Silas did to me. I was burning away our bond just as much as he was."

Asher pulled him close, tucking Blossom's head under his chin as he wrapped his arms around him. "Like you said, you didn't know. You have nothing to be sorry for, Flower. We're bonded now and he's not around to stop it."

Emma cleared her throat, and Blossom peeked out at her from where he was pressed against Asher's chest. "You've said that a few times now, Petal. What do you mean when you say bond? It doesn't sound like you're talking about marriage."

Blossom shook his head, effectively rubbing his face against Asher's tunic. "No, I don't mean marriage, I'm talking about our spiritual bond. You've said before that our spirits are resonant and you're right. Resonant enough that I joined them together when I flooded Asher with my power. We're connected now."

The four adults looked baffled, turning to one another as though to check they weren't the only ones at a loss.

"But that's...that's not possible," Edwin whispered, causing Blossom to pull back from Asher's embrace with a frown.

"What do you mean?" He asked, "I know it's rare for souls to be so closely linked but it's not like its unheard of, right?"

Emma and Edwin looked at each other. "Have you ever heard of something like that?" Emma asked her brother.

Edwin shook his head. "No, never. I've never read anything about it in the archives either. How did you first learn of it?" Edwin asked, turning back to Blossom.

"I nearly bonded with Ash the first time we met, then Silas broke the connection. He was the one who told me about bonding."

The hall fell silent as everyone became lost in their own thoughts, until Edwin snapped his fingers. "Your Majesty," he said, causing Lila to look at him in silent question. "Is there a servant's passage that will take me close enough to the king's private library for me not to get caught?"

"The what?" Blossom and Asher asked in unison.

Queen Lila rolled towards them, waving a hand at Edwin when he opened his mouth to speak. "Silas kept a private library. Only accessible through the royal quarters. I've only ever been inside once when Silas explained his plans to me. After seeing some of the things he kept in there, I knew the time had come for me to disappear. It seems that he and Evelyn have very similar theories about you Blossom, about what your existence means, and I think most of it is stored in there." She took hold of Asher's hand, "and if he knew about your blessing, my son, then there may be information about it there as well."

She sighed again and returned her attention to Edwin. "As for your question, it may be possible. There is no direct route to the royal chambers from here but there is an escape route to the outside. After that you can take the servants halls up to the royal chamber, but you will have to go through the sitting room and the bedroom to reach the library."

"I want to come too," Blossom said suddenly, causing four pairs of eyes to turn to him, "if there is information in that library then I need to see it, and it is far too valuable to leave in the palace for..." He took a deep breath. "...Evelyn to get her hands on. I don't know much about the Blossomites, but their beliefs don't seem like the type that will benefit humanity, only destroy it. We can't give them any advantages."

Emma and Kara both shook their heads vehemently. "No," Emma said, her voice hard, "no Blossom, it is far too risky. You're too valuable to risk getting caught and you stand out like a sore thumb. Kara and Edwin will go, and they can retrieve the documents. You may still be able to study them, but down here where it is safe."

"But..."

"No buts, Petal, this isn't a request."

Blossom opened his mouth to argue but stopped when Asher touched his cheek, turning his face towards him. "She's right Flower, and besides, your mother will recognise you instantly," the prince said, ruffling Blossom's pink hair.

"She's not my mother," Blossom replied with a frown, causing Asher's brows to knit in concern.

"Blossom," he chided, "you know as well as I do that someone doesn't need to have birthed you to be your mother, it's about…"

"It's about the person who raised you," Blossom finished for him. "Exactly. A mother is someone who cares for their child and does what's best for them. Not someone who steals a child away because they have delusions of grandeur. Evelyn isn't my mother, Emma is." He looked back over at his mother as she let out what could only be described as a squeak, her eyes filling with tears as she clamped a hand over her mouth.

Emma pulled him away from the prince and into a tight hug. "Oh Petal, I love you so much," she said tearfully, clasping his face between her hands as she beamed up at him. "You're still not going though."

Blossom groaned theatrically but didn't argue, he could see the logic in their plan and knew he was far too conspicuous to attempt a successful infiltration. "Fine," he said, "I guess I'll have to content myself with helping Asher learn how to control his power."

Asher shifted uncomfortably on the spot. "I don't know, Flower. I don't want to hurt you again."

Blossom smiled at him. "All the more reason to learn. Your blessing lives within you whether you want it to or not, my love. Better to know how to harness it than have it explode out of you again."

He took Asher's hand and led him away from where the others had already begun to plan their infiltration of the king's library. Partially to give them ample room to practice and partially to stop himself from interfering and demanding to join them again.

"Also, this gives me a chance to practice too. We'll be learning this together, my love. This blessing is as unknown to me as it is to you." He sat crossed legged on the floor, motioning for Asher to copy him. "Now, I want you to say Shadow's word again and focus on how it feels when you do," he instructed, finding comfort in returning to something familiar.

Asher smirked at him, obviously reading Blossom's contentedness through their bond. "Once a master, always a master, huh dear heart?" He asked, grinning fully when Blossom flushed.

"I think we're going to need a rule about not using endearments during lessons, Ash."

Asher chuckled, "whatever you say, Master Blossom." His laughter grew louder as Blossom's flush grew even darker.

"Okay no, we're not doing that either. Just call me Flower like you normally do."

"Why? What's the matter, Flower? Do you feel embarrassed when I call you Master Blossom?" Asher asked, the fake innocence in his voice ruined by the wicked grin on his face.

"I have no idea what you mean," Blossom said with false nonchalance, keeping his expression neutral as he finished with, "Your Majesty." He tried and failed to mask his own glee when Asher turned red, his eyes widening as he sputtered. "Now are we going to focus on the lesson, or do you need a moment to compose yourself, my king?" Blossom asked, and he was fairly certain Asher nearly choked on his own saliva at the name.

"Okay, okay I get it. Curses Flower, you're a menace."

Blossom laughed at that. "Says you," he replied before trying to regain some semblance of seriousness. "Okay, deep breath and speak Shadow's word."

Asher shot him a look before doing as he was told, closing his eyes, and breathing in deeply. "Keshanil," he said, frowning when nothing happened.

"That's perfectly normal Ash. It will take time to learn how to call your blessing when you are not under threat. Until now you've only used it when your conscious mind was overrun by your survival instincts."

Asher nodded, keeping his eyes closed. "I did feel something, but it just...I don't know, felt like an itch. Like I was trying to remember a dream."

"Okay, try again."

They tried for over an hour, stopping only when Asher grew too frustrated to concentrate properly.

"This is hopeless!" The prince shouted, throwing his hands up in exasperation.

"It's not, my love," Blossom soothed, taking his hands and pressing his thumbs into the center of his palms the way he did when they were children, hoping it would still calm the prince in the same way. "Different blessings require different levels of dedication and different approaches to master. Shadow appears to be even more picky than Water. I wouldn't be surprised if it requires extra time before it will respond to you."

Asher pulled his hands free and crossed his arms with a huff, clearly not convinced. "You haven't tried to do it yet, I thought we were learning this together," he groused, causing Blossom to roll his eyes.

"I have fewer steps to take than you, my love. I only wanted to focus on getting you started, but if you insist." He glanced over to the wall, focusing on the small pool of shadow cast by it and spoke Nature's word. He felt a subtle tug but nothing more and frowned. He hummed in thought before remembering that he'd only managed to absorb Asher's blessing after using Shadow's word.

He tried to think back to when he was a small child, trying to remember if he'd had to use each deity's word until he became familiar enough with their power to call it using his own. The problem was, he couldn't remember a time when he hadn't been able to ask for and receive a blessing. It was so second nature to him now that the mechanics of it were slightly lost on him. Even children that came to his school unable to consciously ask for blessing had at some point or other received it from their deity. It was possible that Asher hadn't received Shadow's blessing since Silas had burnt his connection away, in fact it was almost certain. The power he'd been using so far was the build-up from nearly 20 years of having Shadow's blessing locked inside of him.

He thought back to the placement of the scar on Asher's neck, right at the top of the spine and focused his attention on that spot in his own body. It was barely more than an inch below the seat of Water's blessing, and only a few inches above the seat of his own well of power. He looked again at the shadow and spoke the word Asher had discovered, feeling a gasp escape him as darkness poured into him. He looked back over to Asher who was quite openly pouting at him and couldn't help but laugh.

"Oh sweetheart, don't look so depressed. I've had 21 years of practice in asking for blessing, it's no wonder I can do it before you." Asher huffed again but his shoulders lowered slightly. "Besides I think I've got more of a handle on it now. I imagine your next try will be easier," he said, still smiling. He was about to launch into another lesson when Emma called out to them.

"We have dinner prepared. Come and eat and we will explain the plan for tonight."

For the first time since they had arrived Blossom didn't argue about sitting down to eat, mostly so he wouldn't interrupt the explanation of Kara's plan.

"So, we're going to go tonight, when the castle should be asleep," Kara said, pressing her fingertips to the tabletop. "This is mostly a reconnaissance mission; we have no idea whether or not anyone has taken up residence in the king's chambers."

"I have some idea," Blossom muttered around a mouthful of soft-boiled potato.

Kara ignored his interruption and continued. "We will take a few bags with us in case we make it to the library. No point in returning empty handed if we don't need to."

Blossom placed his fork down with determination, the metal clinking loudly against the wood. "I really think I should be coming with you."

"Blossom no, we've discussed this," Emma chided.

"I know, I know. I'm too conspicuous blah, blah, blah," he said, not sure why he was suddenly so irritated. He felt Asher place a hand on his knee and looked at the prince briefly as a wave of confusion and comfort washed over him. "Hear me out, you said there was no direct route to the library, but I can make one. I could use Earth's blessing to create a tunnel between the library and the catacombs, that way we won't have to risk being seen again after the first run."

The table fell silent for a moment, during which time Blossom shoveled another forkful of potato into his mouth.

Kara hummed thoughtfully, "I don't hate that idea," she said and Emma spun to glare at her.

"No," she said sharply.

"Not tonight, my dove, I agree. This mission will remain just Edwin and I," Kara soothed but Emma didn't seem convinced.

"No, not at all Kara. I don't want Blossom anywhere near my sister."

"I'm not a child!" Blossom shouted, standing and knocking his chair over in his anger. "Stop treating me like I'm defenseless. I'm more powerful than Kara or Edwin, or anyone we could bump into up there."

Emma gaped at him. "That wasn't what I meant Petal. But you don't know what she's like now, she's dangerous. All of them are. The Blossomites beliefs are twisted."

"Well, I wouldn't know, would I? You've been keeping everything about them a secret. And if I recall correctly, I was the last one here to spend any amount of time with her, unless you've been having secret family get togethers over the last ten years."

"Alright, that's enough Flower," Asher said, standing and taking hold of his hand.

Blossom looked at him in shock, betrayal clear on his face and through their bond. "You're taking their side?" He asked incredulously.

Asher shook his head. "No, I'm not. Because there are no sides Blossom, and when you calm down, you'll see that."

Blossom bristled and tried to tug his hand free, but Asher's grip was stronger.

The prince stared steadily at him, not breaking eye contact as he addressed Kara. "Lieutenant, prepare for tonight's reconnaissance. I will take Blossom back to our room."

"Yes, Your Majesty," Kara responded, standing and gesturing for Edwin to follow her as Emma began clearing the table, her face pinched like she was trying to hold back tears.

"Come on, dear heart," Asher said quietly, tugging at his hand but Blossom shook his head.

"No, I'm not going anywhere," he replied petulantly. Somewhere in the back of his mind he knew he was being childish but there was so much frustration and anger coursing through him that he didn't care.

The only indication he had that Asher was about to move was the sudden determined set to his jaw and the slightly mischievous glint in his eye. The next thing he knew, Asher had wrapped his arms around the tops of his thighs and lifted him, carrying him over his shoulder like a sack of flour.

"Asher put me down!" He screeched, scrabbling against the prince's back to try and regain some sense of dignity.

8

Chapter 8

Asher elbowed the button in the wall that closed their bedroom door before striding over to the bed and depositing Blossom unceremoniously on the covers. The blesser was doing a very good impression of a spitting, feral cat, which would have been amusing if it wasn't so worrying. They hadn't been connected for very long, but Asher was certain he had never seen Blossom this angry before and the emotions gushing through their bond were giving him heartburn.

He placed his hands on his hips and looked down at his husband with a single raised eyebrow. "So, do you want to tell me why you're acting like this?" He asked.

Blossom sat up with a glare and a huff. "Because everyone's treating me like a cursed be damned child and I'm sick of it."

Asher nodded despite not agreeing with the sentiment. "Okay, you've made that clear, but Flower, no one is treating you like a child. Well, Emma might be a bit, but she's your mother, it's kind of her job. They're just being sensible, safe."

Blossom shook his head angrily and stood up, beginning to pace in front of the bed, gesticulating wildly as he spoke, "but they don't need to keep me safe. Does she seriously think that I'm not going to come face to face with Evelyn before all of whatever this is, is over? It's going to happen sooner or later and I'm tired of feeling useless."

"There's a difference between an inevitable meeting and being reckless, Flower. You can't just go looking for danger. That's not going to help anyone."

Blossom let out a cry of frustration, but Asher could tell that he was getting through. "I hate being stuck down here, Ash. I hate not knowing what's going on," he shouted. One of the torches closest to them briefly flared with Blossom's anger and Asher's eyes widened in realisation.

"What blessings have you taken recently, Flower?" He asked, not sure why it hadn't occurred to him until now.

Blossom paused in his pacing, his anger dimming slightly as the prince's question caught him off guard. "What?"

"Since we've been down here, what blessings have you taken?"

"Earth and Fire, and I guess Shadow now as well. Not like there's much choice underground, Ash," Blossom answered and Asher grinned.

He took both of Blossom's hands in his own and pulled him closer. "No wonder you're so irritated," he said, and Blossom looked up at him in confusion. Asher rolled his eyes, still smiling. "Look, I might not have that much experience with blessings, but I've listened to you talking about them enough to have some knowledge. You always talk about the need to maintain balance, right? You once told me that there are hard and soft blessings."

Blossom nodded. "Yes, hard blessings are concrete and fierce. Easier to use but tough on the body if you're not used to it."

"Earth and Fire are the hard blessings, am I right?" Another nod. "And as there are 3 soft blessings already and like you said, nature is all about balance, I'm guessing that Shadow is another hard blessing." Blossom's eyes widened slightly as the meaning of Asher's words sunk in. Asher nodded encouragingly, "you've only been taking hard blessings since we got down here and it's making you angry."

"Fuck," Blossom said, causing Asher to laugh.

He pulled his husband into a hug and pressed a kiss to his hair. "Come on beautiful boy. It's my turn to help you relax. Let's go and have a bath."

Blossom sighed heavily but didn't pull away. "Not everything can be solved with a bath, Ash," he grumbled, causing Asher to laugh yet again.

"You're the one who's always harping on about the curative effects of warm water." The prince tipped Blossom's chin up with the tips of his fingers. "Will it be more persuasive if I bathe with you?"

Blossom snorted but Asher could feel his pulse quickening. "Oh, go on then. But you have to promise to wash my hair like I did for you."

"Deal," Asher said quickly before leaning down for a proper kiss.

∞

Blossom instantly felt calmer the second he submerged himself into the steaming water of the bathing room, Water's blessing soothing his frazzled nerves. He hadn't realised just how tense he'd been these past few days, but it was like a fog had already begun to lift from his mind. He was still annoyed and didn't think all his points were unreasonable, but he could now see that he'd blown most of it out of proportion. His feelings towards Evelyn also seemed to be calming; he was now unsure why he'd suddenly taken such a vehement dislike towards her. Granted, from what he'd heard, and from a few memories that were resurfacing, she wasn't the best person, but the near hatred he'd felt wasn't there anymore.

"Sit here, Flower," Asher murmured, perching on a step a few inches below the waterline so that only his bottom half was submerged. He gestured to the spot in front of him and held up a bar of soap.

Blossom complied, leaning into the prince's touch, and sighing happily when the first jug of warm water was poured over his head.

"I understand why you're so frustrated, Flower. I hate being cooped up down here as well, but there's nothing to be done about it at the moment," Asher said, his tone light and conversational, like he was just filling the silence. "We'll be able to be more proactive once we hear from the Balance. We can make plans then."

Blossom sighed again, "I know that, but we don't even know what's going on up there. We don't know what the Blossomites are doing, or if they're even still in the palace." He traced idle shapes in the water as he spoke, pulling his knees up to his chest.

Asher dug his fingers into his scalp before running his hands down the back of his neck and massaging out the tense knots in his shoulders, smiling as Blossom moaned quietly. "I think it's time we quizzed Emma again about the Blossomites and their beliefs. We've never really asked about them."

Blossom thought back to his conversation with Emma in the school a few months earlier. She'd been hiding the truth from him then as well, but it was possible that she would be more candid now. He pushed the thought away as he felt irritation growing in his gut again and turned so that he was looking at the prince. He gave Asher's knee a light tug and the prince followed the silent request, slipping further into the water.

"You're right, my love. We'll ask her when we're done here," he said, putting an end to the conversation as he climbed into Asher's lap and rocked against him.

Asher let out a gasp but gripped Blossom's waist with a grin. "I take it we're done talking for the time being," he said, smiling into the hungry kiss that Blossom pressed to his lips.

Blossom didn't respond verbally, just wrapped his arms around Asher's shoulders, deepening the kiss with a hum.

They exited the bathing room in their sleepwear sometime later, holding hands as they chatted quietly between themselves. Blossom looked over to the table where they had all eaten their meal to see Emma sat with her shoulders hunched, the subtle trembling to them giving away the fact that she was crying.

Blossom gave Asher's hand a squeeze and inclined his head towards his mother silently. Asher nodded his understanding and made his way back to their room, leaving Blossom and Emma alone.

He padded over to Emma, his bare feet making almost no noise on the stone floor. "Emma," he whispered, watching as Emma grew suddenly rigid, wiping her eyes before turning to him.

"Yes, Petal?" She asked, her voice quiet but surprisingly calm considering how red and puffy her eyes were.

Blossom bit down hard on his bottom lip to stop from crying himself, before flinging his arms around her shoulders. "I'm so sorry Emma. I shouldn't have snapped at you like that," he apologised, squeezing her harder as soon as Emma returned the embrace.

"And I'm sorry too, Petal. Sorry for keeping so many things from you. I swear it was only to protect you, but I understand how frustrating it must be."

Blossom pulled away from the hug only so that he could look Emma in the face, stroking his thumbs under her eyes and giving out pulses of Moon's blessing to sooth and repair the sore skin. "How about we promise not to keep secrets any longer?" He asked, tilting his head slightly, "and we talk to each other about what we're feeling."

"You've never been very good at hiding your feelings, Petal," Emma said with a quiet laugh, causing him to smile.

"Not from you I haven't. You're much better at it than me."

Emma looked away at the barbed comment but didn't argue. "You want to know the truth, Blossom?" She asked and he nodded, "the truth is that I'm terrified. I always knew this day would come. Ever since we found you, I knew it would lead to something like this, but now that it's happening, I feel so unprepared." She slumped back into her seat and looked down at her hands. "Do you want to know why I was so against you going to the king's library tonight?" She asked.

Blossom pulled one of the chairs around so that they could face each other, pressing their knees together to help keep them both grounded. "Yeah, you said I'm too important," he answered, his voice still holding a hint of exasperation.

Emma smiled at him and shook her head, her eyes once again growing watery. "No, that's not why. I mean yes, you are too important, but the real reason is there is quite a large chance that Edwin and Kara are going to be caught. It's hard enough reckoning with the fact that I might lose my brother and my wife tonight, I couldn't lose my son too."

Blossom groaned as the weight of that statement hit him. "I'm such an asshole."

"You're not an asshole, darling," Emma squeezed his knee. "You can be a bit hardheaded, but you are not an asshole."

9

Chapter 9

Asher walked back into the main chamber a little while later to see that Emma and Blossom were still sat in the same place, hands clasped between them, their heads bowed towards each other as they kept company in silence. "May I interrupt?" He asked as he drew close to them.

Emma smiled up at him, "of course, your majesty."

"Is my mother asleep?" He asked, taking a seat to Blossom's right.

"I think so, it's been a tiring day, and I doubt she would have had the strength to wait up till Kara and Edwin return."

"We should talk about something else while we wait, to keep our minds off it," Blossom said, like it had only just occurred to him, but Asher knew he had been waiting until they were both there to broach the topic of the Blossomites.

"That sounds like a good idea. I'm sure you still have a lot of questions. I'll answer what I can," Emma said, standing up, "but first I think we could all do with a hot drink. I'll make us some tea."

Asher bumped his shoulder against his husband's and took hold of his hand, "are you okay?" He asked. Blossom's emotions had evened out during his bath and the strong bundle of rage that had previously burned through their connection was gone, but there was still a faint undercurrent of something unpleasant. It felt more like sadness than anything else, a deep well of melancholy that Asher suspected had been there for a while.

"Yeah," Blossom responded, "it's just a lot." Asher hummed in agreement, just as Emma returned, carrying a tray laden with cups and a steaming teapot.

"Here we are. Now, what do you want to know?" Emma asked as she poured the tea.

"Can you tell us everything you know about the Blossomites?" Blossom asked, not bothering to beat around the bush.

"Edwin has been studying them since we found out about their existence, so he knows more than me, but I'll tell you what I can." Emma took a sip of tea, letting out a satisfied 'ahh' at the soothing warmth before continuing. "Now, as I'm sure you've guessed, Evelyn was the one who formally created the Blossomites, but most of their beliefs have roots in the common creation pact. They're mostly twisted versions of the deities' stories that you've both heard."

Asher watched Blossom nod out of the corner of his eye. Clearly the blesser didn't want to interrupt for fear of stopping the explanation. Asher knew of the creation pact, just like everyone in Vaten. Whilst the story varied slightly depending on the kingdom and who told it, it was a widely held belief that the Earth had been formed many centuries ago after some kind of cataclysm. Some said that the deities were the cause of the cataclysm, and it had simply been the release of their powers into the ether that resulted in the Earth as they now knew it, but Asher and by extension Blossom, had been taught that the cataclysm itself created the deities. A great burst of life and energy into the universe had resulted in the power that the deities controlled, and that they then gifted to the people who existed within their sphere.

Asher had never been fully convinced of the story. For one thing it didn't explain why some people weren't blessed, but mostly it seemed almost too clean. Personally, Asher believed that the universe, the world, and their place in it had all happened at random.

"Well, the Blossomites believe that before the world was created there was another world, one where everyone was blessed, not by one deity but by all of them." She gestured to Blossom, "they think that everyone was like you, Petal."

Blossom frowned in confusion but still didn't speak.

"And they believe this world formed because of a disaster in the previous world. That there was a curse that began to infect people, until one day the last unaffected person gathered as much blessing power as they could and destroyed everything. In doing so, they not only tore the world apart but the blessings themselves, the deities were then born as fragments of a whole." Asher felt Blossom's growing discomfort as Emma talked and tightened his grip on his hand. "They also think that your existence, Blossom, is the signal that this world, as it is, is also coming to an end. That it's a sign that the blessed should take charge and if they work hard enough, they can gain the ability to receive multiple blessings."

Blossom swallowed audibly, "let me guess, the way to do that is through suffering," he said. Emma didn't reply but Blossom knew the answer from the dampness in her eyes.

"That makes no sense," Asher said, exasperation clear on his face.

Emma shrugged, "the fact that it has never worked hasn't seemed to deter them, just caused them to amend their beliefs somewhat. Now it's thought that an event, such as the release of your curse, will cause a surge that will unlock their extra powers. It didn't stop them from abusing and torturing their children though."

Blossom thought back to little Aelius, to his belief that he could only serve Blossom if he had survived the horror of forced blessing transference. The belief that Blossom wanted all blessed to serve him in the first place was ludicrous, but the idea that he wanted their pain was even worse. He sighed and was about to speak again when a hidden doorway slid open to reveal Kara and Edwin. Panting, they stumbled out of the tunnel and dropped two sacks filled to bursting with paper and books onto the floor.

"The castle is crawling," Kara said, brushing herself off and wiping at a smear of dirt on her cheek. "I'm surprised we managed to get so far undetected, but it was a close call."

All three of them rushed over to the two tired and sweaty adventurers, Emma pulling Edwin into a hug before kissing her wife in relief.

"You made it to the library," Blossom said, crouching by one of the sacks and looking back up at them like he was asking for permission to look through them.

Kara nodded, "yeah, that was the easy bit actually. The King's chambers were deserted, I don't think anyone's been in there since the morning of your wedding."

"I'm not sure if Silas had been sleeping in there either actually, the amount of dust and cobwebs was alarming," Edwin added, hefting a sack onto a nearby table. "We grabbed as much as we could but there's still a lot up there," he explained as he began pulling various pieces of paper out, laying them in seemingly random piles.

"Now that you mention it, I think my father once said those rooms reminded him too much of my mother. I never guessed that he'd stopped using them altogether though," Asher said quietly, and Blossom wrapped an arm around his shoulders to try and quell the sadness flowing through their bond.

"What is all this?" Blossom asked, picking up a book with unfamiliar letters etched into its cover.

"What it is, is something that can wait until tomorrow," Emma said definitively, taking the book from him and placing it back on the table, "we should all rest now."

Blossom huffed but didn't argue, even if he did slip one of the sheets of paper into the pocket of his night shirt before they returned to their rooms.

"What did you just steal?" Asher asked once they were alone.

Blossom pulled the parchment back out and looked at the writing, frowning when he realised he had no idea what it said. "Nothing useful," he muttered, handing it to the prince when he held out his hand for it.

"This is Shotsa," Asher said.

"You can read it?" Blossom asked in surprise.

"I can," Asher replied with a smile, "why do you seem so shocked? I didn't spend all my time sparring and mooning over you."

Blossom laughed and stepped closer, kissing the prince sweetly. "Just most of the time," he said, smiling up at him.

"Just most of the time," Asher agreed.

Blossom rested his head against Asher's shoulder, looking at the paper still clasped in the prince's hand. "So, what does it say?"

"It says 'can wait until tomorrow'," Asher replied, causing Blossom to groan. "Emma's right, Flower. We should sleep. You can spend all day tomorrow reading if you like."

"Not all day," Blossom responded, poking Asher in the stomach, "we've got to do more blessing lessons as well."

It was Asher's turn to groan. "Fine," He groused, "but sleep now, yeah?"

Blossom nodded and they both climbed into the bed, laying close together as Blossom extinguished the torches with a wave of his hand. "We could sleep, or we could do something a little more fun," he whispered against Asher's cheek, smiling when the prince turned to him and grabbed the hand he'd been trailing lower as he spoke.

"You're insatiable," the prince said, but his tone was light as he rolled so that his body was blanketing the blesser.

"If this was our marriage tour, would we be doing any different?" Blossom asked, running his fingers through the prince's soft hair. The answer to his question came in the form of a kiss that left him breathless and even more eager than before.

10

Chapter 10

Everyone else was already eating breakfast by the time the boys emerged the next morning. Emma and Kara were chatting quietly between mouthfuls of food. Edwin was already reading one of the books they'd stolen yesterday, and Queen Lila looked more exhausted than Blossom could ever remember seeing her. It was then he realised that due to the commotion caused by Asher's power and the plan to infiltrate the library, he'd completely forgotten about his promise to help soothe her.

"Good morning, Your Majesty," he said, sitting in the unoccupied chair to her right and smiling briefly at Asher as he pushed a bowl full of chopped fruit in front of him.

"Lila please," Lila responded with a tired smile, "and good morning to you, darling boy."

"After we've eaten will you allow me to soothe you? I replenished my stores of Water's blessing last night and you seem more worn than ever."

Lila smiled wider and squeezed his hand in answer. They ate breakfast mostly in silence and Blossom was surprised to find that he had no

73

trouble eating, in fact he was ravenous. It was after he'd devoured his second bowl of fruit and a few slices of toasted bread that he followed Lila back to her room. Asher accompanied them to help Blossom lift the queen onto her bed but left to give them some privacy soon after that.

"These last few days have been more trying than I thought," Lila sighed, closing her eyes as Blossom ran his hands down her right arm, soothing the sore muscles with gentle pulses of Water's blessing before doing the same with her left. "Aside from weekly visits from Emma I don't remember the last time I was around people for this long. It's surprisingly tiring when you are not used to it," she continued as Blossom moved to her torso, pressing his hands to the soft skin of her abdomen.

"I think Asher takes after you in that regard. There have been times in the past where he couldn't stand the clamour of court, and not just because the nobles are all loud and spoiled."

Lila laughed at his words, the sound peeling off into a hiss as Blossom finally moved to her legs.

"Sorry," he said, wincing in sympathy, "the muscles here are very tense, it will hurt a bit, but not for much longer." He kept the flow of Water's blessing strong and consistent as he returned to their previous topic, trying to distract the queen with chatter as he found a particularly hard knot. "I also didn't enjoy court all that much, but I think people tire Asher out, even those he wants to be around."

"You don't feel the same way?" Lila asked, her brow slowly smoothing out as her legs relaxed.

"No," Blossom said with a smile, "it depends on the people, but I feel more energised when I'm with others. For example, when school is in session. I'm always happiest when the children are there." He gently placed Lila's left leg back on the covers. "I don't do well on my own," he said, his voice dropping to a whisper.

Lila opened her eyes and looked over at him. "Were you often left alone?" She asked, "I know Silas tried to keep you and Asher apart by sending him to the barracks and out with his knights, but you were never truly alone, were you?"

Blossom could feel tears pricking at the backs of his eyes and took a few deep breaths. Water's blessing often broke down emotional barriers and his old hurts were using this to their advantage. "I often felt like I was," he said, "treated like a curiosity by the nobles and other unblessed, or like some king or higher being from older blessed. It was only Asher and the children that treated me like a normal person. Oh, and Emma as well, even if she mostly treated me like a naughty child."

Lila pushed herself into a sitting position and held out a hand, which Blossom took. "I am sorry you felt that way, my dear. I'm sorry for so many things really, but I will admit this, I am not sorry you were bought to the palace."

Blossom tilted his head in question.

"I'm not sorry because it meant my son got to grow up. He got to grow into the wonderful man that he is today. He got to grow up alongside someone he loved, someone who loved him back. And you got to grow into the person you are. You got to help so many young blessed learn how to harness their powers, how to use it with kindness and for the good of all of those around them."

Lila took a deep breath, squeezing at the hand in her grip. "Before you were born, Blossom, the blessed were treated very differently from how they are now. Oftentimes the poorer blessed were sold to rich families who used their powers for their own gains, and most rich born blessed used their powers not for the good of their community but for their own selfish desires."

Blossom felt the food he'd eaten suddenly sit uncomfortably in his gut. He remembered the conversation he'd had with Silas about the little Sun blessed girl in the meadow. His obvious disdain for the idea that she should be taught in his school because she was poor, and because she would only use her power to help her family.

"Did Silas agree with the way things used to be?" He asked and Lila looked away from him, which was answer enough. He let out a bitter laugh. "No wonder he saw nothing wrong with trapping Asher's power when it was inconvenient for him, or in stealing blessed children for his own gain." He sat down on the queen's bed, his back turned to her as he stared at the wall. "I just don't understand how someone can view another person as an object to be used," he looked back at her, "and he was blessed too, surely that would have given him some sympathy when it came to other blessed."

Lila squeezed his arm, her eyes mirroring the sorrow that Blossom felt. "I think that when you are raised in a place like the royal palace, when you are told that you are better than everyone else, as he was, it would be very easy to view people who are not at your level as something close to a different species. As something not quite human. It's one of the reasons why I was always so adamant that Asher mix with regular soldiers when he entered the army, not just other knights."

They sat in silence for a while before Blossom heaved another sigh and stood back up. "So do you want me to help you back into your chair or do you think that one session was enough for you to walk again?" He asked, his tone light despite knowing that after so many years it would take quite a while before Lila could walk again.

Lila smiled at him and swung her legs over the side of the bed, pulling her chair towards her and sliding into it with practiced ease. "You are powerful, my dear, but not that powerful," she said as they left her room.

Blossom joined Edwin and Asher where they were crowded around a paper strewn table. "You've been roped into this as well, Ash?" He asked, resting a hand on the prince's shoulder, and looking at the open notebook slowly filling with Asher's messy scrawl.

Asher huffed and flexed his writing hand like he was working out a cramp. "Yeah, apparently I'm the only one here that can read Shotsa so I've been tasked with translating. I feel like I'm back in school." He groused, watching as Blossom took hold of his hand and pulsed Water's blessing through the tight tendons.

"And if you weren't doing this then you'd be complaining about being bored," Blossom said as he sat down, smirking as Asher stuck his tongue out at him. "We'll do real lessons after lunch," he added, grabbing the closest book, and pulling it towards him, disregarding it when he realised he couldn't read it.

"I've split them by language, Your Highness. This is the pile in Vaten." Edwin gestured to a stack by his left elbow just as Asher groaned at Blossom's last statement, dropping his head on the table.

"Thank you, Edwin," Blossom said, reaching forward to take a stack of paper but freezing when he realised what he'd said. "Wait, what did you call me?"

"Your Highness," Edwin replied, blinking owlishly at him. "Now that you and the prince are married you are royalty too. I can go back to calling you Master Blossom if you wish."

Blossom blinked rapidly as that thought sunk in. "I'm..." He trailed off, staring into the middle distance.

"A prince," Asher finished for him, lifting his head, and resting his chin on his hand. "Didn't you realise, Flower? You're royalty now."

Blossom opened his mouth to respond but couldn't think of what to say. After a moment he turned back to Edwin and cleared his throat. "As you're my uncle I think just Blossom would be better," he said finally.

Edwin smiled shyly at him and returned to his book with a small nod. They fell into a studious silence, broken only when one of them found something of interest or when Emma interrupted with tea or coffee. Blossom's original pile of paper appeared to be a collection of Vaten fables, most of which he was familiar with, even if the tone and a few of the specifics were different. The fables he was reading were far darker than the ones he remembered hearing as a child, often ending in death or bloody wars.

He gave them up as not that important and moved on to a leather-bound book with no title. As soon as he opened it Blossom discovered that it was a journal of some sort, and after reading a few lines he also realised it had been written by Silas. He looked at the date on the first page and did some mental arithmetic. This journal had been started two years before he and Asher were born, or found would probably be a better description. It was that thought that sparked another, his and Asher's birthday may no longer be accurate. There was also no way of knowing if he and Asher even shared a birthday anymore.

He pushed the thought away. It wasn't important in the grand scheme of things. They were close enough in age that there would be no point in focusing on it now. He returned his attention to the journal and read the first entry, trying to ignore the similarities between Asher's handwriting and Silas'.

∞

12th day of the Harvest Moon, 10th year of my reign

Lila has told me all she can about the location of the Blessers' isle, but she has never seen it herself, and so I only have vague directions and descriptions to help me. I have narrowed it down to a few places and will go through them one by one. I'm using the expansion of Vaten's borders as cover and so we will push into the weaker countries first.

Blossom turned the page, it was just as Lila had said, Silas had been searching for the source, had begun a crusade because of it. The second page was dated 3 weeks after the first and written in a different pen, the ink of lower quality and the page smudged with dirt.

1st day of the Rising Winter Moon, 10th year of my reign

The first two boundaries were a bust, but the men are happy as we have been victorious in battle. They have been celebrating long into the night with stolen ale and conquered bedwarmers. If I was not so focused on the next push, I would join them. The island is close, I can almost taste it, there is a power in the air that must come from it. We are near the Castillan border and plan on crossing into their lands through the valley where all four kingdoms meet. If there is any place where the island should be it will be there. Now, perhaps I should join in with the revelry, it would be good for the men to see their king in high spirits.

Blossom felt a sourness in his stomach that only grew the longer he read. The way Silas spoke of people as though they were simply the spoils of war made him feel sick, and he was surprised by how shocked he was. Silas had never failed to make Blossom feel like an object so why should he have viewed others any differently?

5th day of the Rising Winter Moon, 10th year of my reign

It was as I thought, the island is at the crossroads of the four kingdoms. The men refused to go near it, saying the shroud of shadow bathing the lake was a bad omen. I allowed them to camp on Vaten territory over the crest of a hill, better that I alone approach the island. I would not want to have to battle with my own men for the power that resides there. I will go tonight. I have ordered a cease in the drinking and cavorting under the guise that I want my men levelheaded and rested before the push into Castilla but truthfully, I wish them asleep before I go.

The next entry was only a day later, and Blossom felt his heart speeding up. He already had answers to so many questions and only hoped he would get more as he read.

6th day of the Rising Winter Moon, 10th year of my reign

I did not reach the island, the shadow is not just a fog, it is a barrier. My foot would not leave the shore no matter where around the lake I tried. However, the night was not lost. I stumbled upon something that I had not prepared for. At the shoreline I found two infants, they could scarcely have been more than an hour old and despite the chill in the air they were not crying. I thought them dead at first but then one of them moved, stretching his arm as though reaching for the other. They looked to be the same age but could not have been related as one had the strong pale skin of my people, whilst the other had the bronzed tan of our Castillan enemies. I had just reached for the Vaten child when I heard a noise and looked up to see a Castillan woman approaching. I recognised the sigil of the Balance on her tunic from the one that Lila had shown me and quickly spoke the word that would show me as a friend. Her guard was instantly lowered, and she turned her attention to the children. I had been planning on the best way to kill her without making too much noise when she said something that caught me off guard.

"It seems the Blessers have given us both a gift." I was unsure what she meant but then she gestured to each child. "A child of my ancestors and one of yours. I am sure that they will each grow to be powerful if we accept the trial the Blessers have given us, though I know not which deities have given them their colours."

I too was unsure of the meaning of the Castillan child's pink hair and eyes, but my gift carried Shadow's colour. I didn't think it wise to enlighten the woman of this, very few people have read the old stories and even fewer believe in the lost deity. So, I simply wrapped my prize in my cloak and bid her farewell. However, I soon realised she was following me and had left the other child on the lakeshore. When I pointed this out, she told me her brother and sister were on patrol that night and that it would be better if they found the child as she was not supposed to be out. She also said something I found quite cruel, that the child would be made stronger for the suffering he would endure on the cold ground. Whilst I do believe that a firm hand is needed with children, that did seem unnecessary.

She asked to accompany me and misunderstanding her meaning I took her to my tent. She did not resist my attempt to bed her, only told me afterwards that she genuinely just wanted to talk.

11

Chapter 11

Blossom had to take a break from reading, he wasn't at the end of the entry but the image of Silas and Evelyn lying together had seared itself into his mind so strongly he couldn't focus on the important aspects of the diary. He placed a smaller sheet of paper between the pages to keep his place before excusing himself to the bathroom. He wasn't there for very long before Asher joined him.

"What's the matter, Flower?" He asked as Blossom splashed cold water on his face.

"Silas and Evelyn fucked," he said bluntly, almost laughing at the dumbstruck look on the prince's face.

"Beg your pardon?" He asked, his voice coming out slightly squeaky.

"They fucked. Silas found the island the night we were born. We were together on the shore and Evelyn found us too. She said that Silas should take you and that she should take me and then they...you know," he waved his hand vaguely in the air.

Asher blinked rapidly as he tried to comprehend the information being thrown at him. "How...? What...? Okay I have a lot of questions," he said finally, and Blossom laughed, a hint of mania in the sound.

"Yeah, me too," he responded, "I've found his journal. One he kept whilst looking for the island. It's...there's a lot going on in it, but it might just be the most useful thing we've got."

Asher nodded slowly, his nose crinkling in disgust. "Please tell me it didn't go into detail."

"It hasn't so far, but I stopped reading when I got to that part." He shivered and the movement reminded him of the fact that, at the point in the journal he'd gotten to, his newborn self had been left cold and naked by the water's edge. "Come on," he said, taking Asher's hand and leading him back into the hall. "This is the closest we've gotten to knowing where we came from."

He picked up the journal and was about to sit back down again when he realised everyone in their little group needed to know the information that lay between its pages. "Everyone," he raised his voice loud enough that it echoed slightly, waiting until all eyes were on him before speaking again, "I've found something that I think we all need to hear."

Emma and Kara looked at each other quizzically before wandering over to the table and taking the last two unoccupied seats. Queen Lila joined them a moment later, after tidying away whatever it was she had been tinkering with.

"This is a journal written by Silas. It starts during his campaign to find the island. I've read a few pages, but I think I should start from the beginning and read aloud so that you can all hear it." Blossom glanced over at Lila. "I'm afraid some of it may be uncomfortable," he warned and Lila looked back at him steadily.

"If you think I don't know what my husband got up to with other women whilst he was on crusade, then you are wrong."

He swallowed the bile that filled his throat and opened the journal, stopping when Asher placed a hand on top of his. He looked up at the prince, eyebrows raised in question.

"I know it's not the most important thing right now, but I want you to know that I have never and will never lay with someone else."

Blossom smiled at him, "I know, my love," he said simply. He didn't need the reassurance, he'd never worried that Asher might have been unfaithful to him, but he appreciated it, nonetheless. He returned to the book and read the passages he already knew, stopping only when he got to the part that he had abandoned beforehand. He looked up to gauge the feeling in the room. Emma and Edwin both looked furious.

"I knew it," Edwin spat, his face red. Blossom had never seen the quiet man so angry before, he'd almost thought Edwin incapable of such intense emotions. "I knew she was doing something that night. She claimed that she'd been in the library studying for her advanced protector exam, but she was out doing this shit."

"Advanced protector?" Asher asked.

"It's one of the highest levels within the Balance, the last step before becoming an Elder. Emma and I had both sat the exam the year before which was why we were out on patrol that night. Normally only protectors or guardians are allowed to travel to the island fortress, it's why the queen had never been there. The Elders waved that rule for us because we had always been a tight knit family and we were 3rd generation within the Balance, so Evelyn was allowed to come with us under the proviso that she also take one of the exams as soon as possible."

"Did she ever become an advanced protector?" Blossom asked, breathing a sigh of relief when Edwin shook his head. He could only imagine the sensitive information she would have been privy too if she had.

"She ran away with you before she sat the exam."

Blossom cleared his throat and returned to the journal, picking up where he left off.

∞

7ʰ day of the Rising Winter Moon, 10ᵗʰ year of my reign

It turns out the woman, Evelyn, knows some of the old stories, but not enough to know that the child that sleeps in my tent is the first Shadow child to be born in centuries. She believes in the resurrection of the old world and hopes that these children will bring it about. I agree with her, I do think these children may be the start of another cataclysm, but unlike her, I plan on stopping it. I will use the Shadow child to secure my place at the top of this world. If the Castillan infant is another blessed child, it will be for the best that they are kept apart. The separation of the blessed into their individual deities was what caused the last cataclysm, hopefully the separation of these two will prevent the next one.

Blossom took a breath and turned the page, pausing again to look up.

"So, Silas was a Blossomite," Kara said, her eyebrows creased in confusion.

"In a sense," Lila added, "it looks like he believed the same things but wanted to subvert them."

"He kept us separate because he wanted to stop the end of the world," Asher said in disbelief, "but we've been together for 13 years, he couldn't still think that, right?"

Blossom wasn't convinced. "After I released your power he said, 'look what you've done'. I think he believed it till the very end."

"But he said he wanted to 'use' my power, so why did he block it?"

"I imagine it was because he couldn't control it. Although we might find the answer in here." Blossom looked around at each person in turn. "Do you want me to go on?" He asked, turning back to the page when everyone nodded.

10th day of the Rising Winter Moon, 10th year of my reign

This child is impossible. I have left the army to return to the palace and he has not stopped squalling since we left the valley. My head is splitting, and I can still hear him crying from my tent. I have picked up a wetnurse to feed and look after him during the trip back, but that has done little to quiet him. I will have to kill her once we are back within the royal ring and hire another, I cannot have anyone knowing where the child has come from. He will be the miracle child born of my wife. Lila will agree to it I'm sure, she has craved a child for so long and she is loyal to me. That, of course, is if I make it back to the palace without murdering the child. He has yet to show any signs of calling his blessing but that is not worrying, he is only 4 days old after all and I did not receive blessing until I was several months old.

Asher was chuckling at the entry but there was a dark undertone to it. "Nice to see that I tried him right from the off," he said, and Blossom smiled at him.

"I imagine you were pining for Blossom," Emma said causing both boys turned to her. "Blossom was much the same, he cried almost constantly for the first week after we found him. If you two are as closely connected as you seem to be, I imagine you were feeling each other's emotions and loss. I wonder now if the bond you had was broken through distance. You stopped crying around the time that Silas announced the birth of his child."

It made sense to Blossom, it probably also explained why they had connected so quickly when they were reunited. "Did he really kill the wet nurse do you think?"

"He didn't arrive at the palace with one," Lila said by way of answer.

14th day of the Rising Winter Moon, 11th year of my reign

The child has finally stopped crying. Almost the second we crossed through the inner ring he fell into a deep sleep and only awoke again this morning. Lila has refused to relinquish the child since I handed him to her, he has slept with her in her bed, and she has named him. I will announce the arrival of Prince Asher to the kingdom at the end of the week.

1st day of the Midwinter Moon, 11th year of my reign

Asher has finally received blessing, thankfully it happened during my time alone with him. I asked Lila to allow me to be alone with the child for two hours per day, so that I can form a paternal 'bond' with him. I have been stimulating the blessing pathways in his little body with Fire's blessing during this time. I know that it hurts him, but Shadow is the blessing of defense, so pain is probably the best way to spark it. Maybe that woman, Evelyn, was onto something. Maybe suffering is the way forward. A dark plume of Shadow oozed from him today and it was only from my quick reaction that I didn't succumb to its power. I will need to train him strictly to ensure that he doesn't use this blessing against me in the future.

"The next one is three months later," Blossom said as he turned the page, running his finger over what looked like a blood stain.

"I imagine that this was around the time the death mark appeared," Lila responded, and Blossom made a noise of agreement because from a quick scan of the page he could see she was right.

5th day of the Renewal Moon, 11th year of my reign

I have had to resort to extreme measures. The child's power is uncontrollable, and it is hard to even get close to him. Thankfully the Shadow has yet to reveal itself to anyone but me and so, until he is old enough for logical thought and can be trained properly, I have sealed his power within him. The old stories told of where Shadow's blessing resides in the body, at the top of the spine, and so I have cauterized that place. The boy squalled so loudly that he attracted Lila's attention but thankfully I already had a lie in place to explain his new scar. The Moon blessed healer soothed the boy but as he did not know what I had done the seal held. I will endeavor to learn how to reverse this act when he is older.

1st day of the Solstice Moon, 11th year of my reign

An unforeseen hurdle has appeared to thwart my plan. By sealing his power, I have inadvertently caused a build-up of blessing energy in the boy. It is starting to affect his health, and a black mark has appeared on his neck. I now wonder if death marks have always been a result of people being Shadow blessed. Maybe they were simply unfit to carry Shadow's power and therefore it ate them alive. Either way I have tried to reverse the cauterization but have so far been unsuccessful. Lila has asked that we try other blessed, maybe one of the lesser blessings can help. I have my doubts but will announce the request to the kingdom tomorrow.

5th day of the Harvest Moon, 11th year of my reign

Nothing has worked and the boy grows weaker and more sickly by the day, I fear he will die before I can make use of his powers if we are not successful soon. It has begun to occur to me that perhaps I was too hasty in leaving the other child with that woman. I will wait one more month and then under the guise of finding more blessed will return to the island.

5th day of the Rising Winter Moon, 11th year of my reign

The neighboring kingdoms have been sending their blessed to help the boy, but nothing is working. I am now convinced the pink haired child is the only thing that can save him. Thankfully the Castillan barbarians have refused to help so I now have the perfect excuse to force their borders. I have begun to bolster the army, and they are excited to be in the field again. We will raid multiple villages at once to further seal the lie.

Blossom felt a sigh escape him and rubbed at his eyes. "So, the raids were always a lie. They never had an actual point." He looked over at Asher to see the prince frowning down at his hands and Blossom could feel a confused melancholy permeating from him. "Ash?"

"Did he ever love me?" Asher asked, his words barely more than a whisper, "or was I only ever a tool for him?" The prince looked up at his mother who smiled at him, her eyes watery with unshed tears. "He's referenced me by name once so far. It's just boy or child every other time."

"I think he did that to remain separate. He never used my name either," Blossom said, knowing it probably wasn't all that helpful.

Lila didn't say anything for a long while. "He was frantic trying to find a cure for you Asher, it couldn't have just been because of your power. He must have loved you in his own way," she said, but she didn't sound sure.

"Do you want me to continue? I could stop for now if you want. We could try some blessing lessons again."

Asher nodded wordlessly and pushed himself to his feet, striding over to the edge of the cavern where they'd sat yesterday, resuming the same position. Blossom closed the journal and placed it back on the table. He felt Emma squeeze his shoulder and looked over at her. "I feel like I should be more surprised at how cold he was, but I'm not," he said, keeping his voice low so it wouldn't carry to where Asher sat. "This is the Silas that I knew, and for so long I wanted everyone else to see him for what he was but..." He trailed off, once again looking over to the prince.

Emma pulled her chair closer and slid her hand down his arm until it rested on his knee. "I know how you feel, Petal. There were so many years when I yearned to tell you the truth about Evelyn, but when you finally found out about her, I hated every second that I'd spent hoping for it. It's never nice to see a loved one hurting, even if it's because of a truth that hurt you in the past." She pushed gently at his knee and inclined her head towards Asher. "Go and be with him. He's strong, he'll get over this, but it will be easier if you're there."

Blossom pressed a kiss to the top of his mother's head and rose to join his husband.

<h1 style="text-align:center">12</h1>

Chapter 12

Asher made more progress this time around, and after what felt like only a few hours he was able to call a small amount of Shadow's blessing to his hand. He was not yet able to wield it the way other blessers did, but it was a start.

"Well done, my love," Blossom said with genuine pride, taking hold of the prince's hand as soon as the shadow dissipated.

"It's something I guess," Asher replied grumpily, closing his hand, and calling his blessing again. "Not sure what it's good for at the moment though."

"We'll find out soon enough, I'm sure. Silas kept referencing the old stories, if they talk of Shadow's blessing then I'm sure they say what it can be used for."

Asher leant back on his hands, stretching his legs out in front of him with a wince. He pressed his foot against Blossom's knee. "Do you think that if I could have controlled it, he would have loved me?" He asked, his voice deliberately devoid of emotion as he looked down at where his boot rested against the pale material of Blossom's robe.

Blossom took hold of the toe of his boot and pulled gently, resting his leg on his lap. "My darling prince, he refused to let me release your power, knowing full well that it would have healed you. There is nothing you could have done to make a man with no heart love you."

He felt Asher's emotions retreating again and pushed his affection through their bond to compensate. Asher smiled back at him, and Blossom could see the odd disappearance of light in his eyes that he was slowly becoming accustomed too. He couldn't help but chuckle, causing Asher's brows to furrow in confusion. "You're using your blessing now, my love," he said, which did nothing for Asher's confusion. "You've been using it internally for a long time I'd wager. The blessing of protection has been shrouding your painful emotions to stop them hurting you. Can I try something?" He asked, holding out a hand.

Asher sat forward and placed his hand in the blesser's open palm. Blossom pinched at the sensitive skin of his inner wrist, keeping hold of his hand when the prince tried to move away. The blackness of Shadow's blessing surged to the surface and still Blossom held onto him.

"Blossom let go, you know that I can't control it yet," he cried but Blossom shushed him, watching as the mist like substance curled up his own wrist.

He felt it wrap around him, the sensation strangely solid, and they both watched as it pulled his arm away from Asher before releasing him and disappearing back into Asher's skin. He grinned at the stunned prince. "Just as I thought, Shadow's blessing isn't inherently harmful. I imagine it was a mixture of build-up and your anger at what Silas was doing that caused such a strong reaction the first time. I'm sure you won't be able to release a lethal dose again unless you really want to."

Asher looked from his hand to Blossom and back again. "I thought you didn't know anything about this blessing," he said, and Blossom shrugged.

"I don't know about this specific blessing, but I've been around the children of the other deities long enough to make some educated guesses. You've been doing the same, we can guess that this is a hard blessing, so I'm betting it means that you will be able to make solid formations when you can produce more physical shadows. You might be able to form a shield of some kind, like the walls that the Earth blessed soldiers make on the battlefield."

Asher rubbed at the skin on his wrist in thought, still pouting slightly at the sting of it. "You're being surprisingly chipper today, Flower. About this whole thing."

"You say that like I'm not normally chipper," Blossom responded, smiling when Asher nudged him with his foot.

"You know what I mean."

"Well, what else can I do? We're learning important information here. It may not be pleasant but it's a step in the right direction, and it's better than sitting here twiddling our thumbs."

Asher suddenly flopped backwards onto the ground, covering his face with his hands, and letting out a groan. It caused a brief flash of memory to cross Blossom's mind, of a young Asher doing something very similar when he was tired or bored during their lessons.

"Do you want to keep going or take a break?" Blossom asked, he wasn't going to push the prince to keep practicing today. He could tell that Asher wasn't in the right mindset for too much right now, and truthfully, he felt exhausted, like he'd been concentrating for a lot longer than the few hours they'd sat there.

"No. I think we should get the journal reading over with, no point in stringing it out," Asher said with a huff, sitting back up.

Blossom stood with a nod, leaning down to help the prince to his feet. As they made their way back over to the document-laden table it became clear that none of the others had moved, doggedly continuing to churn through the documents. They had made a surprising amount of progress, the 'read' pile now much higher than the 'to read' pile. Blossom had known that Edwin was a fast reader, but this seemed like a lot to have gotten through in only a few hours.

The journal, however, remained untouched where Blossom had left it. As he sat back down Edwin smiled up at him and pointed to the little leather book.

"Why don't you continue to read and let us know of any important passages, Master Blossom?"

"Are you two hungry?" Emma interrupted, a worried look on her face that puzzled Blossom. "I can make you something to eat whilst you read. You were practicing for quite some time."

Blossom could feel Asher's confusion mixing with his own as he looked back to where they had sat. Sure, they had been practicing for a while, but nothing close to the full school days that Blossom was used to.

"Uh sure, thank you Emma," Asher said by way of reply, and Blossom nodded, despite not feeling overly hungry himself.

Blossom felt Asher pull his chair close to him and glanced out of the corner of his eye to see the prince peering over his shoulder. He opened the journal to the last page he'd read and tilted it so that the prince could read as well.

15ʰ day of the New Year's Moon, 12ʰ year of my reign

The woman is no longer in the valley. I shouldn't be that surprised but unfortunately none of the Balance members seem to know where she has gone either. Apparently, she absconded with the child only weeks after I found them. The Balance are more wary of those they do not know this time around and it is hard to get any information from them. Or perhaps this is what high-level members have always been like, and it was only a stroke of luck that Lila was so trusting. I have no idea where to even begin my search for Evelyn and the child. The only thing I can be sure of is that she must be within the Castillan borders. I cannot rely on witness accounts as I'm sure she must have hidden the child from sight. We would have heard tell of a boy with such unusual colouring before now if she was out in the open. I think it best to focus on isolated farmhouses. I may form a contingent of trusted men, three at the most, under the guise of an infiltration unit and begin raiding in earnest.

Blossom checked that Asher had finished reading the passage before turning the page. This one was dated five months later.

18th day of the Lambing Moon, 12th year of my reign

No luck so far, but that is to be expected. Castilla is about three times the size of Vaten and most of it is unmapped farmland, so there is no shortage of isolated cottages. The army has wholeheartedly embraced the lust for blood, and I have engaged a well sought after propagandist to inspire more young people to join the fight. I will take this as an opportunity to mount a full invasion, no point in wasting a good siege.

Blossom paused; his thumb poised to flip to the next page. "He speaks of war so casually," he said, turning to Asher, who was frowning so deeply that Blossom would be surprised if he didn't leave this place with a permanent crease between his brows.

"I knew he was war hungry; he never hid that from me. I think he hoped that I would grow to be just as blood thirsty, but there's something about watching a person lose their life before your eyes, or by your hand, that always feels wrong. I never understood how he could crave it so much."

Blossom placed the book on his lap and squeezed his husband's hand, he had never asked Asher about the battles he'd been in. He'd tried hard not to think of his gentle prince ending someone's life. Blossom felt a wash of guilt at the thought that he had willfully ignored a part of the prince's life that may have caused Asher pain, and all simply because he himself found it hard to deal with. He felt Asher's grip on his hand tighten and leant forward until their foreheads touched.

"It's not something you have done, Flower. Why should you feel guilty?"

"Because I should have been a support for you, someone you could come to if you needed to unburden yourself."

Asher smiled at him, rubbing against his forehead like a cat. "We were together so rarely that I didn't want to sour that precious time with talk of battle and death," he reassured him.

Blossom hummed and turned back to the journal. "Let's skip ahead, I doubt there will be much of interest in the next few entries, we know he didn't find me for several years."

Asher halted him with a disagreeing noise. "There might still be important information. We should skim it at least."

The next few passages did not yield much and in fact seemed to skip large chunks of time. Silas returned every few months to the palace to check on Asher and there was a passing remark about him being stable but weak, practically comatose for long stretches of time. The journal's largest time skip was three years, leading to the time where both Blossom and Asher were five years old.

4th day of the Solstice Moon, 15th year of my reign

I have found a lead on where the child may be. This morning we entered a small village in the mountains that appears to be unaware of the war be-

tween Vaten and Castilla. This has resulted in a warmer welcome than we have been used to, we took full advantage and have experienced the luxury of sleeping in real beds for the first time in months. Whilst we were enjoying a good hearty meal, I overheard some locals talking about 'that woman with the demon child'. After enquiring further, it was revealed that there is a woman and small boy living over the mountain. The woman sometimes visits the village to gather supplies but never brings the child. Apparently, he has a strange air and colour to him. I am now convinced that this is Evelyn and the pink-haired child.

"This can't be about you though, can it? He didn't find you for three more years," Asher said, his question causing the others around the table to look up.

Blossom shook his head, silently stating his own confusion. He turned to the next entry, dated two days later and began to read aloud again.

6th day of the Solstice Moon, 15th year of my reign

We have summited the mountain and have an almost perfect vantage point to watch the isolated cottage unseen. So far, I have seen Evelyn returning to the house but no sign of the child, we will wait until he comes into the open to confirm but she would not have let him go easily. He is in the cottage, and we will take him.

8th day of the Solstice Moon, 15th year of my reign

I had my first sighting of the child, that pink hair is easy to spot, and we witnessed him receiving Sun's blessing. There is a wildflower meadow between us and the cottage where he appears to play. What has astounded me is that not an hour after receiving Sun's blessing he made his way to the stream on the west side of the meadow and received Water's blessing as well. That may explain the unusual colouration. He can receive multiple blessings, I am yet unsure how many, but it is possible this child is the beginning of the return to the old world. That mixed with my own Shadow child does inspire an awe that disturbs me. I will still take this child back to the palace but there is a feeling in my gut which tells me that he and the prince should not be allowed to remain together for long. I must make plans on how to use this child to keep my son alive, but I am now hesitant to unlock his Shadow gift.

9th day of the Solstice Moon, 15th year of my reign

We have claimed the child, that woman named him Blossom which is one of the most ridiculous things I've ever heard, but these Castillans have odd naming conventions. Like the need for twins and triplets to have names that start with the same letter. Either way Evelyn gave him up surprisingly easily and disappeared off into the mountains before I had a chance to kill her. I wonder if she had a plan and wanted me to take him, but it aligns with my own plans so as long as I remain vigilant, I'm sure I will be able to stay ahead of her.

The child is odd, he's surprisingly trusting for someone who has been so sheltered, but he also seems to have trouble remembering things. He has been having nightmares about his mother but when he wakes, he doesn't seem to remember that I was the one who stole him. I will be using this to my advantage, but first I need to see how far this memory problem goes. We will take a leisurely path back to the palace and I will use it as an opportunity to test him and his powers.

"I don't remember you having memory problems when you were young," Emma said, and Blossom couldn't help but smile at her accidental joke. She sighed good naturedly before continuing, "in fact, I remember you having a very good memory. You've always been very good at absorbing and retaining information."

Blossom shrugged, "I don't remember much of my childhood, actually the only thing I remember before coming to the palace was being taken, but like Silas said, I didn't know it was him." He thought back to the nightmare he'd had before the wedding, the fact that the king had replaced the unknown soldier. "I've never really questioned it. I guess I thought that it was because I was young. I mean you don't remember much from before I was with you, do you?" He asked, turning to Asher as he spoke.

Asher shook his head. "No, but all I remember was pain, so I figured that I was just too ill to remember much more."

Blossom hummed and returned to the journal.

11th day of the Solstice Moon, 15th year of my reign

I'm not sure what Evelyn has done to this child, but he appears to believe that he will be punished if he uses his blessings in front of people. When I ask him to show me, he is more than willing but if I catch him using Sun's blessing to grow flowers he cowers as though I will strike him.

5th day of the Red Moon, 15th year of my reign

We have reached the palace. We arrived during nightfall, and I smuggled the child past my wife and into my son's room. Already he seems better, but I had to restrain the over-blessed child from touching Asher or from using his blessings to heal him. Hopefully their simple proximity will allow him to heal. I have hidden the child in my library and have made a bed for him to sleep in. I have instructed him to remain quiet, but he still wakes shouting in fear. Thank-

fully the library is mostly soundproof and what little noise comes through I have convinced Lila originates from Asher.

"You were in the palace for three years before we knew about it," Emma said, her voice a mixture of surprise and disgust. She looked over at Lila. "Did you know anything about this?"

"No, I did not even suspect. Yes, Asher grew a little healthier but not by much. He could simply stay awake for longer periods of time, but he still couldn't move much and rarely spoke."

Blossom looked up at the prince. "I don't remember any of this, do you?" Asher shook his head.

The next few entries included much of the same, Silas growing impatient with Asher's lack of improvement but still unwilling to allow Blossom to be within touching distance of him. He only allowed Blossom to visit Asher when he was asleep, and after Lila questioned the sounds coming from the library he was moved to another secret room. Blossom's eyes widened as he read the description of a small storeroom sequestered beneath the royal hearth. As the king wrote of it a memory began to rise to the surface, one of deep discomfort, of feeling trapped in a sweltering cage, begging to be let out.

This was the first time Silas wrote of punishing Blossom, in his frustration and desperation to unlock both children's powers he began to experiment. Harming one to see if it caused a reaction in the other. He had some mild success as the first strike that Blossom witnessed inflicted upon Asher caused him to burn the king with Fire's blessing.

Blossom snapped the book shut with a definitive noise; a hand clamped over his mouth like he was trying to stop from being sick. "I can't read anymore," he said, putting it back on the table and standing.

"Master Blossom, it is an important piece of information," Edwin said, reaching for the book.

"You read it then. All I see is the rantings of a cruel man who tortured children for his own gain. If there are revelations within its pages, I don't want to see them." He pushed the book towards the man and leant back against his husband who instantly wrapped his arms around him. "How long do you think it will be before the Balance finds us?"

"It's only been a few weeks, Petal. It's going to be at least a few more."

Blossom frowned at Emma's statement. They had only been beneath the palace for a few days, a single week at the most. He sighed, Emma must have just spoken wrong, and he was too tired to correct her.

"How are they planning on getting to us? How are they going to get a message to us with the palace 'crawling with Blossomites' as you say?" Asher asked, waving his hand towards the ceiling. "Shouldn't we be trying to leave this place? We can't exactly plan an attack or regroup with supporters from down here. I don't even know how the soldiers and my knights are doing, have they joined the Blossomites? Did they fight back?" He addressed most of his questions to Kara who opened her mouth to respond but Emma beat her to it.

"We can't just wander out into the Vaten wilderness. Blossom is far too obvious and so are you, Your Majesty. No one in the world has your colouring. We've already gone through this..." She snapped her mouth shut with an audible click as Kara laid a hand on her arm.

"We will be leaving and regrouping soon, I promise. And I would not worry about your knights Asher, they will have retreated to the barracks to await your orders."

Blossom looked over at the queen, sensing that she wanted to interject.

"I actually have something that may help with that," she said chipperly, her tone at odds with everyone else.

Blossom got the feeling she was simply trying to lighten the mood, but he stood and followed her over to one of her invention tables anyway, the prince following closely behind. Lila took hold of a pair of bronze framed spectacles and held them out to him. The glass in the eyewear looked similar to the unusual piece of glass that Lila had been fiddling with when they'd first arrived, casting everything he could see through it in a different colour.

"Try these on," she said, gesturing for him to take them.

He looked at her skeptically before complying. "Not sure that spectacles will be enough to hide my identity," he said but Lila was grinning proudly, and the queen gestured for him to turn towards Asher. He did so, eyes widening when the prince gasped. "What?" He asked, suddenly self-conscious.

"Your eyes," Asher said, awe in his voice, "they've changed colour."

Blossom frowned. "What?" He repeated, although now that he thought about it the room did look a little different, like there was a tint of colour at the edges of his vision, everything bathed in a mixture of pinks, purples and blues. He removed the spectacles and looked back at Lila.

"Give them to Asher and see for yourself."

Blossom handed the prince the spectacles and watched as he put them on, his own gasp leaving his lips as Asher's pure black eyes became a dark brown instead. "How is this possible?" He asked, taking hold of Asher's face and turning him from side to side. On a close inspection it was clear to see that something was wrong with his eye colour, a gloss to it that wasn't natural, but a quick glance wouldn't raise suspicion.

"It's a type of crystal that I found down here, it bends light rays in such a way as to shift colour," Lila explained, the same excitement in her voice that Blossom remembered from childhood. "I originally used it for the lanterns, it causes the light to come out with a pink tint which makes it easier on the eyes."

"What colour does it turn my eyes?" Blossom asked, reaching out to take the spectacles back.

"Blue. Like a really light blue," Asher said.

"That doesn't change the colour of his hair though," Emma said as she walked over to him. "Blessers hair can't be dyed, it doesn't stick. I'm still not sure how the Blossomites manage it."

"There's your fix. We pretend that Blossom is a Blossomite, we can modify one of his robes to match the Blossomites uniform."

Emma looked like she desperately wanted to argue but even she could see the logic in this plan.

"It makes sense," Blossom said tentatively, "and Edwin knows enough about their ways that if we all pretend to be one of them, we might not get caught."

"That's not a very large certainty, and Evelyn will recognise Edwin and I instantly. As well as you, Petal."

"Evelyn will recognise us regardless of what we do, this isn't about trying to mystify her, it's about getting out of the palace and Kilan. Once we're in the wilderness we can focus on reaching the Balance." Blossom paused as he tried to figure out if he should say the next thing. "The more I've been thinking about it the more I think we shouldn't wait for the Balance to come to us. We need to go back to the island." There was a silence that fell over the room as everyone mulled over his words. "I can't explain why, but I think Asher and I need to go there."

Emma made a distressed noise and Kara wound an arm around her shoulder. "I know you want to keep him safe, dove, but we can't stay down here forever," she said soothingly, pressing a kiss to the top of her head.

"I know, but we need an actual plan," Emma replied with a pained sigh.

"We make our way to Shotsen. Princess Cassandra is one of us so she will give us refuge. We regroup there and take the convoy to the island," Kara said instantly, and Emma squinted up at her.

"You came up with that very quickly."

Kara shrugged. "What can I say, I've also been thinking about it. It's not like I haven't had the time."

"Wait, Shotsen doesn't have a princess...do they?" Asher asked and Blossom had to wonder why he was focusing on that.

"You danced with her during your coming-of-age celebration Asher, but of course she was Prince Karken then."

Asher and Blossom made twin 'ohhh' sounds of realisation before returning to the subject at hand.

"So, were you ever planning on bringing us into the Balance? Princess Cassandra is younger than us so it couldn't be an age thing," Asher asked, steering them towards something that Blossom had been wondering as well.

Blossom joined in before Emma had a chance to respond. "Yeah, you were planning on raising me in the Balance anyway so why did you never mention it?"

"Because of Silas," Emma said simply, "it was far too dangerous to try and recruit the both of you with him around. We also had no idea where Evelyn was, so we thought it safer to keep you both in the palace. He may have been a brute, but Silas knew how to keep you safe from outsiders."

Blossom grumbled quietly to himself, but he could see the logic in what was being said. "What about now? Are we trustworthy enough to be brought in now?" He knew he was poking at open wounds and really hoped his own bitterness towards the situation would dissipate soon. Intentionally hurting others, especially those he cared about, went against every fiber of his being, but he couldn't seem to stop himself.

Emma took the barbed comment in her stride however and simply nodded. "You now know about the existence of the Balance. We've told you our purpose and our secrets. You're already half-way there."

Kara nodded with authority, crossing her arms over her chest. "And taking you to a high-ranking member before joining the convoy is the first step towards proper initiation."

"You've said that twice now, what's the convoy?" Asher asked.

"It's a pilgrimage that members take when they are deemed trustworthy enough. To visit the island is a big honor and the convoy ensures that it is kept a secret. Members are kept in darkened carriages so that they don't know the exact location, only guardians are given that privilege." Kara spoke of the tradition with pride and Blossom wondered vaguely if she had been part of the convoy before coming to the palace, one of the members that took new pilgrims to the island perhaps.

Emma sighed deeply, her shoulders drooping. "I see that we have come to a decision. Do I even need to ask whether or not you've already contacted the other guardians?"

Kara smiled, pressing another kiss to her wife's cheek. "Of course you don't. They're expecting us by the end of next week. Which means we have three days to prepare before we bolt." She looked over at Blossom and Asher. "Do you think your shadows will be of any help in an escape?"

"Not unless you want me to kill everyone we come into contact with," Asher grumbled, mostly to himself it seemed, discomfort flowing through their shared bond.

Blossom hummed, causing everyone to look over to him. "I'm not sure, but I do have some ideas. Three days might not be enough to master it though."

"I'm afraid that's all you're getting Blossom."

Blossom nodded, sliding his hand into Asher's and tugging him away from the group. "In that case, we have more training to do."

13

Chapter 13

"I'm still not sure I understand, Flower," Asher said. It was the next morning, and Blossom had been trying to explain his ideas about a 'shadow shield' since breakfast. "How would cloaking myself in the shadow do anything but draw more attention to me?"

Blossom hummed in thought, tapping his chin as he tried to think of another way to word what he meant. "Maybe I should just show you. I'm not sure it'll work but it's better than trying to explain it."

Asher gestured for him to do so with a smug little smile, settling back on his hands like he was certain this was going to be highly amusing.

Blossom glared at him, muttering something under his breath before disappearing from view, his entire being blinking out as though it had never been.

"Blossom?" Asher asked tentatively, worry surging through him. "Blossom where...?" He startled from where he sat, a hand clutched to his chest in shock as Blossom suddenly appeared again, right in front of him. "How did you do that?" He asked, his voice breathless and almost embarrassingly high.

Blossom grinned at him, clearly pleased by his reaction. "Shadow's blessing," he said, before disappearing again, "it can conceal you from a person's view. That's what I was trying to say. Cloak yourself in shadow and people can't see you."

Asher looked around in an attempt to pinpoint where the blesser's voice was coming from, only to squeak in surprise when he felt warmth cupping his cheeks and something soft press against his lips. He blinked as Blossom reappeared; his eyes closed serenely as he kissed him.

"See?" Blossom asked once he'd pulled away.

"No," Asher responded, grinning when his husband looked at him in confusion. He wrapped his arms around Blossom's waist and tugged him close, causing him to stumble from his crouch and land on his knees. "I literally do not see, but that's the point, right?" He chuckled when Blossom groaned and slapped playfully at his shoulder, ending any complaints with another kiss.

Now that Asher had successfully asked for Shadow's blessing by himself the rest began to flow easier. The flood gates had opened, he'd heard his deity's voice and so was able to better listen for it. That didn't mean he was instantaneously able to cloak himself the way that Blossom could, but instead of the many days it had taken for him to even call his power, this took two nights. Two intense but fruitful nights where they barely slept and instead subsisted on black coffee and the sugary cakes that Emma made.

During this time Kara and Edwin mounted more excursions into the castle. Kara to take note of the various guards and their movements, Edwin to see if he could get his hands on any more information from the King's library. Their initial raid hadn't gone unnoticed though and had in fact caused the Blossomites to conduct their own sweep of the library.

"They're burning the books," Edwin said when he returned one night, his voice so quiet and sad that Blossom couldn't help but reach over to comfort him. "In the gardens, they're burning all of the books, and not just the ones from the library either. They've taken everything from the school. Master Blossom, all of your lessons, all of the children's work... It's all gone."

Blossom swallowed, unsure what to say to comfort his uncle as his own chest clenched at the words. All of their hard work, everything that he and the other Masters had built together, everything that his children had been so proud of.

Gone, just like that.

"As long as they aren't burning people, we still have hope," he said instead, "the words we wrote can be written again, but people are not so easily replaced."

"I think I've managed to determine the safest route out of here," Kara interrupted, her tone stern and emotionless, "and I've managed to get in contact with some of the knights still in the palace. The ones that continue to be loyal to you, Your Majesty."

"How can you be sure? If they've stayed, then surely they're working for Evelyn?" Asher asked.

"Because I've fought and trained alongside these people for years, as have you," Kara explained like it was as simple as that. "I know where their loyalties lie, and they have only stayed because they hoped that we hadn't left yet. I have managed to coordinate a plan with them, they are going to create a diversion, two nights from now, to allow us to escape. I've drawn the map here, Blossom can you use Earth's blessing to tunnel us to this point?" She gestured to the crude map on the table, tracing a line from where they were now to the inner cloisters, the barrier between the palace and the gardens.

"That should be fine," Blossom replied despite the unease gnawing at his gut. The reality of what they were about to do was finally dawning on him. It had almost felt like a dream up until now, or a nightmare. Something he could hopefully wake up from and forget once the day grew warm.

The sensation of Asher's hand in his and the strength he felt through their bond calmed him somewhat and he smiled at his husband. "If we are to do this in two days' time then you need to learn how to cloak more than just yourself," he turned to the rest of the group, "I'll need your help now, in order to let Asher practice."

Blossom wasn't sure if it was due to their bond, or if Asher was just naturally gifted in calling his blessing. After succeeding in cloaking himself it didn't take long for Asher to be able to spread that power to encompass the whole group. The difficulty came in the energy it took to do so. Whilst calling Shadow and using it internally seemed relatively easy, making those shadows manifest enough to cover himself was draining. By the end of the first day Asher was able to hold the Shadow Shield for a full half hour before he collapsed, but cloaking everyone caused him to grow cold and weak within minutes.

Blossom would have liked to cultivate this technique with the same time and care as he did the rest of his teachings but knew that they didn't have the luxury of that. So, he pushed Asher harder, trying to ignore the uncomfortable churning in his gut watching how increasingly weak he became.

The second night was a little better, with Asher managing to hold the shield for ten minutes, and after Blossom joined him, pulsing his own stores of Shadow's blessing into Asher, they managed to extend that to a full half hour. The problem was that this technique required Blossom to ask for Blessing almost constantly, and he couldn't imagine doing that whilst they ran for their lives.

"Okay, we're done," Blossom said, shooting Kara a glare when she opened her mouth to object. He knelt by Asher's prone form, pulsing just enough Water's blessing into him to rouse him again. "We've practiced as much as we can, the best thing now would be rest. There's no point in pushing if it means that we're unable to move tomorrow."

Blossom bundled the prince into their room, spending the night pulsing Water's blessing into his tense muscles until Asher grew warm again.

"I overdid it, didn't I?" Asher whispered when he woke, stroking his hand down Blossom's cheek.

Blossom nodded, curling up next to his husband with a yawn, "you did."

"Sorry."

Blossom smiled, letting out a slightly delirious giggle. "You'll learn to notice when you're overdoing it. That cold emptiness, the feeling like there's a pull behind your eyes. You'll learn to recognise it." He sighed, closing his eyes as the heaviness of his eyelids grew too much for him to fight. "We should sleep, we've got to get going in a few hours. Do you think you'll have enough energy to keep us cloaked on the way out?"

Asher nodded hesitantly, "what about you? You haven't had any sleep so far."

"I'll be fine. I've done more on less sleep before," Blossom said, his words getting quieter and quieter until he slipped into unconsciousness.

14

❧

Chapter 14

The group prepared in silence the next morning, the weight of what they were about to attempt hanging over each and every one of them. They packed as much as they could, with the understanding that they probably wouldn't be returning to the underground sanctuary again. Even still, Blossom felt a strange ache in his chest when he looked over everything they had to leave behind. He hadn't realised how much emotion he'd attached to the things he owned. As he ran his fingers over one of the small ornaments that had sat by his bedside since before he could remember, he couldn't help but feeling like he was in mourning. Perhaps not for the items themselves but for the life they had represented. The life he was leaving behind.

They gathered near the wall that Blossom would use to create their escape tunnel just after breakfast, holding hands as Blossom centered himself and gathered as much Earth's blessing as he could. He opened a hole in the wall, and they began their escape.

Excitement and relief was coursing through Blossom at the knowledge that they would be outside soon, that he would be able to breathe the fresh air and see the stars, but it was fast overshadowed by a somber seriousness. An aura of trepidation and unease surrounded the whole party, which was not helped by the closed, claustrophobic tunnel that Blossom was creating around them, piece by piece. He couldn't risk a cave-in by creating too large a tunnel and so they moved slowly, only ever in an area barely larger than a closet.

"How close are we?" Asher asked, right by Blossom's ear sometime later.

"Nearly there," Blossom replied through gritted teeth. It was using almost all his energy and concentration to get them through this, and he couldn't waste any of it on speech. In addition to creating the tunnel, he was also illuminating the small space using what was left of his reserves of Sun's blessing, and whilst there was an abundance of Earth and its power around them, Blossom hadn't seen the sun in weeks. He was having to pull from his own limited resources to get this done, and just hoped that when they reached the outside, he'd be able to take a moment and replenish.

He had no idea what time of day it was, but Kara had indicated that they would be making their escape once the sun had set, and if he had his dates correct, the moon would be nothing but a sliver in the sky tonight, barely enough to keep him going. Even still, it would be better than nothing.

After what felt like hours, they emerged into the darkness of the inner cloisters and Blossom took his first breath of fresh air since his wedding day. He hiked his pack higher on his back and followed Kara into the open when she gestured that the coast was clear. Looking up he spied the smallest glitter of the moon and closed his eyes, a smile of relief crossing his face as Moon's blessing surged through him, filling him as though he were asking during a full moon and not just before it was new again. He could feel some strength returning to his legs, his sore muscles loosening slightly and the chill that had crept into his bones began to dull into something more bearable. He was still exhausted, and nothing but a long day of sleep and multiple blessings would ease that, but he felt a little less like he was about to collapse.

"Now Your Majesty, Blossom," Kara instructed with a hiss.

Blossom took hold of the prince's hand, feeding his own well of power into him as Asher began to shield them. They hurried across the courtyard, pausing only when they reached the inner ring and Asher turned and looked back at the castle. His face was carefully blank, but Blossom could feel the conflict and yearning warring inside of him.

"We will be back, my love," He said with a squeeze to Asher's hand, "I promise."

He wasn't sure if Asher believed him, but the prince took a deep breath and nodded, turning back towards their escape, pausing again as a thought struck him. "The road," he said, gesturing to the dirt path ahead of them, "it's not paved, how is my mother supposed to move over such terrain?"

"There are horses waiting for us at the royal ring. Until then I will carry her," Kara said with determination. "Edwin, you take her chair. I apologise for the indignity, Your Majesty." She crouched in front of the queen, who waved her worries away with a smile.

"Dignity is of no concern right now." She grasped Kara by the shoulders, holding tightly as she was hoisted onto her back. "Let's go," she ordered, and they all took off again, running as swiftly as they could.

On foot the royal ring was an hour and a half's sprint from the palace, but they couldn't move as fast as they normally would and within 30 minutes Asher was beginning to grow pale, stumbling over gravel and twigs as he panted.

"We have to stop," Blossom gasped, his own reserves of Blessing power beginning to run dry. "We can't keep the shield up for much longer if we don't rest."

The group ducked into a thicker copse of trees, Kara settling the queen back in her chair. Asher glanced around quickly and, determining they were not being watched, let the shadow shield drop. Blossom pulled the prince into the darkest shadow he could find, coaxing him through the process of receiving blessing until the coldness of overexertion began to ebb.

"I'm not sure I have it in me to hold that thing up until we reach the gate," Asher confessed, slumping back against a tree trunk. He was drenched with sweat, the circles under his eyes somehow even darker than they had been before they'd started. In truth, he looked ill.

"Then we can swap. It can give you a chance to practice Blessing transference."

"Is now really the time for lessons, Flower?" Asher asked wearily.

"Life is a lesson, my love. Now come on, let's see if the others have caught their breath." Blossom took hold of Asher's hand and pulled him to his feet. He knew that his husband could feel his exhaustion as much as his own, but they didn't have time to dwell on it.

They returned to the group, who had taken the small break as a chance to eat and drink. Blossom accepted the dried fruit that Emma held out to him wordlessly, swallowing it down with a gulp of water.

"We think we should be safe enough for the next few miles to go without the shield," Emma whispered, "better to save your strength to get through the gate; they're more likely to have patrols on the wall than in the woods."

To Blossom's surprise Asher didn't argue, simply cautioned that they would have to move even slower.

Kara looked up at the sky, muttering something under her breath which sounder like numbers before nodding. "We have time, but we'll have to move away from the road and cut through the hunting forest instead." She hoisted Lila onto her back and headed deeper into the trees.

"It's... surprisingly dark in here," Edwin murmured a little while later. They were deep in the hunting forest now, the tree canopies above them serving to block out most of the weak moonlight. He flinched as something rustled up ahead, causing Blossom to walk straight into him as he stopped. "What was that?"

"I imagine it was a deer," Kara responded, her voice sounding surprisingly far away. "Come on, we can't stop now."

"Should I... I could use Moon's blessing to give us a little light," Blossom said.

"And signal exactly where we are to anyone that might be in the forest?" Kara snorted, "no, I'm afraid you're just going to have to do this the unblessed way. Besides, we're nearly there, I can see the wall."

"Then you must have the eyes of an owl," Edwin grumbled, swearing seconds later when he caught his foot in a tree root and landed face first in the dirt.

They arrived at the edge of the forest just as the first rays of dawn began to peak over the horizon, the towering walls of the royal ring shrouding the palace under the veil of night for half an hour longer than the rest of the country.

"Okay Your Majesty, time to put the barrier up again. If you can, drop it for a few seconds once we let out the signal, just so they know where we are," Kara's voice was barely more than a whisper, but it carried through the silent morning air easily.

Asher nodded silently, taking hold of Blossom's hand and calling his blessing to him. They moved cautiously despite the shield, not wanting to attract the attention of the guards on top of the wall. Blossom waited until the coast was clear and let loose his last reserve of Sun's blessing, shooting it into the sky where it exploded into a thousand tiny shards of light.

The group held their breaths for a few moments whilst they waited for something to happen, some responding signal from the Balance. Anything that wasn't arrows or Fire's blessing being rained down upon them by the Blossomites. Blossom winced as he heard shouts from the patrol on the wall; they had seen the signal. Thankfully the doors began to creak open seconds later and a young woman's face appeared on the other side.

"Now Asher," Emma whispered, her voice urgent. The prince dropped the shield. "Shadow's trail," she called to the unknown woman before disappearing again as Asher raised his blessing.

The woman nodded and stepped aside. "Follow me," she said, barely loud enough for them to hear, and they took off after her as the shouts continued to grow louder. The group raced through the door and across the open ground to where another woman stood, holding the bridles of several horses.

"I've got to...I've got to drop it," Asher gasped, and the shield disappeared suddenly as they ran.

"There!" One of the guards shouted and the ground suddenly exploded behind them.

"Shit!" Blossom stumbled as something sharp and heavy hit his ankle, feeling a warm bubble of blood begin to track down his foot as he continued to run.

"I've got you flower," Asher tugged on his hand, pulling him along, "nearly there."

"Get the horses ready!" Kara screamed, hiking the queen higher up on her back.

"Edwin!" Emma's own scream caused Blossom to stop in his tracks. Looking over his shoulder he saw Edwin sprawled on the ground, the queen's chair laying in pieces around him.

"Emma, no." Kara grabbed at her wife as she made to run to her brother.

"I'm not leaving him."

"Get on the horse, I'll get him," Asher shoved Blossom forward, turning on his heel and sprinting over to where Edwin lay, the ground beneath him turning dark with what Blossom didn't want to admit was probably blood. Asher lifted the shorter man up easily, slinging him over his shoulder despite the pained moan Edwin let out.

"Hurry!" Kara called, having mounted her steed and settled Lila onto her own horse.

"Get on that horse!" Asher repeated desperately as Blossom just stood there, paralyzed with fear and shock.

It was the sharp stab of Asher's panic through his own chest that finally forced Blossom to move, and he swung himself up onto the nearest horse, holding his hand out to pull Edwin up after him.

The ground exploded again, closer this time and with a wordless shout Kara kicked her horse into action, the rest of the group following close behind.

15

Chapter 15

"Is he okay?" Emma called across the space between them, her words almost getting lost in the wind as they galloped through the Vaten countryside. If they were being followed their pursuers were far behind them, the expanse of the land around them empty, the buildings dark as the kingdom continued to sleep.

"I don't know," Blossom replied truthfully, he couldn't tell if Edwin was even still alive let alone heal him whilst moving. Especially because Edwin was slumped against his back, and he couldn't see his wounds. "We need to stop; I need to check him over properly."

"We can't stop yet," Kara shouted back, "we need to get to the first safehouse, Evelyn's minions are still hot on our trail, I know it. We can't risk it. The second we stop they're liable to come crawling out of the woodwork."

"He could die, Kara!" Emma said, her voice cracking in her desperation.

"He could and probably would still die if we stop and the Blossomites catch us, along with everyone else. We can't stop."

"I can try and heal him," Blossom said, "or at least...at least I can keep him alive long enough to heal him." He reached behind himself, placing his hand on Edwin's back, wincing when he realised how cold his uncle felt. Without knowing which area to focus on Blossom simply pulsed Moon's blessing through his whole body, unable to concentrate enough to feel out the wound.

Edwin let out a gasp of pain, which Blossom took as a good sign as it was the first noise he'd made since getting on the horse. This was followed by a groan as he regained consciousness and began to stir against Blossom's back.

"No, no, Edwin, sleep now. It'll be better if you sleep," Blossom soothed, adding a sliver of Shadow's blessing to the stream of power now pumping into the other man, just enough to rob him of his consciousness. Blossom could feel the yawning emptiness that always came from using too much power at once, numbness creeping into his fingers, and he let his hand drop. The small amount of Moon's blessing that he had received when they'd first emerged above ground wasn't enough, and the exertion of holding the shadow shield up for so long was weighing heavily on him. "He's stable...for now," he whispered, unsure if anyone heard him over the sound of hoofbeats and wind.

"Flower," Asher called, worry evident in his voice and through their bond. He steered his horse as close to Blossom as possible whilst they were still moving so fast, his face pinched with a mixture of worry and his own tiredness.

"I'm fine," Blossom replied. He knew why Asher was asking, there had been something pushing against his blessing when he'd tried to heal Edwin, something unnatural that had siphoned his power and drained him quicker than it should have. He wasn't surprised that Asher could sense it.

They rode in silence until they reached the outer ring of Kilan, weaving through streets and squares in an attempt to lose their pursuers. The two women that had collected them knew their way around the capital city, and after about an hour they pulled the horses to a stop. The great stone wall loomed above them almost protectively, but they were still miles away from the main gate.

"Why have we stopped?" Asher asked, stroking his hand down his horse's neck as it panted and snorted.

"We can't leave the city just yet Your Majesty," the woman they had first met said, "we have to time it properly. We have Balance members amongst the outer guards, and we need to wait until they are on duty to escape through the gate. We have a safe house a little way away, but we need to leave the horses here and go on foot."

"Just leave them here?" Blossom asked, dismounting as he spoke and helping Kara guide Edwin down. "What will happen to them?"

"I will take them Master Blossom," a voice replied, and Blossom turned to see a young child emerging from the shadows. "They're my horses anyway. I'm glad they were of service," he said, bowing low to the group.

"Thank you..." Blossom trailed off, gesturing to the boy.

"Sitan. Master Blossom."

"Thank you Sitan," Blossom turned to the two women who had helped them escape, "and your names?"

"I am Elana, and this is my sister, Gita," the first woman answered, gesturing to her sister who was helping to guide the queen down from her horse as they spoke. "Now, I'm afraid we have to move again, there is no time to lose." She looked up and down the street as she spoke, checking for signs of their pursuers. But the street was empty, the early hour causing the usually bustling city to appear almost deserted.

Blossom nodded, taking hold of Emma's hand and preparing to walk.

"Oh, one more thing," Gita said, her voice surprisingly high pitched despite her gruff exterior. She pulled a dark blue scarf from her pack and stepped up to Blossom. "Do you mind?"

"Are you going to blindfold me?" Blossom asked, taking a cautious step back.

Gita smiled at him. "No. But your hair is quite the giveaway, I was going to wrap it."

"Oh, oh yes, that is a good idea." Blossom bowed his head, allowing the woman to wrap the scarf around his hair in a manner very similar to the way the people from Krestaza wore it. Most Krestazans had skin similar in colouring to the Castillans, so most onlookers would simply assume that Blossom was from that small desert kingdom to the south.

"There, now we can go," Gita stepped back and motioned for everyone to follow her. They moved at a much slower pace now, not wanting to draw undue attention by running, and as promised they stopped by a non-descript stone building only a short time later.

Elana knocked on the door, waiting until a small hatch opened and a pair of green eyes peered out at them. "Shadow's trail," she said, and the hatch snapped shut again. There was the sound of bolts being pulled aside before the door swung open, and an Earth blessed man gestured them inside.

"Did everyone make it?" He asked.

"Yes, but we have one injured... badly," Kara responded, shifting the queen higher on her back and gesturing to Edwin with her head. "Please clear a table, we need somewhere flat to lay him."

Emma rushed to help the man clear the kitchen table so that Asher could lay Edwin down upon it. "Blossom can you...can you heal him now?" Emma asked, letting out a pained noise as she pulled aside the ruined material of Edwin's shirt to reveal an angry, open wound.

"I will try," Blossom responded, "I'm running low on Moon's blessing, so if you know of any Moon blessed that could help, it would be most appreciated."

The man nodded, "my son, Hanwell. He is Moon blessed. He is only young though."

"Bring him here," Blossom commanded, returning his attention to his uncle, who had grown cold and grey again since Blossom's last healing attempt. "There is something about this wound that is...unnatural," he whispered, mostly to himself. He spread cautious threads of Moon's blessing through the wound, trying to feel out the most damaged parts, frowning when he encountered that resistance again.

"Here he is, Master Blossom." The man had returned, his hand resting on the shoulder of a young boy who couldn't have been older than 12.

"I didn't catch your name," Blossom said, addressing the man.

"Tristan, Master Blossom," Tristan said, almost seeming surprised that Blossom was asking.

"Thank you, Tristan." Returning his attention to the young boy, Blossom crouched in front of him. "I'm surprised we've never met before."

"We...we were not permitted to send Hanwell to your school, Master Blossom," Tristan explained, looking away sheepishly. "The king...he rejected our request."

Blossom frowned, remembering the conversation he'd had with Silas months ago. His statement that only the rich and well placed in society had been allowed to attend the blessing school. "I'm sorry about that, I didn't know."

"It is not your fault, Master Blossom," Tristan replied, his smile genuine.

Blossom returned his attention to Hanwell. "Hanwell, have you healed many large wounds before?"

Hanwell shook his head, "only broken bones and a few cuts."

Nodding Blossom held out his hand. "When was the last time you asked for blessing?"

"Last night."

"Okay good, I have a big and potentially difficult request to ask of you Hanwell. I'm going to ask to take some of your blessing, would you be willing to let me?"

"Anything, Master Blossom," Hanwell replied quickly, placing his small hand in Blossom's outstretched one.

"Thank you. It will feel weird to begin with, but it shouldn't hurt. If it does hurt, please tell me." Standing again, Blossom closed his eyes, feeling for the well of power that lay within the child. Once he found it, he took a deep breath and began to slowly draw from it. Hanwell let out a gasp, his grip on Blossom's hand tightening. "Am I hurting you?"

"N-no...it just...it just feels weird," Hanwell replied quietly.

Blossom drew as much as he could without hurting the child, leaving him with enough reserve that he shouldn't feel the uncomfortable coldness of overexertion. "Thank you," he said, opening his eyes and letting go of Hanwell's hand. "I would advise you to ask for blessing again tonight, refill your stores so you are not overdrawn."

Hanwell nodded and stepped back to his father's side, cradling his hand against his chest.

Blossom returned his attention to Edwin, placing his hands on his chest, one on either side of the gaping wound. He sent stronger pulses of Moon's blessing into Edwin, watching as the skin began to knit itself back together again. But the process was a lot slower than it should have been, like his uncle's flesh was fighting him. "There's something wrong," he gasped, releasing his hold and stepping back. "I can't...I can't heal him. Not properly."

"What do you mean you can't heal him?" Emma asked, her desperation causing her words to come out with an edge to them. "Do we need to get more Moon blessed here?"

"I don't know," Blossom snapped back, softening his voice when Emma looked at him in shock. "More Moon blessed might help but I'm not sure. This seems like it was designed to...I'm not sure...prevent healing?"

Emma looked at her wife. "Can we get more Moon blessed here?"

Elana answered instead of Kara. "I'll send out word that we need healers."

"I can get him stabilized," Blossom said, his voice quiet. He knew it wasn't enough, but he could already feel the pull behind his eyes that told him he'd used too much of his power. He wasn't about to take more from Hanwell, the child was too young for that.

Emma nodded, biting her bottom lip as she sat next to the table where her brother lay, taking his hand and squeezing it. "Anything you can, Petal. Just keep him alive."

"I can do that," Blossom sent one more rush of Moon's blessing through Edwin's chest, knitting the skin together through sheer force of will. He managed to stem the flow of blood, closing the wound to the outside world even if it wasn't completely healed on the inside. As he felt the very last of his reserves leaving him, he slumped against the wood, exhaustion seeping into his bones.

"That's enough," he heard Asher's voice on the periphery, feeling someone moving him but unable to open his eyes to see who it was.

"Bring him here, we've a bed waiting." Tristan's voice also sounded far away, and it was the last thing Blossom heard before he fell into unconsciousness.

∞

Asher watched the colour slowly returning to Blossom's cheeks as he slept. He'd felt the emptiness of Blossom's overexertion, so similar to how it had been all those months ago when he'd burnt his room down, and it worried him. How often had Blossom done that to himself in the past? He glanced at the shadows in the corner of the room, wondering if calling his own blessing would help with the chill he could feel in the tips of his fingers.

He whispered Shadow's word, coaxing the darkness to him and smiling slightly as it wound around his arm before disappearing into his skin. Returning his attention to his husband, he placed his hand on Blossom's neck, stroking his thumb over the soft skin, trying to mimic the way Blossom had healed him before. He had no idea if Shadow's blessing could be used to heal but it was possible that he could gift Blossom some of his own energy, something to bring him back to consciousness.

He let out a gentle pulse of Shadow's blessing, trying to send it into Blossom but unsure how. The shadow danced over his fingers, spreading to Blossom's neck, but instead of sinking into his skin it simply sat there, like cloth.

Blossom's eyes fluttered open, and he gave Asher a wan smile. "That tickles," he whispered, sounding drawn and tired.

"I was trying to give you some of my blessing," Asher replied, returning his smile and removing his hand.

"Thank you, my love," Blossom caught hold of Asher's hand and returned it to his neck. "Right now, I just need rest, and your touch is nice."

"Then I'll stay here."

"Petal?" Emma's voice floated over from the doorway, where she was hovering uncertainly, wringing her hands. "Are you okay?"

"I'll be fine," Blossom replied, attempting to push onto his elbows.

"No, no. You said you need to rest. Lie back down, Flower." Asher pushed at Blossom's chest until he gave in and flopped back onto the bed.

"I'm sorry I pushed you so hard, Petal. I shouldn't have shouted at you like that." Emma made her way into the room, pulling a small chair from the corner over to them so she could hold Blossom's hand.

"You were scared, I understand. How is he?"

Emma sighed, resting her chin on her knuckles, Blossom's hand still clutched between both of hers. "He's still alive, he hasn't woken up, but he does look better. There are a couple of healers downstairs, but they said the same thing as you. There was something in whatever they threw at us that is fighting against their blessings."

Blossom stared up at the ceiling, a small frown on his face. "I don't understand what it could be. If only we'd seen who had sent the blessing, or whatever it was that hit us. If we knew who had blessed them then it would give me somewhere to start."

"I don't think they were blessed," Asher said, sitting straighter as both Emma and Blossom looked at him. "When I grabbed Edwin, I caught a glimpse of the guards that launched the attack. They were setting something up, getting ready to launch again. It was mechanical, there was no blessing involved."

16

Chapter 16

"What do you mean mechanical?" Kara asked. Asher had insisted that Blossom try to get some sleep, which hadn't taken much cajoling considering how exhausted his husband already was. Emma had stayed in the room to watch over him and so Asher had convened with the other women in the small living space of the house, hoping that he might be of some use.

Edwin was still lying on the table, two Moon blessed twins alternating pulses of their blessings as they tried to heal him. He still hadn't woken up, but his cheeks had regained some of their original bronzed hue and his breathing had evened out.

"I don't know. There was something mounted on the wall, and whatever it was, it shot the ground. There were metal shards all around the crater, and I think some of them may have gotten lodged in Edwin. They're definitely the reason for his wounds."

Kara shook her head slowly, a mixture of fear and - if Asher wasn't mistaken - awe on her face. "If they've developed something like that, something that can't be healed through blessing, then we're in big trouble."

"You said you saw some of the shards in Edwin?" Tristan asked as he walked down the stairs and into the main room of the house. "Are they still there?"

Asher blinked, shaking his head and shrugging his shoulders at the same time. "I don't know. I didn't see Blossom close him up, it's possible I guess."

Chewing on his thumb in contemplation Tristan made his way over to the Moon blessed. "Would you be able to open his wounds again?"

"Why would we do that?" One of the healers replied, Asher still hadn't been introduced to either of them yet and didn't know their names. "We want to heal him, not make his wounds bigger."

"If he still has those shards of metal inside of him, couldn't that be stopping him from healing?"

There was a pregnant pause as everyone digested that information. The second Moon blessed hummed in thought before turning to their sibling. "It's a possibility...but I'm not sure..."

"You're right. If we opened his chest again now, he would die. He needs to heal more before we could even think about that. He's stable right now, he's returning to the world. After a week or so, where he can remain conscious for multiple hours at a time, it might be possible then."

∞

"Do you think Edwin should be moved?"

Blossom had awoken an hour or so before the sun set and now sat with the rest of the group as they attempted to make their final preparations before they left the capital city. Kara had taken point, organizing everyone with the same military precision with which she trained her knights, but it did little to put him at ease. Blossom could sense the tension in the air as they planned; everyone's tones were hushed, and he couldn't help but feel like the escape from the palace had been a breeze in comparison to what they were about to try.

"He needs to move," Emma replied, sitting straighter in her chair when Kara smiled gently at her. "Not because of the reasons you're thinking Kara. Yes, I want my brother to escape with us. Yes, I don't want to leave him because he's my brother and I love him, but there are other reasons as well. We can't leave anyone in this city that knows of our plan, we can't leave him here to be recaptured and tortured. Edwin is also the only one of us with enough knowledge of the Blossomites for us to competently fight them."

"We can put him in the cart with Queen Lila," Gita said, turning to the queen, "As long as you don't mind, Your Majesty."

"Of course not. That way I can look after him as we travel. He shouldn't be left alone in his state. Even if I can't heal him, I can keep him company."

Tristan walked back into the small house, followed by Hanwell who was pushing a wheeled chair very similar to the one the queen used before. "The convoy is here your majesties, Master Blossom." He gave a little bow that Asher waved away. "We hope this will serve as a suitable replacement for the chair that was destroyed."

"It will do wonderfully," Lila replied, sliding into it and squeezing Hanwell's small hands in thanks.

"Okay, let's get moving then. Elana, Gita, help me with Edwin. Emma, you and Blossom get the packs. Asher, help your mother," Kara ordered, already making her way over to the kitchen table.

Gita and Elana followed, holding up a door they had removed from the bedroom to use as a makeshift stretcher. Kara slid Edwin onto the door, shushing him gently when he let out a moan of pain.

"Thank you, thank you for all your help," Blossom said, resting a hand on Tristan's shoulder. "And thank you Hanwell, I hope one day we can meet again, and that we can learn more about Moon's blessing together."

Hanwell smiled up at him, looking exhausted in a way that wasn't just due to the lateness of the day. "Thank you, Master Blossom. May you be blessed."

"And you, little one."

Kara, Elana and Gita loaded Edwin into the back of a covered wagon, helping Lila up afterwards. They then loaded the rest of the supplies into the small space, strapping them down in such a way as to give Lila and Edwin a few hiding places should they be stopped and inspected.

Emma and Blossom sat at the front of the wagon dressed in clothing provided by Tristan, with Blossom's hair still wrapped and the queen's glasses obscuring the pink of his eyes. With the wagon, clothes, and their tired, bedraggled appearance, they made the perfect image of a travelling merchant family. Kara and Asher rode alongside the cart as it trundled down the street, playing the role of hired guards who would help Blossom and Emma through the wilderness and the more dangerous areas near the Vaten border.

They arrived at the outer gates only a few minutes into their journey; they really hadn't been as far away as Blossom had originally thought. As the towering door came into view Blossom felt his palms grow clammy, sure that they would be instantly recognised, but then he remembered that the guards stationed at the door were supposed to be members of the Balance. Even so, he shrunk back against the canvas of the wagon as the guards approached them, staring down at his lap as Emma handed over their forged trading papers.

"Travelling to Shotsen are we? And what cargo do you carry?" The guard asked.

"That which will restore Balance," Emma replied, and Blossom furrowed his brows in confusion. The continued strain of using so much of his blessing was muddling his thoughts and he couldn't begin to understand what that meant.

But the guard nodded and handed back the paperwork. "Then blessings on your journey."

Blossom waited until they were a few miles away from the city before he turned to his mother. "What was that?"

"That is the code we use to identify one another. There are five phrases that members of the Balance may use, and we learn them when we are initiated."

"What are the other four?"

Emma smiled at him, resting a hand on his knee. "You'll learn them when you are initiated." Blossom huffed and slumped down in his seat, crossing his arms over his chest. "Don't pout Petal, you know why we have to be careful. We can't make exceptions, even for you."

They travelled through the night, meeting only a few other travelers on the road, making it a good distance from Kilan. Enough that Blossom could feel himself relaxing, his eyes fluttering shut as the sun began to peek above the horizon.

"Don't fall asleep yet Petal, we're nearly at our first base camp. You'll get to meet more Balance members in a little bit," Emma said, her voice gentle and smooth like she didn't really mind if Blossom slept or not.

Blossom hummed in response, looking over at his husband who was slouching slightly in his saddle. "Do you want me to ride for a bit, my love? You can sit on the wagon if you want to."

"No Flower, I'm okay. It's just been a while since I've ridden. I've gone for longer than this without rest before," Asher said, betraying himself somewhat as he yawned widely soon after.

"Let's stop for a little while," Kara decided, "we'll be no good to anybody if we reach the village in this state, and besides we should check on Edwin and the queen."

They pulled the wagon over to the side of the dirt road, far enough into a copse of trees that passersby wouldn't spot them straight away. Asher hopped down from his horse and stretched his back with a groan, which turned into a sigh when Blossom joined him and pulsed a small amount of Water's blessing into his sore muscles. He hadn't had a chance to replenish himself fully yet, but now that they were in the open, he didn't feel the need to ration his power too much.

"Thanks," he said, tugging Blossom close and kissing him deeply. "How are you faring, beautiful boy?"

"You know how I'm faring," Blossom replied, but his smile was indulgent and loving.

"I do know, but weren't you the one who said we should still talk about our thoughts and feelings even with the bond?"

"Oh, now you decide to listen to me?" Blossom rolled his eyes, pushing playfully at Asher's shoulder and receiving another kiss in response. He looked over his shoulder at the sounds of cloth swishing, seeing Emma climbing into the back of the wagon, handing the queen's chair down to Kara. "How is he?"

"Much the same as when we left," Emma replied.

"He hasn't regained consciousness yet, but he is starting to respond to me a little," Lila clarified, "he squeezes back now when I hold his hand."

Blossom nodded, "let me give him some more blessing, just to ease him a little."

As the rest of the group set up an impromptu camp of sorts, pulling out their water gourds and some of the provisions they'd been given, Blossom climbed into the wagon and settled down next to his uncle.

"I'm sorry I can't fix you," Blossom said quietly, resting his hands over Edwin's chest. He'd taken as much of Moon's blessing as he was given whilst they rode, but the moon was still waning, growing closer to its new form and there wasn't much power to spare. Instead of trying to heal him the way he'd learnt to, Blossom focused on soothing Edwin's pain, mixing Moon's blessing with what was left of his Water's blessing.

Edwin let out a gasp, his eyes fluttering as Blossom's power flooded through him. He didn't wake, but it was more than he'd managed to do before now. Perhaps soothing was what Blossom should focus on, instead of healing. After they got Edwin to the point where he was conscious, and strong enough to withstand it, then he could try removing whatever was still lodged in Edwin's chest.

Once he was sure Edwin wasn't going to wake, and realising that he'd nearly overexerted himself again, Blossom left the wagon. He gazed around at their surroundings, wondering if there might be a stream nearby where he could replenish his power reserves. Just as he was about to give up and return to the rest of the group, Blossom saw movement out of the corner of his eye.

"Kara," he called, gaze trained on the spot amongst the trees where he'd seen movement. It was too dark amongst the foliage to be sure, but he was fairly certain someone was there.

"Yes?" Kara walked up to him, following his finger as he pointed wordlessly.

"I think we're being spied on," Blossom dropped his voice, speaking as quietly as he could.

Kara's hand went to the hilt of her sword, and she nodded, before turning on her heel and returning to where everyone else sat.

After a few seconds of confusion, he also returned to the group, but when he reached them, Kara was nowhere to be seen. "Where...?"

His question was answered a second later when Kara emerged, holding a small, very familiar, child by the collar of his tunic. "I found the spy," she said chipperly, like she wasn't currently scruffing a kid the way one would a cat.

"Aelius?" Blossom asked in disbelief.

"I'm...I'm not a spy Master Blossom, I promise," Aelius responded, hugging himself as he shivered with fear.

"You know him?" Kara asked.

"He was one of Blossom's students," Emma replied for him, her easy smile dropping seconds later as she seemed to remember something. "One who comes from a Blossomite family."

Aelius' face drained of colour, and he started to shake. "M-Master Emma, I swear I'm not..." he swallowed loudly before bursting into tears, hiding his face in his hands. "M-my mother...she said that I was bad because I wouldn't let her hurt me anymore. I ran away, I'm not a spy."

"Hey, hey," Blossom said soothingly, crouching in front of the child. "Let him go Kara."

"You believe him?" Kara asked, releasing her grip on Aelius' tunic.

"I do. We had a good chat about how best to treat people and how it was wrong that your mother hurt you, didn't we Aelius?"

Aelius sniffed, nodding as he wiped his eyes with his sleeve. "I...I tried to hide. When school ended, I wanted to stay in the palace, but they found me."

"How long have you been by yourself Aelius?" Asher asked, joining Blossom in his crouch.

"I'm...I'm not alone," Aelius confessed, "I found some of the other students, one's that didn't get back home before...before the attacks."

17

⚬⚬⚬

Chapter 17

"Attacks?" Blossom looked up at Kara and Emma, hoping to see some form of recognition on their faces, but they looked just as confused as he felt. Kara shook her head and looked down at Aelius.

"When we left at the end of the school year," Aelius began, looking down at his feet, "the convoy that always took us home, those of us that live close to the border, it was attacked...by Blossomites."

"Come and sit with us Aelius, tell us everything." Emma guided the small boy back to their makeshift camp, handing him a cup of water and a chunk of bread.

"They tried to take us, I'm not sure where but they were saying something about the time of the blessed and the fall of the false king," Aelius explained, tearing through the bread like he hadn't had any substantial food in a long time.

"So, Evelyn is rounding up blessed children," Emma said with a sigh, rubbing her forehead with a look of exhaustion on her face.

"Where have you been staying Aelius?" Blossom asked, taking in the sight of the Sun blessed's bedraggled appearance.

"With Skyla. She took me back to her village, it's only a little way from here. Her family has been looking after me."

"Where is Skyla now?" Blossom remembered the strong, steady, Earth blessed girl. She'd graduated at the end of the year, ranking very highly in her protector's exam. He'd expected to see her back in the palace as soon as her initial army training was completed. She was definitely talented enough to be raised to the level of knight.

Aelius swallowed his last mouthful of food, looking almost sheepish as he responded. "In the village, she's fighting today."

"She's what?"

"Fighting. There's a tournament to celebrate the changing of the seasons and its good money if you win."

Blossom could feel Asher's interest peek at the mention of a tournament, but the way Aelius said those words made him think it wasn't going to be like the royal tournaments held at the palace. The mention of the changing season also struck something, an itch in the back of Blossom's mind that had been there since they'd escaped.

They should have been in the depths of winter, Blossom had been counting the days as well as he could whilst they were underground, but the weather was far too warm for that to be the case.

"What season are we moving into?" Blossom asked, suddenly reminded of his travel clothes. He hadn't been wearing his robes for days now, had almost missed their heavy weight on him. Suddenly being so unsure which robe he should be wearing right now was more unsettling than he'd anticipated.

Aelius gave him a strange look, glancing down at the plain brown tunic and trousers Blossom was clad in. "Summer," he said, "the long day is in a week."

∞

Asher looked at Blossom, his own shock mirrored on his husband's face. "How...how is that possible? We were only in hiding for a month at the most." He turned to survey the rest of the group who were also looking confused, but he soon realised that their confusion was directed at him, not the child.

"No Ash, we were beneath the palace for a lot longer than that," Kara said, sitting down next to Asher and resting her hand on his knee.

"What?" He could feel Blossom's ratcheting panic mixing with his own and stood, taking a step closer to the blesser. "What are you talking about?"

Kara and Emma looked at each other, like they were hoping the other had the answer to that question. It was Lila who spoke next, and her words only added to his growing sense of unease.

"The bonding," she said, rolling forward when everyone stared at her blankly. "All those times they sat and attempted to learn Asher's gift, the days you two would spend in silence together. Do you not remember those?"

Blossom shook his head. "I don't understand what you're saying. We never trained for days on end; our lessons were only hours at a time. Asher couldn't handle more than that."

"No Petal," Emma said soothingly, "the queen is right. Did you never wonder why you were always so tired and hungry after? It was because the two of you had been locked in your own world for days."

Asher met Blossom's gaze and shrugged, unable to comfort him because he was just as lost. Now that he thought back, it did make a strange kind of sense. The training had always sapped him, had left him feeling like he hadn't slept in an age, ravenous and shaky with hunger.

Blossom also had no trouble eating during that time, something Asher had tried not to dwell on, worried that if he brought it up, he could reignite the difficulties his husband had struggled so much with.

But if Blossom was eating because he too had starved for days then that made more sense than him suddenly being cured of his mental demons, even if that realisation did nothing to comfort him.

"How..." Blossom looked down at where his hands lay in his lap. "How could we not know? How did we not see it?" He stood, shaking his head. "Asher would have grown a beard if that was the case, we would have smelt, would have...would have needed to relieve ourselves."

Asher scratched his cheek, at the shadow of stubble already growing after a day and a bit of riding. Blossom had a point, even though the blesser had never really been able to grow facial hair himself, Asher had needed to shave daily since the age of 15 if he didn't want to begin looking like a wild man.

"I'm not sure," Lila said with a shake of her own head. "It's hard to explain, but you always had a kind of...aura around the two of you when you were together, similar to the one that came about whenever you tried to bless away Asher's death mark. It was like the world moved around you whilst you stopped. Like maybe time was moving differently for the two of you."

"This is insane." Blossom ran a hand through his hair, turning on his heel and wandering a little way from the group, stopping just at the tree line where he had spotted Aelius.

Asher followed after him, wrapping his arm around Blossom's waist and pulling him into his side. "I'm not sure how to explain it but I think they're telling the truth."

"I know they are," Blossom replied, "that's what scares me."

Asher pressed a kiss to Blossom's forehead, not sure what else to do to comfort him.

"I'm used to being different, Ash," Blossom said, gaze trained on the floor, "but it's like all we're doing is finding out just how different we are. I'm starting to wonder if we're even human, you and I."

Asher hummed, he'd been thinking the same thing. Everything they'd read, all they'd discovered over the last couple of weeks, or months as it turned out, made him question their origins even more. "I think we need to go to the island, actually get onto the island itself. Hopefully returning to where we were born will help us figure this out."

"Yes, you're right."

They stood in comfortable silence for a few minutes more until Emma called to them. "Petal, Asher, we need to get going. You should change now as well."

Blossom disappeared into the covered wagon, returning a short while later clad in the Blossomites version of the blessers coat. He'd forgone the scarf wrapped around his hair since they'd left, and his curls were sticking up haphazardly.

"Okay, I'm ready," Blossom said, tugging at the sleeve of his coat uncomfortably. Asher could feel the unsettled emotions swirling through their bond, his stomach clenching with nerves that weren't his. He understood why his husband was feeling this way, he didn't like the sight of Blossom dressed as one of the people that had caused such unrest either.

∞

They rode to the village in silence, a tension now hanging over them that hadn't been there before. Even little Aelius was quiet, like he could sense the heaviness of what was happening. It seemed like such a stroke of luck, that the first Balance safe house outside of Kilan would be in the same village that two of his students were staying in. Blossom had yet to decipher if it was good luck or bad.

"We'll leave the wagon here. I'll go and signal that we've arrived," Kara said, helping Emma down from her seat, "you stay with Edwin and the queen."

"I'm going to go with Aelius to find Skyla," Blossom said, taking the child by the hand.

"I'll go with you," Asher stepped close to him, looking at Kara like he was daring her to stop them. "Aelius said there was a tournament of some kind going on, we can blend in with the crowd, we won't be seen."

After a few seconds Kara nodded, she then kissed Emma on the cheek before turning and disappearing down a small side street.

"Be careful Petal," Emma said, looking around as though to check that they weren't being overheard, "and don't interact with anyone who isn't Skyla."

Blossom nodded and began following Aelius through the dusty village streets. Whilst the capital city had been quiet due to the time of day this village's silence felt unnatural. The sun was now high in the sky, and they had passed quite a few farms on their approach. Blossom had been under the assumption that farmers always rose early, and he'd expected some form of market or something but instead there was nothing.

"Is this normal?" he asked, looking between Asher and Aelius, "shouldn't there be more activity here?"

"Since you disappeared things have...changed," Aelius said quietly, staring off into the distance. He seemed so much older than the last time Blossom had seen him, as though he had lived years in the months they had been parted. "The Blossomites have been taking children, the ones that are left are kept inside now. And...well, the unblessed don't trust us anymore."

"Why?" Blossom could feel a coldness travelling down his spine. Perhaps he shouldn't have dressed in the Blossomite robe, if they were making a name for themselves as child snatchers then him walking through the streets with a Sun blessed child couldn't be a good idea.

Perhaps he should have just kept to the brown travel clothes and head-scarf.

"The Blossomites keep saying that the blessed should be raised up and rule over the unblessed...and they don't like that. Especially when we were always the ones meant to serve the unblessed."

Blossom wasn't sure which part of that statement distressed him the most. He vaguely remembered Lila telling him that the blessed were treated like commodities before he was born, but he had assumed that had stopped.

He'd assumed a lot of things. He now wondered how many of those assumptions were dead wrong.

"Should we go back to the wagon so that I can change?" Blossom whispered to Asher, but any response the prince could make was cut off by the sounds of shouting and cheering.

"Hurry, the fight is about to start," Aelius said, tugging Blossom's hand until he began to run.

They turned a corner to see a fairly large crowd of people, all unblessed and all in various states of dishevelment. They looked far poorer than they should have given the state of the village, and again Blossom felt his heart clenching painfully.

They pushed their way to the front of the crowd, an easy feat given Blossom's current attire, to find Skyla and an unknown Fire blessed in a crudely drawn sparring ring.

There was a man who appeared to be in his early 40s also in the ring, standing in the very center. He held his hands out, addressing the crowd. "Honored guests, welcome to today's fight. Today we have an Earth blessed that was trained at the royal blessing school by Blossom himself." He gestured to Skyla and the crowd booed, causing Blossom to look around in shock.

"And our competitor, a Fire blessed who learnt his craft the way all their kind should, at the hearth of his master." This statement was met with a cheer.

Blossom was wrenched to the side as someone grabbed his arm, coming face to face with an angry looking woman who snarled up at him.

"You see? This is all they're good for," she hissed, spitting at his feet. "You delusional Blossomites need to get that through your thick skulls. Especially one's like you, how can an unblessed voluntarily lower themselves the way you have?" She grabbed at his hair, yanking on the pink locks.

Blossom let out a yelp of pain as his scalp protested the rough handling, drawing the attention from the fighters in the ring over to him.

Skyla's eyes widened and she took a step forward. "Master Bl..."

"Get off him," Asher snapped, smacking the woman's hand away and pulling Blossom behind him.

The woman straightened her spine, readying herself to snarl some more nasty words if her expression was anything to go by, but then her eyes widened as she looked more closely at Asher's face. "Your...Your Majesty," she gasped.

"Curses," Asher replied with a hiss, grabbing Blossom by the hand and gesturing for Skyla who was making her way over to them. "Come on." He shoved his way through the crowd that had instantly turned to them, pushing closer as they shouted.

"Aelius," Blossom called, his grip on the child's hand tightening to the point where it had to hurt, but he couldn't risk losing him in the rush.

"I'm...I'm here Master Blossom," Aelius shouted back, causing Blossom to wince as several members of the crowd gasped in unison.

"It is him!"

"He's a Blossomite?"

"Of course he is, he's probably their leader."

There were hands on his clothes, pulling at him to the point where he was worried that he would get sucked into the gathering mob. Just as he stumbled and nearly fell, a large wall of earth erupted between him and the crowd.

"This way Master Blossom," Skyla called, waving them over to an alleyway a little way away from them. They made it over to the alley as the crowd grew louder and Skyla erected another wall, effectively blocking them from the mob in the square. "Master Blossom, what are you doing here?" She asked, wiping a smudge of dirt from her forehead.

"No time to explain. We need to get back to Kara," Asher said, sounding out of breath, "Aelius do you remember how to get us back to the wagon? And can you do it without us being seen?"

Aelius nodded and looked up at Skyla. "We need to get to the bakers."

"Master Blossom, can you help me? I know the way, but it would be better to go underground."

Blossom nodded silently, still shaken up from what had just happened. He took a second to center himself, asking for Earth's blessing to replenish his stores. They worked together, creating a hole in the ground beneath their feet and then resealing it once they were all inside. Aelius lit the way this time, spreading a glow over his skin so that he could work as a walking lantern.

Their destination wasn't far away but they remained in place beneath the street for a little while in the hopes that they wouldn't emerge and find themselves face to face with the angry villagers. After at least fifteen minutes, if Blossom's internal clock was working correctly, although he wasn't sure he could trust it anymore, they began their ascent, opening a hole directly below the wagon.

As the smallest one, Aelius scrambled out first. "It's all clear," he whispered, crawling out from under the wagon and keeping watch as the rest of the group followed him.

Asher checked inside the wagon, only to find it empty. "They must have moved to the safehouse already. How are we going to find them?" He asked, but his question was answered only seconds later when Emma emerged from another side street.

"What in blessing's name is going on?" She hissed, waving them over, "get over here."

Her tone was so similar to the one he'd heard numerous times as an unruly child that Blossom almost smiled, but he knew that now was definitely not the time and followed the order silently.

Emma took them down a series of streets to a nondescript house, but this time Blossom noticed the mark on the door. It was in the top corner, two mirrored triangles, one on top of the other with their narrow tips touching. There had been a similar mark on the door of the house where they'd hidden in Kilan, but with everything that had been happening at the time he'd not thought to question it.

Before knocking or entering the house Emma turned and peered at Skyla. "Do you believe that we can trust her Blossom?"

Skyla answered for him, "that which is set in motion will have consequences."

Emma blinked in surprise, the corners of her lips twitching like she was trying not to smile. "It is up to us to prepare for those consequences." She smiled properly now as Skyla nodded. "So, you are a member then."

"More than that," Skyla said, knocking three times on the door. "I'm the daughter of the housekeeper."

The door swung open and a woman who shared the same familial colours as Skyla waved them inside. "Are you unharmed?" She asked, checking first Skyla and then Aelius for injuries.

"We are, but they know that Master Blossom is here," Skyla said with a sigh, "and now they think he's the leader of the Blossomites."

"Well can you blame them?" Blossom asked, gesturing angrily to his clothes. "How could no one tell me how awfully the blessed are treated out here? That woman spoke of us as though we were animals!"

"The people are scared, ever since the Blossomites started stealing their children it's..."

"Don't act like this is a new thing, Reena." Kara admonished the woman from her place by the kitchen table. She had a large map spread out over the wood and returned her attention to it as she continued to speak. "Things got better when Blossom arrived and began to look after the blessed children of this land, but Vaten has never treated its blessed as anything other than tools."

"I don't...I don't understand," Blossom said desperately, "Why? Why are they treated this way?"

"Hundreds of years ago, before the kingdoms that we know, the blessed and unblessed were in constant combat with each other. Due to their differences each group thought that they should be the ones in charge." Emma sat down next to the fire as she spoke, holding her hand out until Blossom joined her, sitting on the chair opposite. "This was before the Balance was formed. The blessed believed that because the Blessers had given them gifts, that made them better than the unblessed. And the unblessed believed that their vast numbers meant that they were supposed to rule. There were many wars fought over it, but the final one ended with the unblessed victorious."

Blossom rubbed his hands over his face. It had never made sense to him, the human preoccupation with viewing differences as something to fight over. That different somehow meant wrong.

"But if that was hundreds of years ago then why is it still happening? Especially if, as you said, the blessed were beginning to be treated more equally?"

"You have to understand Blossom," Kara sat down next to him and placed a hand on his knee. "That when someone has spent years with their boot on another person's neck, it's very hard for them to remove it. Because they worry that they will then be stepped on."

"That doesn't make it right!" Blossom shouted, standing back up in his shock and indignation.

"I wasn't saying that," Kara tried to explain, "I'm saying that bigotry isn't logical, it's built on emotions, fear, and ignorance. Saying that it isn't right doesn't stop it from happening."

"Then what? I'm just supposed to accept that it does?"

"In a way," Emma joined in. "Understand that it does, and then you're better equipped to fight it."

18

Chapter 18

The group, now in the company of Skyla and Aelius, waited until nightfall before moving again. The mob that had discovered their presence had mostly died down, however there were still a few angry village members wandering the streets, so until they left the village Blossom and Asher hid in the wagon. It was quite a squeeze, but it also allowed Blossom to continue to sooth Edwin as they moved. They had made good progress their first night and so reached the border between Vaten and Shotsen just as the sun was beginning to rise.

Blossom was exhausted, a state he was rapidly growing used to being in, and he knew that it was more than the lack of sleep that had him feeling this way. He had always thought that the blessed and unblessed lived in harmony with each other, as Nature wanted it. The realisation that his own worldview was so at odds with what seemed like the rest of society had sapped him more than he'd thought possible.

He slumped forward, resting his head against Asher's back. They were both riding the same horse now, the introduction of new members of their little traveling pack meaning that they needed to get creative with how they arranged themselves. Blossom wasn't complaining though, their bond was stronger when they were close, and he'd found that Asher's physical presence was able to sooth him almost as well as Water's blessing.

"Nearly there, Flower. You'll be able to sleep soon," Asher murmured, the words accompanied by a wave of adoration that had Blossom rubbing his cheek against the rough cloth of Asher's travel clothes.

"It's not that," he replied, followed by a yawn which caused Asher to chuckle.

"I know, but it'll help. A good sleep, a warm bath and some decent food, it will all help."

"The bath sounds nice," Blossom conceded, sitting up straighter as they reached a border checkpoint. He had changed out of the Blossomite robe and back into his original travel clothes, his hair once again wrapped and concealed so he wasn't that worried about being recognised.

Kara handed the guard a small handful of papers with an air of indifference. The guard's eyes widened as he read them, and he looked at each member of the group in turn before handing them back.

"Please proceed and may the Blessers guide you on your way," the guard said with a bow, gesturing them through grandly.

"What did you show him?" Asher asked, pulling their horse closer to Kara so that it was easier to speak.

Kara smiled. "Royal invitations. We are noble members of an old Shotsen house, one that is known to have Vaten and Castillan blood as well as Shotsen. It was the easiest way to get in without arousing suspicion, as we are all clearly from different kingdoms."

"How long till we reach the palace?" Blossom asked, once again resting his cheek on Asher's back, tightening his grip on his husband's waist just to feel the rush of mirth that it produced.

"A few more hours yet. I'm sorry Blossom but it will still be a little while. If you're that tired why not go back into the wagon?" Kara asked, smiling at him the way she had when he was small and refusing to heed his bedtime.

"I'm fine," Blossom mumbled, only further proving Kara's point, "but I should check on Edwin anyway."

The group slowed to a halt and Blossom slid down from Asher's horse. He stretched with a groan, even if he wasn't tired enough to sleep, he certainly ached. Unlike his husband, Blossom had never ridden for more than a few hours at a time, one of the side effects of never leaving the palace grounds. He stumbled over to the wagon, climbing very ungracefully into the back and nearly falling on top of Edwin's prone form.

"How's he doing?" He asked, settling down on a soft pack next to Lila.

"About the same," Lila replied, smiling tiredly at him.

"How are you doing?" Blossom asked, taking in the gray tinge to the queen's skin. He might have been aching from riding all day, but traveling in the back of a wagon designed to haul products instead of people couldn't have been much better.

"Better than Edwin," Lila replied, wincing as she shifted slightly. "Don't worry about me little flower, just focus on our fallen friend."

With a sigh and a nod Blossom shuffled forward, placing his hands on Edwin's chest and spreading a mixture of Moon and Water's blessing through him as he had every few hours since they'd begun their journey. After doing this so many times with the same person Blossom was becoming attuned to the way Edwin's body was hurting. He could feel the shards of metal lodged in his chest, the way his lungs were struggling to expand properly.

He couldn't imagine how this felt and was really quite glad that Shadow's blessing was still lingering in Edwin's mind, keeping him unconscious as they moved. Blossom knew that he needed to allow Edwin to wake up, but with the sway of the caravan and the bumps of the rocks in the road, Blossom couldn't bring himself to do so. He would remove the shadow once they reached the palace, allow Edwin to return to consciousness in the safety and comfort of a proper sickbed.

"There. He's getting stronger, I can feel it." Blossom slumped back against the wall of the wagon. "Are you sure you don't want soothing?"

Lila smiled, slightly bashfully if Blossom wasn't mistaken. "Well, if you insist."

Blossom laughed lightly. "Where hurts the most?"

Lila gestured to her legs and then her lower back, wincing again as she kneaded at the top of her hips.

Blossom hummed in thought, looking around the small space. "This would work better if you could lay down, but I don't think we're going to be able to do that. Okay, how about this?" He took each of Lila's legs in turn, stretching them whilst pulsing Water's blessing through the tight muscles. He then moved to her back, shuffling so that he was sat behind the queen. He traced the outline of her pelvic bone, feeling for where the muscle was the most painful and finding a bundle of trapped nerves right at the base of her spine.

Lila gasped as Blossom used Moon's blessing to loosen them, her back straightening at the sensation.

"Feel better?" Blossom asked, smiling as Lila nodded, tears beading at the corners of her eyes. "Are these tears because I hurt you or because you're relieved?"

"Relieved," Lila replied, her voice trembling slightly. "That ache has been getting worse these past few months, I can't remember the last time it didn't hurt."

Blossom hugged Lila close to him, feeling the gentle rocking of the wagon as they continued to roll through the countryside. He must have fallen into a doze at some point because the next thing he knew the back of the wagon was opening and Emma's head peeked through.

"We're here," she said, smiling softly as Blossom sat up. "Looks like you did need to sleep after all."

Blossom rolled his eyes as he climbed out of the wagon, taking Asher's hand to steady himself. He looked around once he'd straightened, they were in a grand courtyard of white stone, people who were clearly servants bustling to and fro carrying a plethora of different items.

Two of the servants approached them with a stretcher, a Moon blessed following closely behind, and Blossom stepped to the side to allow them into the wagon.

"What can you tell me of his injuries?" The Moon blessed asked, placing his hand on Edwin's chest.

Blossom began to describe what had happened, the attack and his subsequent attempts to heal his uncle, following as the servants carried him into what he could now see was a palace.

"Thank you, thank you for all you have done. I'll take it from here," the Moon blessed said, squeezing reassuringly at Blossom's shoulder before disappearing down a long hall where the servants had already gone.

"Come on, Flower," Asher coaxed, sliding his hand into Blossom's and tugging him gently away when Blossom simply watched the retreating form of the healer. "Let him do his job, let's go and meet the princess."

Blossom swallowed thickly, suddenly overcome with a feeling of uselessness. "Okay," he said finally, glancing down at his and Asher's appearance as they approached a set of dark, wooden doors. "Shouldn't we change first?"

"Why? Afraid I wouldn't recognise you?" A voice sounded from just behind them and the whole group spun to see a smiling Shotsa woman with shining black hair and sparkling brown eyes. She had changed since they had last met, her hair longer, her figure fuller, but her smile was the same.

Blossom remembered it well, watching her dancing with Asher during his coming-of-age ceremony. She had seemed happy then, but already he could tell that she felt lighter now, more centered and secure in herself.

"Princess Cassandra," Asher bowed reverently, an action which Blossom quickly copied.

"Prince Asher, Master Blossom," Princess Cassandra replied, her smile widening, "or should that be King Asher and Prince Blossom?"

"I haven't been coronated yet princess," Asher said, his light tone hiding the pain that Blossom could feel surging through their bond.

Cassandra hummed, tilting her head to the side as she took in everyone else gathered there. "I see you have met the great leveler."

"Time makes dust of us all," Kara, Emma, Lila, and Skyla replied in unison.

"How many of those phrases did you say there were?" Blossom asked with a sigh.

"Five Petal. You've heard three of them now," Emma replied, stepping away from the door as Cassandra walked forward and swung them open.

"I'm sure you wish to rest, and I will have some of the servants show you to your chambers as soon as we are done here, but first I must introduce you to my parents."

∞

The king and queen of Shotsen had the same kind eyes as their daughter, even if they didn't share their colour. The king was a large

Earth blessed, the queen a willowy Water blessed, and they greeted everyone like they were old friends.

Like Asher wasn't the son of the man who had stolen their kingdom's blessed.

He knew that he hadn't had a choice in the matter, that Silas had used him the way he had used the blessed, but that didn't make him feel any better. He looked down as Blossom squeezed his hand, his husband's worry emanating through their bond seconds later.

He smiled at Blossom and returned his attention to the royal family. "We are honored to be received here, Your Majesties."

"Not at all," King Hawk replied, raising his hand to silence any protests, "we are only happy that we could help. The Balance has been silent on these matters for far too long, they should have stepped in when this all started. When our children were taken from us. When the blessed were beaten down. When the blessed and unblessed were pitted against each other so that they wouldn't focus on the real enemy."

"We're stepping in now," Emma said with determination, "and hopefully, with Blossom as a real part of the Balance we can begin to create a truly equal world."

King Hawk nodded and Queen Meela stood up with a small smile. "You have travelled a long way, you need rest. We will send food to your rooms tonight and tomorrow we can plan properly."

The group were taken through the light, airy hallways of the palace towards the bedchambers. This palace was so different from the one he'd known his whole life that Asher found himself staring as they walked, his head turning quickly from side to side in an attempt to take it all in. The royal palace of Vaten was grand, filled with opulence, but to the point where it was oppressive - the dark reds and golds sometimes feeling stuffy and suffocating. In comparison, the Shotsen palace was all light stone and wide-open spaces. The climate of Shotsen was warmer than that of Vaten, with mild winters and long summers, so the palace was built to remain cool and relaxed.

Asher and Blossom were shown into a large bedchamber, the bed in the center of it round instead of the rectangular ones they were used to. The room was also round, with large windows taking up the majority of the space. The windows were open, the warm breeze from outside causing the light blue curtains to flutter inwards, casting the room in a glow that rippled like water.

"This place is beautiful," Blossom breathed, hands clutched to his chest.

"Thank you, Master Blossom," Cassandra replied, her almost constant smile widening with pride. "There is a bathing room just through here, I will have the servants send up some food in an hour or so. Please take this time to relax and recuperate."

Asher closed the door behind him as Princess Cassandra left, turning to Blossom when he sighed.

"Guilt won't do anyone any good, my love," Blossom said gently, cupping Asher's cheek and placing a sweet kiss on his lips. "Now come, let's bathe and then sleep. That bed looks far too comfortable for us to waste it, don't you think?"

Asher couldn't help but chuckle lightly. "Is this to be our marriage tour then?" He asked, following his husband as Blossom pulled him in the direction of the bathing room.

"Why not? I get the feeling that the time for lightness and brevity will soon be over. Let's enjoy it while we can."

19

Chapter 19

Blossom fell asleep almost as soon as his head hit the pillow. The bed was one of the most comfortable ones he'd ever been in, and the slow rise and fall of Asher's chest next to him was just as soothing as it had been on their first night together. For the first time in months, or perhaps even years, he slept without dreaming.

They were awoken in the morning by a gentle knock at the door. A young servant girl entered silently and rested a tray laden with warm bread, honey and yogurt on the vanity. "Princess Cassandra instructed me to tell you that they will be gathering in the royal library in an hour," she said with a bow, before backing out of the room just as quietly.

"Did you sleep as well as I did?" Asher asked, stretching with a groan.

"You know I did," Blossom replied, smiling and kissing Asher's cheek. "Would you like honey or yogurt with your bread?" He asked, making his way over to the tray. The scent of the freshly baked bread was enough to make his mouth water, and he popped a small chunk into his mouth before bringing the tray over to the bed.

"I've never had bread with yogurt before," Asher said, tearing off his own piece and dipping it in the creamy substance. He groaned happily at the taste, reaching for another slice before he'd even swallowed.

Blossom ate at a much slower pace, making his way through half of his own roll before standing and disappearing into the bathing room. He cleaned himself quickly whilst Asher finished his breakfast, pulling on his summer robe and sighing happily at the comforting familiarity of the cloth against his skin.

It had only been a few days but already he had missed his traditional blessers robes.

"There's my pretty flower," Asher cooed when Blossom emerged again, taking his face in his hands and pressing a kiss to his forehead. "It was odd seeing you in those other clothes."

"It felt odd being in those other clothes," Blossom replied, tracing the outline of the new black threaded pattern that had joined his robes since their marriage. "Let's go down and see if we can make a proper plan now."

They walked, hand in hand, through the open, airy halls of the palace until they reached the library, where they found themselves to be the last to arrive.

"We're not late, are we?" Asher asked, sitting next to Kara at the large table.

"Not at all Your Majesty, we were just discussing the best way to go about your initiation," Princess Cassandra said with an almost mischievous smile, her dark eyes sparkling with excitement.

"Please, we are both royalty. Call me Asher."

"Okay Asher, but only if you call me Cassandra."

"The traditional initiation would take too long and requires years of study on top of that, so we've been trying to come up with something that would work instead," Kara began, pausing and looking at her wife when Emma huffed.

"Emma?" Blossom asked.

"I think, considering what the two of you have already gone through, and all that we have already told you, you're basically honorary members of the Balance as it is. We should simply give you the oath to recite and then get to what is actually important." Emma looked around the gathered group, rolling her eyes when nobody spoke. "Confronting my sister, dismantling the Blossomites and restoring balance."

"But that is not the way we normally do things," Cassandra said.

"Forgive me Princess," Lila cut in, "but can't we concede that these are not 'normal' times, and Blossom and Asher are not and have never been 'normal' people?"

"We need to go to the island of the Blessers. If Asher and I need to complete some kind of initiation in order to get there then I'm willing to do it, but we have to get there and we have to do it soon." Blossom looked down at his lap once he finished, curling his fingers into loose fists. "Things are changing rapidly; I can feel it. The world may have already been out of balance but what happened on the day of our wedding, whether it was Silas' death or Asher and I bonding, it's shifted something. We need to fix it, and the only way we're going to be able to do that is to go to the island, I just know it."

After a beat of silence Cassandra nodded. "A test then, let us test you the way we always test fledgling blessed members and then you can recite the oath. Once you've done that you will be true members of the Balance." She spread her hands expansively, looking around the table for any kind of disagreement.

"Okay, Emma, Lila and I will stay here and prepare for the next pilgrimage. You take Asher and Blossom to the training grounds and give them their test," Kara stated definitively, resting her hand on Emma's shoulder to keep her in her seat when she made to rise. "You know that they should do this alone, dove. We are in a hurry but that doesn't mean that we need to throw away all of our traditions."

"It's okay Emma," Blossom said, squeezing at her knee, "Kara's right, we should uphold at least some traditions."

Despite wanting to stay and help with the planning Blossom followed Cassandra back out of the library, smiling over his shoulder as Asher lingered by the table. "Come my love. You need to do this as well."

Asher sighed but did as he was bid, following them out of the library and further into the palace until they reached an open courtyard. The sun was shining, and the weather was warm enough that Blossom could almost believe that they were simply on their marriage tour, and not on the run.

That they weren't on the precipice of a fundamental shift in the way that Vaten, perhaps even the world, functioned.

He could feel it, deep in his gut. None of them were going to come out of this the same. No one was going to be able to go back to the way things had been before this. And he couldn't find it in himself to be sorry for that.

"So, what is it we need to do to prove ourselves?" Asher asked, an underlying current of offense travelling through his bond which caused Blossom to chuckle lightly.

"Oh, come on Asher. You had to go through an initiation to enter the knight's guild," Blossom said when Asher glared at him, "this is just the same."

"Fine," Asher agreed begrudgingly. He shook out his hands and rolled his neck as though he was preparing for a fight.

"Not exactly the same," Blossom clarified, before looking over at Cassandra, "is it?"

"I'm not sure what the knight's guild initiation is but I'm not going to ask you to spar or anything," Cassandra replied, her smile easy and open. "I will ask you to showcase your blessings. I've been told that you have also discovered a blessing Asher?"

Asher nodded, "we discovered that I wasn't cursed at all. My blessing was being suppressed which was what was making me ill." He pre-emptively reached out and squeezed at Blossom's shoulder. "Silas knew about it and made Blossom suppress it, he had no idea what he was doing."

"Which Blesser has given you their gift?"

"Shadow."

Cassandra raised her eyebrows, "Shadow? I've never heard of Shadow's blessing before."

"No one has, at least as far as we know. We're still not sure why. Edwin was going to research that when we reached the Blessers island but now..." Blossom trailed off, gazing into the distance. "He's not going to be able to make that trip."

"We'll care for him Blossom," Cassandra interjected, "I've already spoken with queen Lila, and she is also going to stay here. We will both look after him. We have many talented Moon blessed in our kingdom who will be able to help, I'm sure." When Blossom nodded she took a deep breath and stepped to the side, gesturing towards the center of the courtyard.

"Asher, please step into the center circle and show us the truth of your blessing."

Asher followed the gesture and walked out into the sunlight. He looked around, turning in a small circle. There weren't a lot of dark spaces in the courtyard, which would actually serve as a good challenge for him. They had yet to reach the point in their training where Asher had to ask for blessing when the Blesser's presence was only tangentially there.

Asher focused on a shadowy corner of the courtyard, closing his eyes and reaching his hand towards it. Blossom watched his lips move as he used Shadow's word, and a thin tendril of darkness crawled from the corner and up his hand. He allowed it to spread over his arm, turning it invisible as he employed the shield technique that they had learnt together.

"Oh wow, that is really something! What an unusual blessing," Cassandra said, clapping her hands together in front of her in excitement. "Blossom, your turn now. Please show us the truth of your blessings."

Blossom smiled and took Asher's place in the center. He had replenished his stores of all the blessings this morning and now felt much closer to his old self. This would just be the same thing that he'd done during the long day and night celebrations back at the blessing school.

He took a deep breath, taking stock of where the Blessers dwelled in the little courtyard. There was a small fountain behind him, enough for Water's blessing to be felt, the floor appeared to be heated, the warmth of Fire's blessing glowing beneath his feet. And of course, the sun which beat down upon him, the stone of the walls, and the same shadow that Asher had called from.

He opened his eyes again, reaching behind himself to call a thin stream of water. He flicked his wrist, causing the water to twirl in a ribbon around his body. With his other hand Blossom raised a wall of earth. He dropped both hands and took another breath, this time when he raised them a spiral of fire followed. With a clap the fire extinguished, and as he slowly spread them apart he formed a small ball of sunlight.

He lowered his hands, keeping the ball of light between them. He then called forth his store of Moon's blessing, turning the light from a warm orange to a cool blue. Finally, he mimicked Asher's actions, surrounding himself with Shadow's blessing and disappearing for an instant.

"Well done, well done!" Cassandra said gleefully, practically bouncing as she clapped. "I've always wanted to watch the way you manipulate all of the blessings. It is my honour and pleasure to tell you that you are now officially members of the Balance."

20

Chapter 20

By the time Asher and Blossom returned to the library the majority of the plan for their journey had already been agreed upon. Asher could feel himself growing incensed again as Kara outlined the pilgrimage, he wasn't used to not being included in things like this. He had always been at the forefront of planning, and this feeling of being treated like a child that couldn't be trusted to be involved was really grating on him.

He glanced over at Blossom as his husband sighed, catching his eye and mimicking his wry smile. He knew that this wasn't a new feeling for Blossom, even if it had never been this bad before.

"The pilgrimage to the island is a well-worn but secret journey, it will be the safest way to get to our destination without being caught," Kara explained, glancing up at Asher. "There really isn't much in the way of war planning that can be done at this moment, Your Majesty. We need to see what information the archives at the balance headquarters can provide, and what Blossom discovers at the island before we make real plans."

"I didn't say anything," Asher replied snippily, causing Kara to chuckle.

"You didn't have to. I've trained with you long enough to read your feelings on your face. You needed to be inducted into the Balance, we needed to talk dates and the other mundane acts that are needed for the great pilgrimage. We weren't excluding you."

"Fine. When do we leave?" Asher asked, crossing his arms and rolling his eyes dramatically.

"In two days," Emma replied, straightening when Asher and Blossom blinked in simultaneous surprise. "The pilgrimage happens twice a year, starting on either the long day or the long night. The long day is in two days, so we will leave then."

"Do you have a solstice celebration?" Blossom asked, turning to Cassandra.

"We do. It is mostly a feast the night before, we then rise with the early sun and give our thanks to the Blessers in the royal gardens. Would you like to join?"

"I would."

"The feast will be tomorrow night," Cassandra said clasping her hands together in front of her, "we will also use it as a goodbye feast, to wish you well on your journey."

"So, what should we do until then?" Asher asked, shifting on his feet.

"You could relax. Spend the day exploring the palace, walking the gardens, whatever you want," Cassandra said, shrugging like she didn't care either way.

"Or you can join me in the training arena and work on the techniques that we've both been letting slide for the past few months," Kara interjected with a meaningful look at the prince.

Asher straightened, feeling a rush of excitement through his body at the thought of returning to something familiar, something that he could do in his sleep. Working his body until he fell into bed, satisfied and aching in a way that he could be proud of. He felt a flicker of something else through his bond and looked over at Blossom.

But Blossom simply smiled at him, leaning up to press a kiss to his cheek. "Go if you wish. I need to speak with Skyla and Aelius, we can both train in our own way. As long as you return to me with enough energy to celebrate our escape, my love."

Asher couldn't help but flush at the insinuation, but he hid it with a smile of his own. He wound his arms around Blossom's waist, tugging him close and kissing him properly. "I love you."

"And I you. Now go," Blossom slapped lightly at his chest, stepping back and turning to Emma. "Where are the children?"

∞

As much as he would have loved to spend the day relaxing as Cassandra had offered, Blossom knew that he had more important things to do. He needed to find out from the people who had experienced it first-hand what had happened after his disappearance.

Emma took him to a smaller courtyard than the one that he and Asher had performed in, finding Aelius and Skyla sitting in a huddle on one of the stone benches that jutted from the walls.

"Skyla, Aelius, how are you today?" Blossom asked as he made his way over to sit down on the empty bench next to theirs.

"Master Blossom." Skyla almost looked like she wanted to stand up, but she contented herself with bowing her head slightly. "I'm well Master Blossom, how are you?"

"Mostly okay, if a little confused," Blossom confessed, smiling when Skyla and Aelius shared their own look of confusion. "I'm confused because I had no idea how my blessed children were living outside of the palace walls. How you were being treated. I'm so sorry, I should have been doing more to..."

"Master Blossom," Skyla interrupted, her cheeks turning pink when she realised what she had done. "None of us blame you for that, we know that you didn't have the power to change things. We also know that you were never allowed outside of the palace, how could you know what was going on?"

Blossom curled his hands in his lap, feeling the silky material of his robe slipping through his fingers. "That doesn't make it okay," he said quietly before straightening. "I want you to explain to me exactly what it was like before you joined my classroom, how you were being raised and how you were treated as blessed children."

Aelius and Skyla looked at each other again. "We were raised very differently," Skyla said after a moment of pause.

Aelius nodded, "I told you how mama used to treat me."

"You did, and again, I'm very sorry I didn't help. I hope you believe me when I say that I was making plans to keep you within the palace. I didn't want to send you back to your mother."

Aelius smiled up at him, his eyes large and full of trust. "I believe you, Master Blossom."

"How about you Skyla. How were you raised?"

"Both of my parents are Earth blessed," Skyla said, looking off into the distance. "Or at least they were, the Blossomites killed them a month ago when they tried to take me."

"I'm so sorry."

Skyla's expression was sad and her grip on the stone bench beneath her tightened, turning her knuckles white. "They were strong, they fought to the end, I'm proud of them." She sighed, shifting in her seat, shaking her head like she wanted to physically dispel the thought. "It's rare for an entire family to be blessed, especially by the same deity, so my childhood was unusual. I was able to learn my blessing from a very young age, and in my village at least, Earth blessed were held in quite high regard. We had built all the buildings in the village, we were responsible for guarding against bandits and wild animals, so I was never treated badly. It wasn't until I visited the city with my father that I saw how other blessed were treated."

"And how were they being treated?"

"Like animals…no, like tools." Skyla tapped at her chin in thought. "As though we exist purely as a channel for the Blesser's gifts, like we're just vessels that can be used to build things, grow things." She gestured to the little Sun blessed next to her. "And as vessels we don't have thoughts and feelings. I even saw a few blessed still in bondage."

"In what?" Blossom asked, a stone sinking into his gut at the word.

"Before Silas became king it was common for the unblessed to own blessed people. Rich unblessed brought blessed children from their parents and raised them like pets."

"That's…that's…" Blossom didn't know what to say. "Did Silas outlaw that?"

"He did," Skyla replied, "one of the few good things he did do. He never seemed that interested in the outlying villages, or blessed people who weren't rich, but he did stop children from being stolen from their parents."

"And now they're being stolen by the Blossomites," Blossom sighed, scrubbing a hand down his face in exasperation. "Okay next question. Would you two be willing to help me, me and Asher, take down the Blossomites and restore peace and order to this country?"

"Of course, Master Blossom," Aelius practically shouted, bouncing in his seat. "Skyla's mother inducted me into the Balance a few weeks ago as well."

"She did?" Blossom asked, frowning in confusion. "Wait, I thought you said your parents died?"

"My birth parents," Skyla explained, "but I had two mothers, my parents were a trio."

"Oh," Blossom said, he had heard of a few families that raised children communally, relationships where more than two people shared a bed, but he hadn't actually met anyone from one of those families. "Okay, that makes more sense."

"So, we can come with you on the pilgrimage, right?" Aelius asked.

"Uh...yes I think so."

∞

They set out as the sun set on the long day, filled with good food and wine. Well, Asher was filled with food and wine, he'd watched with a sinking heart as Blossom once again reverted to picking at his plate, staring off into the distance as time wore on.

But Blossom had at least eaten - he'd cleared half of his plate and then finished one of the strawberry tarts that Emma placed in front of him, and Asher couldn't help but feel like tonight's meal was different to the others where Blossom had struggled. Beforehand it had been clear that Blossom had either been scared or felt unable to eat, tonight it was just like he had no interest in it.

He had perked up when the group went to the royal gardens and gave their thanks to the Blessers. Had smiled so proudly at Asher when he'd released some of Shadow's blessing into the sky along with all the other blessed there. Asher had always been aware that the long day and night were sacred occasions, but there was something different about it this time. He felt a deeper connection to the whole thing now, and he wasn't sure if it was because he was now blessed, or if it was due to their bond.

"Are you okay, Flower?" Asher asked, shuffling closer to his husband in the covered wagon that they had been guided into. It didn't matter who they were or what they might be, Kara had made it clear that neither of them would be getting special treatment. They would journey to the island the same way everyone else did, housed in a windowless box, let out only at pre-determined rest stops so that they couldn't track the location of the Blesser's home on earth.

Blossom blinked at him, seemingly coming out of a daze. His face broke into a relieved smile, and he slumped against Asher. "Yes. It finally feels like we're going somewhere. I feel like we're right at the precipice of figuring out who we are."

Asher wasn't sure he agreed, he was glad they were actively doing something, but he wasn't sure that they were going to get all the answers that they wanted by going to the island. He wasn't sure any one place could hold all of the answers to any question.

"Excited to see where we were born?" Asher asked for no other reason than to speak. He laid down on the soft cushions that made up the bottom of the wagon, holding his arm out until Blossom took the hint and followed him, laying his head on Asher's chest.

"Yeah," Blossom said after a pregnant pause, the word holding a weight that Asher couldn't guess at.

Asher bumped Blossom's head with his shoulder, peering down at him when Blossom looked up in confusion. "What's on your mind?"

Blossom pushed himself into a half-sitting position, hovering over Asher. He gnawed on his bottom lip as he thought and Asher stayed silent, letting Blossom figure out how he wanted to say whatever it was that he'd been thinking about. "Is it..." Blossom sighed, shaking his head. "This is going to sound mad."

"Flower," Asher said, tilting his head to the side with an indulgent smile. "It's just me, tell me what you're thinking."

"You said the place where we were born," Blossom muttered, tracing the stitching on Asher's doublet as the prince nodded. "I'm not sure we were born."

"What do you mean?"
"I think we were made."

21

Chapter 21

Blossom had never really taken the time to think about it before. It had always been in the back of his mind, the idea that there should have been at least one other person with the same gifts as him, but he'd never had the time to properly focus on it. Now, with Asher's blessing, with the reveal of the Blessers earthbound home, he was starting to wonder if there was something more to his blessed nature than simple luck.

Blossom couldn't explain what he meant by his statement, and he knew that Asher didn't understand. But the more he'd been thinking about their blessed nature, about the fact that there had never before been someone born with all of Nature's blessings, nor someone that had been gifted Shadow's blessing, the more he became certain that he was right.

The first day and night of the journey passed fairly uneventfully, they stopped in a nondescript copse of trees where Blossom and Asher were allowed out of the wagon, along with the 5 other travelers who were making the pilgrimage with them. They ate quietly, spoke rarely and at a near whisper, constantly on watch for passers-by. There was an air of excitement in the camp, a knowledge that they were taking a sacred journey, but the threat of being discovered dampened any real levity that might have been felt.

As Blossom and Asher lay comfortably among the pillows and blankets the next morning, in no hurry to rejoin the world, they were jolted into wakefulness as the carriage came to a sudden stop.

"Blossom." Blossom and Asher both looked up as Emma's voice floated through the canvas of the wagon, followed by a rapping of knuckles on the frame.

"Yes?" Blossom asked, confusion clear in his voice.

"I think you might want to see this."

Asher and Blossom exchanged a glance before scrambling out through the back of the wagon.

"Emma what..." Blossom trailed off as he finally took in his surroundings. He felt a cold, hard stab of recognition when his gaze landed on the tiny cottage, surrounded as it always had been by thousands of brightly coloured flowers. "How..." He stopped himself again, unsure exactly what it was that he was asking in the first place.

"This is the cottage that you always described, isn't it Petal?" Emma asked, resting a hand on his shoulder. "The one that Evelyn took you to when she stole you away."

Blossom nodded mutely, stepping forward into the meadow that he'd spent so much time alone in as a small child, only this time he was flanked by his husband and his mother.

"How did you find this place?" Asher asked as they slowly descended the hill.

"This is part of the usual pilgrimage route. The convoy has passed this spot thousands of times before, however when I was last on pilgrimage I was in the wagons. That was also years before either of you were born," Emma explained, before heaving a sigh. "And when we went in search of you, well, we never thought to check I guess."

"Do you remember ever seeing a convoy of black, covered wagons Flower?" Asher asked, looking back at the slightly foreboding sight of the line of wagons atop the hill.

Blossom shook his head. "There were days when Evelyn would keep me inside, where she would bar the door and block the windows. She would tell me that she had gotten word that there were people on their way to take me from her. I was always so scared that I never paid much mind to the time of year."

"She wasn't wrong, in a way. If any of the guardians had ever seen a little, pink haired child, then they would have known that it was you." Emma mused as Blossom reached out a tentative hand for the door handle.

The door was stiff but not locked, and with a heave and a shove of his shoulder it swung inwards. The cottage looked exactly the same as it had the day he had been taken, aside from the layer of dust covering everything. Blossom clapped his hands together once, causing a loud boom to echo around the small space. Emma jumped at the noise but whatever exclamation or question she had died on her lips as Blossom called on Earth's blessing and, using the vibrations he'd made with the clap, moved the dust from every surface. Sweeping his hands towards his body he stepped aside, sending the dust motes through the open door.

"I guess Silas never came in here, I can't imagine this place would still be standing if he had," he muttered, mostly to himself as he moved through the space. He bent and picked up a discarded toy, rubbing his thumb over the smooth wood of the duck's painted head. "Did the journal ever speak of what Evelyn did when Silas tried to take me? I can't remember."

"I don't think so Petal," Emma said, she spoke quietly but her voice seemed to echo around the small space.

Blossom slipped the toy into the pocket of his robe as he opened the door to the meadow out the back. The meadow he'd been playing in when they had taken him, and he was suddenly seized with a desperate urge to return to the spot from his dreams. Not checking to see if Asher and Emma were following, he walked the gentle incline until he reached the spot that he remembered from his dreams. He knelt down carefully, taking care not to crush any of the flowers beneath him and reached a finger out to a new bud.

He pulsed a gentle jet of Sun's blessing into the flower and watched as the bright blue petals began to unfurl, just as they had all those years ago. Except this time, Blossom knew enough about his gift to know that he had influenced the colour of the flower as well as its growth.

"Blossom."

Blossom turned on his knees to call back to Emma but froze as he took in the sight of Asher walking towards him, of Emma standing in the doorway of his childhood home. This was almost exactly as his dream had been before his wedding day. The only difference was that instead of the rolling fields that he could now see, in his dream the cottage had been backed by a lake shrouded in fog.

"What?" He whispered to himself, so many questions encompassed in that one word.

Did this mean something?

Had he foreseen this? Or was it just a coincidence?

"Flower?" Asher asked as he drew level with him. "Are you okay?"

"I...I've seen this before," Blossom said, still staring at the cottage.

Asher looked over his shoulder and then back at Blossom, his brows furrowed in confusion. "Of course you have, this was where you grew up."

Blossom climbed to his feet, stumbling slightly when he realised that his legs had gone numb. "No I mean, I've seen this exact scene before. The night before we wed, I woke up from a nightmare remember?"

Asher nodded, reaching out a hand as though to steady him. "Yes, it was after that you told me what Silas had done to you, how he had severed our bond."

"It was this." Blossom gestured to the meadow, to Emma, to Asher. "This was my dream except...except I was afraid, I was worried that something bad was going to happen."

"But you don't feel afraid," Asher stated, "at least not in a way that I can feel it."

Blossom couldn't help but laugh lightly, taking Asher's hand and beginning to walk back down the hill. "No, my darling, I don't. I do have a question for you though."

Asher hummed, gesturing for Blossom to continue.

"Do you notice our bond anymore? I mean, I still feel it and I know when it's your feelings and not mine, but it doesn't feel weird anymore."

"No, I understand what you mean," Asher replied, swinging their clasped hands between them. "I almost don't remember what it was like not to experience your feelings, and I'm not sure how I went for so long feeling so empty."

They reached the bottom of the hill where Emma was still waiting. "We should get going Petal, this isn't one of the scheduled stops and we've already been here for too long. Are there any things in the house that you want to take with you?"

Blossom slipped his free hand into his pocket and grasped the toy duck again as memories of the other small toys and trinkets that he had as a child flashed through his mind. "I think...there was something, if I can find it." He went back into the cottage, heading to the little cubby in the back where he used to sleep and rooting through the old blankets until his fingers brushed against something soft.

He grasped the stuffed animal, stroking the soft grey fur of the little rabbit. "There you are," he whispered, twisting one of the long ears around his finger the way he used to when he was falling asleep.

A loud gasp caused Blossom to look up, frowning as he saw the look on Emma's face. Her eyes were shiny with tears, and she was covering her mouth with her hands like she was desperately trying not to cry.

"Miss Flops...you still had Miss Flops," Emma gasped, tears now tracking down her cheeks.

"Yes." Blossom looked down at the rabbit and then back up at Emma as her statement finally sunk in. "How did you know her name?"

"Because I gave that to you," Emma explained, wiping at her tears with the heel of her hand. "It was my toy as a child, and I put it in your crib the day we found you. I thought it had gotten lost, but Evelyn must have taken it with her when she left."

Blossom felt a swell of love for Emma, enough that he could feel tears of his own building. He stepped forward and pulled his mother into a tight hug, burying his face in her shoulder as she continued to weep.

∞

They walked back to the convoy in a happy silence. Asher could still feel the warm giddiness that Blossom was experiencing at the discovery of his childhood toy, and he couldn't help but smile.

"Come here Flower," he said gently once they had climbed into their wagon, pulling his husband down onto the pillows and holding him against his chest. "Do you want to talk about it?" He asked, stroking his hand up and down Blossom's side.

"I'm not sure what there is to say. It was my home, and it looked the same as the last time I saw it. Knowing that in a way, Emma was with me even after Evelin stole me away, that makes me happy," Blossom whispered, holding the little bunny toy close to his face and inhaling its scent.

"It's a special thing, isn't it?" Asher said, touching the rabbit's head tentatively, almost worried that Blossom wouldn't want him to. "Maybe one day we can give it to our child."

Blossom smiled up at him, pressing a quick kiss to his lips. "This is the first time we've spoken about kids since we've been married."

"Is it so different from when we weren't?"

Blossom shrugged, jostling Asher and causing him to snort in amusement. "Before... I never allowed myself to actually consider it, I never believed that we would get married, that Silas would let us."

"And now?"

"Now do I believe that we could get married?" Blossom asked, joining in with Asher's returning laugh.

"No, what do you think of children now?" Asher kissed Blossom again, stroking a hand through his soft curls.

"I would love to have children with you..." Blossom said, his sentence seeming to trail off at the end as he gazed into nothing.

"But?"

"But I'm not sure how I feel about a surrogate. I know that the people would expect the king's child to share his essence but...I would rather we take in children. Ones without parents, or ones who have parents that can't or won't take care of them."

Asher could feel Blossom's worry, knew that it was worry about his reaction to his husband's confession. To sooth his fears Asher kissed him yet again. "I love that idea, my sweet boy. We can give our children a better life than they would have otherwise had."

Blossom visibly relaxed, returning his attention to the toy, contemplating it with a hum. "We should wait until this is all over, but as soon as we are settled again, as soon as the world is back in balance, we should start our family."

22

Chapter 22

B lossom had expected a pilgrimage of multiple days to get to the island, but as the sun was setting on the second day the convoy drew
to a halt and Emma pulled aside the canvas flaps.

"We're here," she said chipperly. "Come and see the place where you
were born."

Blossom stretched with a groan, stiff from almost a full day of laying
down. The wagon had been comfortable but wasn't really large enough
to sit for any length of time. Asher also groaned as he climbed from the
wagon, clicking his back audibly in the encroaching darkness.

"I'm glad that's over," he sighed, smiling over at Blossom as he
looped their arms together.

"We might need to do it again on the way back."

"Don't worry Petal. Once you've made the pilgrimage, once you've
been accepted by the leaders, then you are free to come and go as you
please," Emma said over her shoulder as she led them towards a large,
but squat, building made of red brick. "Welcome to the headquarters of
the Balance," she said as she pushed open the door, spreading her arms
in a dramatic gesture of greeting.

The inside of the building was fairly nondescript but felt instantly cozy, and clearly lived in. The red brick was hung with a variety of rich tapestries all in warm colours, the ground beneath their feet was smooth with age, and Blossom could hear the indistinct chattering of many voices further ahead. As they walked down the hallway Blossom spied that strange symbol with the two triangles again.

"Emma," he called, jogging slightly to catch up with her. "What does this symbol mean?"

"That is the symbol of the Balance," Emma explained, pointing to another one set below one of the burning torches. "Two identical triangles, the top one balanced on the bottom. The two points of the triangles must be perfectly aligned for this to work, just as the world must be carefully cared for to remain balanced."

Blossom hummed in understanding, taking Asher's hand as the prince lagged behind somewhat. "My love?" He asked when Asher drew level with him.

"Sorry, I was distracted," Asher replied, glancing behind him at a tapestry that they had passed. "They have a tapestry of the night of our birth," he said, "well, your birth. Or at least it depicts Emma and Edwin finding you."

Blossom looked over his shoulder to where Asher was gesturing. "I guess that makes sense, they didn't realise that you were there too."

Emma showed them into a grand dining room filled with long tables. The tables were only half filled, people sitting in seemingly random spots, some chatting in groups, some sitting alone, reading as they ate. "This is the main eating hall. There are smaller places if you want to eat in the quiet, but this is where the food is prepared. We have a constant stream of food being served because we work in shifts, so everyone's days are different."

They joined a line that was moving slowly along the left-hand wall of the room. As they drew closer to the end Blossom noticed a number of cookers and tables with deep bowls in them, and four people stood behind the tables serving food to those in the line.

"Emma, when can we visit the island?" Blossom asked, taking a bowl filled with an aromatic stew that was handed to him.

"Once you've eaten, and once you've met with the Elders. I'm sure they will be happy to take you to the shoreline to see the island, Petal," Emma replied, adding a few small, warm rolls to her plate. "But no one has ever been able to get onto the island, the shroud of shadow prevents that."

"Shadow?" Blossom looked at Asher who shrugged. A realisation hit him so suddenly that he almost dropped his food. Catching his bowl at the last moment he stumbled over to the nearest table and sat down.

"Blossom? What's the matter?" Emma asked, sitting down next to him and pressing the back of her hand to his forehead. "Do you feel unwell?"

Blossom shook his head mutely, waving away her hand. "Shadow is the blessing of protection," he said, almost to himself, "and Asher is the first Shadow blessed person that we know of."

Asher was nodding along with him, but Emma still seemed lost.

"What if Shadow is so particular about its blessing because only Shadow blessed people can remove the shroud and allow someone onto that island?"

"I don't know, I guess it's possible," Emma mused, taking a mouthful of stew.

"We should at least try though, right?" Blossom pushed, clutching his spoon hard enough in his excitement that the metal began biting into his hand.

Asher gently pulled the spoon from his hand and placed it back on the table. "If we're going to meet the Elders after we've eaten then we can ask them," he said, rubbing his hand up and down Blossom's back. "So, eat up Flower, let's get prepared for whatever's going to happen."

They ate in silence, the stew going down surprisingly easily considering the way heavy meals had always been difficult for him. Blossom thought back to the last few days of travel and realised that he hadn't really eaten since first climbing into that wagon, but that didn't fully explain why. He had been finding that he could eat a lot more often since he and Asher had bonded. He wasn't sure if the two were related but he had wondered if Asher's confidence and ease when it came to that part of life was rubbing off on him. There was also all of the little pushes and reassurances that Emma and Asher had been giving him over their months of hiding. He hadn't really thought much of it, but they had always made sure he ate something, sitting with him long after they had finished their own meals until he was full.

Once they had eaten and Emma had said hello to a few Balance members that she hadn't seen in a long time, she took them down the winding halls towards where the Elders worked.

"Where's Kara?" Asher asked as they stopped outside a non-descript wooden door. "And Aelius and Skyla?"

"Aelius and Skyla have been taken to the children's dorm room to settle in and meet the other young ones. Kara is gathering the guardians," Emma explained, knocking on the door with three quick raps of her knuckles.

"Come in." A voice sounded through the wood and Emma pushed the door open, ushering Asher and Blossom inside.

"Honored Elders, this is Blossom, and this is Asher. They have just completed their pilgrimage and wished to meet with you," Emma said, bowing reverently before gesturing to each of them.

There were 5 people in the room, each sat behind a curved desk. Upon their introduction the man in the center rose to his feet, his heavily lined face creasing into a smile. "Greetings Master Blossom, long have we waited for this reunion. And you have brought with you your husband, it is very nice to meet you, Prince Asher." He opened his hands in a gesture of welcome. "We hope your journey was a pleasant one. We are very happy to have you with us. I assume that Emma has explained our role and your own part in our history, but should you have any questions then I'm sure we can find the time to answer them."

"Thank you Elders. We have indeed been told of our origins. Finally." Blossom muttered the last word under his breath but from the disapproving look he received from a few of the seated Elders he knew that it had been heard. He readdressed the man that was standing. "However, Asher is not only my husband." He tugged at his and Asher's entwined hands, causing Asher to look at him. "He is also Shadow blessed, perhaps the world's first."

The elders looked at each other in confusion, muttering amongst themselves for a few moments before the man who had originally spoke addressed them again. "We don't understand Master Blossom, there is no such thing as Shadow's blessing."

"There is, it just so happens that Shadow appears to be even more selective than Water in who can receive its blessing. Asher, do you want to show them what we've learnt?" Blossom asked, gesturing Asher in front of him.

Asher stepped forward, calling Shadow's blessing and winding it up his arm in much the same way as he had back in Shotsen. "It's the blessing of protection, and Blossom believes that it is why the Blessers' island is shrouded in shadow."

The elders didn't seem convinced, but the man in the center nodded. "This is definitely an interesting development. We will have to search through the archives to see if any of the texts speak of a Shadow's blessing." He sat back down, as though to signal that their conversation was at an end.

"We were hoping to see the island. We think that it might hold the answers to some questions about out origins," Blossom said, looking around at each of the Elders to gauge their reactions "and with Asher's blessing we might be able to dispel the shroud, which would allow us to actually get to the island."

A woman to the left of the center shook her head. "I don't think this is a good idea. We are happy for Emma to take you to the shore where we found you, but the island has been protected for a reason and it is not up to us to question the Blessers."

Blossom opened his mouth to retort but snapped it shut again when Asher took his hand and gave it a squeeze, a surge of calming and reassuring emotions flowing through their bond.

"Well, we will let you get settled in, you have had a long journey. Tomorrow we will begin the proper preparations for removing that traitor Evelyn from the throne of Vaten and restoring balance to the kingdom. So, I would recommend that you get some rest. Emma, you have our permission to take Master Blossom and his husband to the lakeside."

Blossom could feel Asher's indignation at the way they were being dismissed and returned his own soothing feelings through their bond. "The king and I thank you," he said as they turned to leave, his mouth quirking up at the corners as Asher snorted.

"They meant no disrespect, Your Majesty," Emma said as they walked back down the winding halls towards the entrance. "It's just that kingdoms are an invention of man, and the Balance focuses on the rule of Nature. Royalty is treated no differently than anyone else."

"Still, even if they don't view royalty as higher than non-royalty, Asher is the first Shadow blessed. Shouldn't that require a bit more respect than being viewed as nothing more than my husband?" Blossom asked. "The idea that someone should exist as nothing but the spouse of someone else is just...an uncomfortable thought."

Emma didn't reply but he got the feeling that she agreed with him. Saying nothing more, Emma took them through a sprawling garden filled with fruits and vegetables. It was so similar to the kitchen garden at the blessing school that Blossom couldn't help but feel at home. Blossom waved to a few Sun blessed gardeners who gasped and giggled when he passed.

"I believe your reputation precedes you," Asher said with a shit-eating grin.

"Well, I am pretty unmissable," Blossom replied, gesturing to his hair.

"Here we are Petal, this was the spot where Edwin and I found you," Emma said as they approached the shoreline. She gestured to a spot on the ground that had been marked with a small stone, on which was painted the Nature blessed symbol that Blossom also wore. "I remember it like it was yesterday."

"Asher," Blossom said quietly, tugging his husband's hand until they both stood on the same spot. "This is where our story began, or at least where our story was documented from."

"This is where Silas and Evelyn separated us, where they began their abuse," Asher replied, dropping Blossom's hand in favour of wrapping his arm around his waist.

"I'll leave you two in peace for a while. You remember your way back?" Emma asked, gesturing behind her to the gardens.

"It wasn't a difficult trip Emma, we'll be able to find our way back," Blossom said, accepting the kiss that Emma pressed to his cheek before she left.

They waited until Emma had disappeared out of sight to speak again, turning their attention to the lake. He wasn't sure what he had expected when Emma had described it as a shroud of shadow, but the thick, dark mist that cloaked the entire lake was breathtaking to behold. It stopped a foot from the shore, the only indication that it was a lake at all being the gentle lapping of the water at their feet.

"Do you think you could clear that mist?" Blossom asked, stepping away from Asher so that he could more easily look at him. "I can use Water's blessing to get us to the island once the mist has gone. Or if not gone, then maybe you can move it around us as we walk?"

"As they didn't want us going to the island, I think we should try the second option," Asher said, before taking a deep breath. Blossom watched that curious absence of light in his eyes that constituted his Blessing as Asher raised his hands, separating them slowly.

Before them the shadows surrounding the lake began to part, creating a tunnel of light, at the end of which was a lush island, green and healthy with a large building right in the center.

Chapter 23

"Wow, it's beautiful," Blossom breathed, taking an unconscious step forward. He looked back over his shoulder to where Asher was still stood, his arm raised to keep the shadows separated. "Let's go." He held out his hand for Asher's as he stepped onto the surface of the lake, the water beneath him solidifying into translucent ice as his skin glowed.

Asher hesitated for a second, his foot hanging over the water, like he was worried that it wouldn't take his weight.

"It's safe my love, just focus on keeping the shadows away and I'll take care of the rest."

Asher paused for a moment more before relenting and stepping forward, releasing a tense breath when he remained on top of the water. They began to walk, and as they moved Asher allowed the shadow to reform behind them, hiding them from the rest of the Balance.

The walk to the island didn't take long and they made it in silence. Blossom could feel Asher's awe the same as his own, there was an aura around the island that felt otherworldly, as though everything pulsed with energy and life. The presence of the Blessers' power was evident in the way everything glittered, as though it was bathed in the strongest sunlight. Despite the fact that it had been twilight on the shore, the island was bright enough that it could have been the middle of the day.

Blossom released a breath once he stepped foot on land. He wasn't sure why, but it had been hard to breath consistently as they'd walked, it almost felt sacrilegious. He could feel the blessings flowing through him, replenishing his well of power without him even having to ask for it. "Asher," he gasped.

"Yeah, I feel it too," Asher replied, and when Blossom turned to him, he could see the way Asher radiated Shadow's blessing. "Blossom, you're glowing," he said, stepping forward and reaching his hand towards him, glancing down at his own hand and gasping when he saw the shadows emanating from his skin. "I'm not...Blossom I'm not doing that."

"I'm not doing anything either," Blossom replied, mirroring Asher's gesture and watching the myriad of colours dance about him. "I think it's the island. The Blessers are doing this."

"Should we...should we go to the temple?" Asher asked, his gaze still focused on his own arm.

Blossom looked up at the large building. Temple was definitely the word to describe it, there was something sacred about the building, about the whole island. They walked up the stone path with a hushed reverence, hands clasped between them, and Blossom couldn't tell where his own awe ended and Asher's began.

Once they reached the door Blossom took a deep breath, hesitating on the threshold.

What if it was locked?

"Go on Flower, it should be you that opens it," Asher whispered, like raising his voice would be disrespectful.

Blossom nodded, finally grasping the handle and pushing it down. The door swung open silently and Blossom gasped... he recognised this place. "Asher," He breathed, grabbing his husband's hand again and pulling him through the door, walking all the way to the center of the circular room.

"This is...Blossom...this is..."

"The blessing school," Blossom finished, turning in a slow circle as he noted where each of the 6 doors of the blessing school would have stood. Instead of doors though, there were towering mosaics depicting the blessings that they represented. He stopped in his circle as his eyes landed on a statue standing in front of the wall directly opposite the entrance.

"This...this doesn't make any sense," he said, mostly to himself as he made his way towards the statue. "Shouldn't there be a statue of each of the Blessers?"

"You're right," Asher replied, looking around, "there's something else on the walls as well, not just the blessings."

Blossom glanced over his shoulder, following Asher's gaze to a panel to the right of the statue. It was another mosaic, but this one showed the kingdoms, except without the dividing lines between the countries. The map was green and gold, showing the rise and fall of the land, the lakes, the forests. And as they watched the mosaic began to change, with dark lines splitting the land into the more familiar shapes of the kingdoms.

"Asher," Blossom said hesitantly.

"I see it too," Asher responded.

They watched as the kingdom boundaries shifted and grew, looking more like cracks in the wall than simple location markers.

Then the cracks began to bleed.

It was the only way Blossom could describe it. Red tendrils emanated from the cracks, growing to encompass the land until only one spot remained green and untouched. The island on which they now stood. The mosaic stayed the same for a long while and only after he was sure that he wouldn't miss anything Blossom dared to glance back at the statue. He startled when he noticed that it had begun to glow.

Stepping round so that the statue was directly in front of them Blossom and Asher watched as the stone effigy began to cry. Rivers of clear water cascaded down its chiseled cheeks, and at the same time flowers bloomed from its outstretched hands. The ground beneath their feet began to shake causing Blossom and Asher to cling to each other.

"Is it an earthquake?" Asher asked, looking around desperately.

"Not a natural one," Blossom replied.

They stared with a mixture of horror and awe as the statue split in two, the two halves falling away and disappearing into the ground, leaving behind the two flowers that had bloomed in its palms.

One pink.

One black.

∞

Asher stared at the flowers as understanding dawned on him. He looked over at Blossom, watching the way he shook as he tried to comprehend what he had just seen.

"It's us," he whispered.

Blossom nodded, swallowing thickly, tears shining in his eyes. "We...Asher... I think we are the Blessers."

Asher knew, deep in his bones, that what Blossom was saying was true. They weren't just born of the Blessers, they were the Blessers. Or perhaps Blesser was more accurate, if what they had just seen was to be believed, there had only ever been one. A single deity with all of Nature's blessings, and as the world split, becoming war torn and covetous, the Blesser had split too.

"But why split?" Asher asked. "And why like this?"

"The blessing of protection, it hadn't been gifted to anyone because of what was happening." Blossom gestured up at the mural again, which had returned to its original state, all lush greens and golds. "We needed to protect the last blessed place on earth, so we made sure that no one but us could use this gift." Blossom locked eyes with him again. "And we needed to make sure that there was a way for us to find one another should we be separated further."

Asher nodded; in some strange way it made sense. Like he was just looking back on a decision that he had made in the past.

"I think..." Blossom trailed off, reaching across the space between them to touch Asher's hand. "If we wanted...we could become whole again."

Asher knew, as soon as Blossom said it that it was true. The energy in the air, in the temple that they were in. It was like it was calling to them, begging them to join again, to become one being. He also knew that he didn't want that, not yet.

"We don't have to, not right now," Blossom said with a reassuring squeeze to his hand, like he could read Asher's mind.

Asher nodded. "One day. We'll join one day, but we need to fix this mess first. I get the feeling that once we become one, we won't be able to leave this place again." He looked down at his hands, feeling almost bashful. "And I want to be with you, as we are now, for at least a little longer."

"Okay," Blossom agreed instantly, his smile bright enough to light up the room. "Then let's go back and fix this."

24

⚜

Chapter 24

It was surprisingly hard to leave the island, as though there was something attempting to keep them there. Or maybe now that they had returned to their true home they simply didn't want to leave.

The island had rejuvenated the both of them and Asher was able to part the shadows covering the lake with barely more than a thought. A thought that Blossom was half-convinced he heard himself. Perhaps they had already bonded more than before, growing closer by simply stepping foot on the island.

By the time they reached the shoreline it was clear that their absence had been noted. Emma was waiting for them, her arms crossed as she shook her head with disapproval.

"The Elders explicitly told you not to visit the island," she said, but Blossom could see the corners of her mouth quirking.

"Well, we discovered something on that island that might show the Elders that we don't really need to heed their 'orders'," Asher replied, turning to Blossom when he giggled internally. "Oh, come on Flower, you really think they're above us now?"

"I didn't say anything," Blossom said, mirth colouring his voice.

"What did you find?" Emma asked, her arms dropping to her sides, "And what do you have there?" She nodded to the flowers that Blossom and Asher had taken from the temple.

"We should say this in front of everyone don't you think?" Blossom asked, head tilted to the side as he contemplated Asher. "No, you're right, Emma should hear first."

Emma looked between them in confusion. "What happened over there? You're acting like you can read each other's thoughts."

Blossom blinked. "Did you not say that we should tell Emma out loud?"

"I don't think so," Asher replied.

Shaking his head Blossom decided to put it aside for now and returned his attention to what was more important. "There aren't five Blessers, there's only one."

"What are you talking about?"

"There is, or at least there was, only one Blesser. Nature itself is the Blesser. There aren't five deities at all, just the one...and that deity split in two just over 21 years ago."

Emma stared at him in disbelief for a few moments as the meaning of his statement sunk in. "Are you trying to tell me that you are the Blesser? You are the source of all the blessings in this world?"

"Asher and I are. As the world grew more divided and chaotic we split in two, the world was out of balance and so were we."

"I know it's hard to believe," Asher consoled, falling quiet when Emma shook her head.

"Actually, it makes a shocking amount of sense. It would also explain this bond that you two have, why it was so traumatizing for you both when you were split apart. But why were you born in these bodies? There are more kingdoms than Vaten and Castilla, so why did you give yourselves these bodies?"

Blossom and Asher looked at each other. "I'm not sure, perhaps it was because Vaten and Castilla were the ones with the bloodiest conflict? Perhaps because their kingdoms are the largest?" Blossom replied with a shrug. "To be honest, I don't remember our past life or the decisions we made in it. These are just gut feelings."

"We need to tell the Elders about this," Emma said definitively, "although they may take more convincing than me."

Blossom nodded, crouching to place the black flower next to the stone marking where they had first appeared in this world. Asher did the same, stroking a gentle finger over the petals of the pink flower with a smile.

"We should do something to make sure that no one disturbs them," Asher said as he stood. "A sign or something."

"This spot is considered an important historical area," Emma gestured to the stone. "I'm sure that once we speak with the Elder's no one will touch them."

Emma was right about one thing. The Elders didn't believe them at all, despite Blossom's insistence that he could prove it to them by returning to the island. He was hesitant to take humans to the island, not only because it felt like a sacred space where only he and Asher should walk, but because he had a suspicion that something bad might actually happen to any human that set foot on that land.

"Even if this was true," Elder Leena said, waving off the complaints that came from her fellow Elders when they sputtered in indignation. "Why are you still separate? You said that you could become one again if you wished, so why haven't you done so?"

"Because there is still so much to be done here. Once Blossom and I take our true form again we won't be able to leave the island," Asher explained. Blossom didn't know how Asher knew this, just as he didn't know why he knew it to be true. It was a similar feeling to when they had first learnt about their origins, not quite a memory but something close to it, something he could feel in the deepest parts of himself.

"Asher is right. We need to restore balance before we can leave this world. We need to fix the mess that we allowed humans to create. We were silent for too long, just as the Balance was. So, whether you believe us or not it is time to begin making plans to take back Vaten and stop this conflict once and for all."

Elder Hasham nodded. "We have sent word that all members of the Balance are to return here. We need to build an army. It is not something that the Balance has done before but we have the numbers, and we have enough military trained people that we should be able to mount a proper attack before winter. It will take at least two weeks for those in the farthest reaches to get here but we can start training with those that already are. We hope that the two of you will help to train our blessed members, much like you did back at your school, Master Blossom."

∞

They both agreed to help with training without complaint. Blossom had experience of teaching even the most inexperienced of blessed children how to harness their power, and whilst there were no other Shadow blessed, Asher was well versed in the art of battle. He was looking forward to returning to training again, something normal that he could lose himself in as he grappled with the knowledge of what he was.

What he and Blossom both were.

It made sense now, how compatible they were, how he had always felt like he loved Blossom from his very bones. But that didn't change the fact that the realisation of their origins had changed something fundamental in how he viewed their relationship.

The first night after their return from the island, when they retired to bed, Asher couldn't help but bring up something that had been niggling at him.

"Is this odd?" He asked, stroking his fingertips down Blossom's bare arm as his husband sat himself in his lap. "As we are the same, should we be doing this?"

Blossom simply smiled at him and ducked forward, placing a gentle kiss on his lips. "What's wrong with a little self-love?" He asked, pulling a laugh from the prince. "And besides, once we are joined again we won't be able to do this, shouldn't we enjoy it whilst it lasts?"

Unable to come up with an argument for that Asher rolled them until he had Blossom pinned beneath him. "Well, when you put it like that."

∞

There was already a large number of people at the balance headquarters due to the long day pilgrimage, so Blossom and Asher decided to get to work immediately.

They waited in the large training courtyard at the back of the headquarters whilst it filled with people from all age ranges. Blossom even spied a few people that had graduated from his school some years ago. He gestured for them to join him at the front with a wave of his hand.

"Well, this will certainly make things easier," he said after they had all reintroduced themselves. "This way I can have some help when it comes to the individual blessing lessons. Who here would be willing to be raised to the level of Master?"

He had enough volunteers that each of the blessings now had 3 dedicated teachers, and Blossom was able to focus more on individual help. He and Asher had split their duties between each of their strengths. Blossom was to nurture and develop each person's blessing, growing it stronger and keeping it under control. Asher was to train them how to harness that power and use it in war, how to fight and train with their hands and bodies instead of only relying on their gifts.

Training was smooth and almost easy. Most of the Balance members had done at least some formal training, be it in one of the kingdoms' militaries or in the Balance itself. It probably also had to do with the fact that whilst some of his new students were children, the vast majority were well into adulthood. Blossom had made it very clear that he would not stand for the young ones to be trained in battle, something that he could see irked some of his more precocious students, but it was a stance he was unwilling to move from.

No human was built for war, not really, and he would do everything in his power to protect his children from something so unnatural.

The Balance was far more regimented in its schedule than Blossom's school had ever been, which was something that he struggled to deal with. Forcing conformity through drills never, in his experience, led to people reaching their full potential. But as Asher pointed out on numerous occasions, both verbally and through the mental bond they now shared, right now they didn't have the time to slowly coax their students into their full form. They needed to create soldiers, as much as that thought pained him.

They returned to the island multiple times over the following weeks as well, an invisible pull luring them back time and time again. It felt more like home than any other place they had been to, but with each visit it was becoming harder and harder to leave again.

"I think we need to stop this," Asher said one day as they lay on the grass by the shoreline.

"Stop what?" Blossom replied, frowning when Asher laughed at him. It took a few moments for him to realise why, because he hadn't spoken the words out loud. Their bond had been growing stronger with each visit, to the point where Blossom often had to remind himself to actually form the words he wanted to say when they were around others.

He looked down at their entwined hands, having to blink multiple times until he could spot where one of them began and the other ended. "Oh," he said softly, "you're right, we're going to become one if we're not careful."

"I know it will be hard, but let's make a pact. This will be our last visit until we are ready to return for good. We'll say goodbye to the island for now and the next time we set foot on it; it will be with the knowledge that we're not going to leave again."

"Okay my love. Then let's say goodbye," Blossom stood, extricating his hand from Asher's hold as he turned to gaze at the temple. He closed his eyes, feeling Asher doing the same as they made their internal promise. The pull to stay grew even stronger, like the island could hear them, and didn't want them to leave again.

"Come on, before we change our minds," Asher whispered, dispersing the shadow enough for them to step onto the water, but not enough to allow anyone on the other shore to see the island.

25

⧈

Chapter 25

Word came from Shotsen a few weeks into their new training regime that Edwin had returned to consciousness, but it was clear that it would still be many months before he could be moved. It seemed like such a logical assumption that Blossom had almost dismissed the Elders summons to their offices to debate the matter.

"He needs rest. He needs to recuperate in a proper sick bed with good healers," Emma protested when the Elder's laid out their plans for Edwin's journey to the Balance headquarters.

"We have good healers here," Elder Hasham stated, stabbing his finger into his desk in emphasis. "Edwin was the only one to conduct such extensive research on the Blossomites, we need him here. We have the numbers to mount a proper counterattack, but without proper intel we'll be going in blind."

"If your healers are as good as you claim then they will agree with me. It would be foolish to moved Edwin now. Yes, he is awake, but it is only for an hour or so at a time. The metal shards of that machine are still embedded in his chest, and they need to be removed. Any amount of travel over rough terrain might cause them to shift and slice his vital organs, we're lucky they haven't already," Blossom retorted, waving the letter that he had received from Princess Cassandra that morning.

Tensions between Blossom and the Elder's hadn't eased much. He was fairly certain that they now believed that he and Asher were the Blesser's, but if anything, that had simply made them less forthcoming. Blossom wasn't sure if it was reverence or distrust that caused it but either way it wasn't helpful.

"That's another thing," Elder Leena said, "We need to know more about this weapon that prevents healing. If the Blossomites come at us with that and we don't know how to counter it, then it will be a bloodbath."

"Then send someone to go and get one."

Blossom almost flinched, he'd forgotten that Kara was in the room with them. She had been loitering in the corner, leaning against a wall with her arms crossed but now she stepped into the light.

"You're right. We're going in with less information than is ideal, and Edwin would be the easiest way to get that information, but he isn't an option right now," She placed a hand on the small of Emma's back as she spoke, looking at each of the Elders in turn. "But you're acting like he's the only option. We have infiltrators, don't we? And as far as I remember, we have some within the Blossomites themselves. Get word to them that we need information."

"That would break their cover and risk their lives," Elder Tarka barked.

"Their cover?" Kara scoffed, rolling her eyes. "You make it sound like you expect the Blossomite cult to still exist after this. Fine, have them break cover. They can break cover whilst they're stealing one of the weapons. They've been trained on things like this, they can extract themselves."

"If you've got spies or…, what did you call them… infiltrators?" Blossom looked over to Kara who nodded. "Then why do you need Edwin so badly? Surely someone who has lived amongst them would know about their ways, possibly even more than my uncle does."

The Elders didn't seem happy about it, but after a few moments of tense silence Elder Hasham nodded. "We will send word to our infiltrators. You are correct Guardian Kara, we should begin extracting those within the Blossomites, if word ever got out that they were there… I would hate to think what those monsters could do to them."

"I doubt all of the Blossomites are monsters, Elder Hasham," Blossom said coldly, meeting the older man's stare. "These are people, just like you and everyone else within my realm. I am sure that some…" He trailed off as images of Evelyn passed through his mind, "are too far gone to be saved, but not all of them. Only a monster condemns an entire group due to the actions of a few."

He could see the Elders bristling but no one argued with him and without waiting to be dismissed, he turned and strode from the room.

"Petal."

Blossom paused to allow Emma to catch up with him. "Are you going to lecture me about speaking more respectfully?"

Emma sighed and looped her hand through his arm. "Normally I would… but this time I think they needed a bit of a dressing down," she said as they left the headquarters and began to walk down towards the lakeside. It had become an almost nightly routine with his mother, a gentle stroll along the beach, and it was something he always looked forward to. "Edwin once said to me that he thinks the Elders get a little stuck in their ways sometimes. They hold power for so long that they get used to being blindly obeyed."

Blossom hummed, "I can see the sense in that. Did he ever say how he thought to counter that?"

"He said that there should be more frequent appointments," Emma replied, squeezing Blossom's arm when he frowned at her in confusion. "The Elders are chosen by the members of the Balance. When one of the five leave their position, either because they can no longer do the job, or because they are no longer with us, we hold a vote. People put their names forward and then whoever gets the most votes becomes the next Elder."

"That... that actually sounds like a very fair and just way of doing things."

"Exactly. That way everyone has a chance to become an Elder. Yes, it's usually an advanced protector who gains the most votes, but we have had guardians, infiltrators, and carers become Elders as well. Elder Leena was a guardian, in fact she was the one who trained Kara."

"But you said that Edwin felt there should be more votes," Blossom said, attempting to stop the conversation from going too far off track.

"Yes. You see, once an Elder has been voted in, they have that position until they choose to step down. Edwin's suggestion was that we have regular votes, perhaps every ten or so years, to decide if the current Elders should remain in power. That way..."

"That way, if they're not serving the Balance the way they should, or simply not fit for the role, they could be replaced earlier." Blossom finished for his mother. "That does sound better."

"And also, it would give the Elders even more incentive to do their best work. Unfortunately, there have been those that, once they gain the title, simply sit on their laurels and don't do much."

Blossom nodded, halting in his tracks as he spotted a small figure near the stone that marked his birthplace. Ever since he and Asher had placed their flowers near the stone other members of the Balance had started doing the same, leaving flowers with their blessings colours next to the pink and black ones. Now the shore was constantly awash with colour, with the few blooms that were carried away by the lakes unusual tide soon replaced by new flowers.

"Aelius?" He asked as they drew closer.

"The sun set two hours ago, you should be in bed," Emma admonished, her voice holding no real heat to it.

"Sorry Master Emma, I just wanted to put some flowers out," Aelius said from where he was still crouched by the stone. He had three little blooms clutched in his hand, pink, black, and yellow. He beamed when Emma nodded at him and tucked the flowers amongst those already there. "Master Blossom, do you think the Blessers can see when we leave gifts for them?" Aelius asked, looking back up at him.

Blossom smiled, it had been decided that news of what he and Asher were should remain secret for now. It was one of the few things he agreed with the Elders about. "Yes Aelius, I do."

Aelius stood, taking one last look at the mound of offerings before sliding his small hand into Blossom's outstretched one and following them back towards the headquarters. "Do you think..." He looked down at his feet, suddenly shy.

"If you have questions Aelius there is no harm in voicing them. You're not going to be in trouble."

Aelius had come a long way since Blossom had first spoken with him at the blessing school, but he still carried a lot of his early life with him. He was never cruel or unkind, and far less shy than he had once been, but he had an air of self-consciousness about him that Blossom found almost familiar. He had clearly taken all of Blossom's lessons to heart, and not just the ones about Sun's blessing. Blossom had even heard him lecturing some of the older children about how to treat one another, which had given Blossom a good laugh the last time he'd been passing the dormitories.

"Aelius." Blossom crouched in front of the young boy, nodding his goodbye to Emma when she squeezed at his shoulder and disappeared into the building. "You can talk to me."

Aelius chewed on his bottom lip as he thought. "Do you think the Blessers are proud of me?" He blurted out, flushing bright red as soon as he spoke.

Blossom's lips spread into a wide grin, his heart swelling with love for this earnest little Sun blessed. "Yes, Aelius. I think they are very proud of you. As long as you continue to be hard working, patient, and above all else, kind, they will always be proud of you."

Once he had seen Aelius safely into his dormitory Blossom joined his husband in their room.

"What was it that had you so happy earlier, beautiful boy?" Asher asked, giving him that lovestruck look that always made Blossom giddy.

"What made me so happy is that I believe we may already have the perfect child to begin our new family with," Blossom replied as he climbed into bed, not bothering to voice the words aloud.

"Little Aelius, am I right?" Asher asked, cupping Blossom's cheek and pressing a chaste kiss to his lips as they both lay back against the cushions. "That seems like a wonderful idea, and very fitting."

"How so?"

"Well, he was the child that first came to your mind on the eve of the long day celebration was he not? When we were on the castle roof and imagining what our future family could look like."

Blossom stared up at Asher in shock. "But how... we weren't even bonded then; how did you know?"

"Because I know you," Asher replied, speaking the words against Blossom's cheek. "The second you told me that you didn't want to send him back to his parents, I could see how attached you were to him. Didn't you realise it, Flower? We've known each other for so long, it doesn't take our bond for me to understand you. You're in my bones, my very soul."

26

Chapter 26

Over the next few months more and more people arrived at the balance headquarters from all over the world. Some from countries that Blossom hadn't even heard of before, further cementing in his mind that he was far more ignorant to what had been happening in the world than he'd initially thought.

When he and Asher weren't training the new blessed recruits, they were in the headquarter library or sat in on war meetings. Blossom didn't often contribute during these meetings, he wasn't very well versed in the art of war and the constant discussions about battle, death and violence were beginning to get him down.

Asher was in his element however, setting out battle plans and formations, discussing with Kara and the other generals the best way to overwhelm the enemy forces. He wasn't exactly delighting in the idea of war, but Blossom could feel his confidence and ease, and it didn't help with his own discomfort.

There was one thing that had been agreed very early on and was often reiterated during the subsequent meetings. Which was that even should the Blossomites surrender, Evelyn needed to die. She had caused far too much harm over the years to be allowed to live. Blossom had fought for life imprisonment for the first few meetings but had been rebuffed to the point where he knew that he was liable to be disinvited if he brought it up again. So, he simply began to tune out.

There were a few times when the meetings delved into the nitty gritty details that Blossom wondered if being disinvited would actually be a good thing. He never left these meetings in a good mood, and often remained sullen for the rest of the day as he replayed scenes of death and violence over and over in his mind. So, in an attempt to lighten his spirits after a particularly arduous meeting, Asher arranged for Blossom to spend the day with Aelius and Skyla.

Blossom agreed gladly. Ever since they had decided that Aelius would be the ideal child for them to take in as their own, he'd been spending as much time with the little Sun blessed as possible. Skyla was also becoming a constant in their lives; Kara had taken a shine to her and the two could be seen training and planning together most days. After retrieving them both from their lessons, Blossom took Aelius and Skyla down to the lakeside where Asher had set up a small picnic, complete with a large blanket and plethora of pillows.

"So, how are you two finding it here?" Blossom asked, handing out the sandwiches that the kitchen staff had made earlier.

"It's okay. I liked the school better," Aelius said around a mouthful of bread. "Your lessons were more fun than the ones we have here. And they won't let me train with you and Prince Asher."

Blossom smiled, ruffling the Sun blessed's hair. "That's because we don't want you training as a soldier Aelius. You're only 9 years old."

"Skyla gets to train with you though."

Skyla and Blossom both laughed. "Skyla graduated and passed her protectors exam last year. She is already a trained soldier, though I have always hoped that my students wouldn't have to see war."

Skyla reached over and squeezed Blossom's hand. "I trained as a protector so that I could join the Balance and look after those I love. War was an inevitability."

"That doesn't really make me feel better," Blossom squeezed back, "but I'm very proud of you."

"Thank you, Master Blossom."

They ate and chatted about light topics for about an hour before Skyla was called back to training by another Balance member.

"So Aelius, when this is all over do you think you'll stay here?" Blossom asked once they'd waved Skyla off.

Aelius looked down almost bashfully, tracing random shapes on the blanket. "I...I'd like to come back to the school," he confessed quietly.

Blossom smiled and was about to say that of course Aelius could come back to the school, but then he remembered what he and Asher had planned for once the war was done. How could he have forgotten that they were going to return to the island? How could he and Asher have spoken so often about bringing Aelius into their family when they were planning on abandoning him? And what about the school, and all the other blessed children that were relying on him? He and Asher wouldn't be returning to Vaten, and if they did it wouldn't be for long. In all the commotion of the past few months, he hadn't had a chance to think about the school, but of course it should continue after he was gone.

He hadn't seen any of the other Masters since his wedding, but he hoped that none of them were secret Blossomites. As long as they were loyal to him and the sanctity of human life then he would be happy to leave the running of the school in their capable hands.

That just left the question of Aelius.

"Of course you can come back to the school Aelius," Blossom said gently, glancing over Aelius' shoulder at the familiar silhouette of his husband. "Oh Asher, has your training finished for the day?"

Aelius scrambled to his feet, bowing to Asher as he made his way over to them. "Your Majesty," he said to the ground.

"Now, now Aelius, we trained together last year, didn't we? Anyone who has sparred with me doesn't need to bow," Asher said with an indulgent smile as he settled down on the blanket next to Blossom. "Are you two having a nice picnic?"

"We are. Aelius was just telling me about how he wants to come back to the palace with us when this is over," Blossom leant over and placed a quick kiss on Asher's cheek.

"I...I didn't..." Aelius flushed to the roots of his golden hair but before he could stammer another apology Asher beat him to it.

"That's a great idea. Weren't you telling me before Flower that you wanted to take in children without homes?" Asher said as though they hadn't been speaking about this literally the night before.

"Master Blossom?" Aelius asked, his eyes glistening with barely contained excitement. He leant forward on his knees, practically vibrating as he waited for Blossom's answer.

"I'd love to have you living with us, Aelius."

Blossom couldn't fight the smile that broke across his face as Aelius launched himself into his arms. He hugged the child back, stroking through his fine golden hair as Aelius thanked him profusely, trying to ignore the guilt already gnawing at his stomach. They held one another for a long while until the bell rang, signaling the end of the Balance's first shift.

"I believe that you have some lessons to go to," Blossom said, still smiling. "Master Emma wouldn't want you to skip her class."

Aelius nodded and stood, his face flushed with happiness. "Thank you again Master Blossom, and you Master Asher. Thank you."

"There is no need to thank us Aelius, it is our pleasure," Asher answered, waving the young Sun blessed away. Once they were alone again he turned to Blossom, his smile faltering as Blossom slumped against him. "What's wrong?"

"How can we take in children when we're planning on leaving? How can we abandon him?" He whispered, staring despondently at the spot where Aelius had sat. "Wouldn't that be more cruel than never bringing him in in the first place?"

Asher stroked through Blossom's soft hair, humming in thought. "Once we have restored balance, I would have to appoint an heir to Vaten anyway. I don't see why it couldn't be Aelius, you already care for him so much. We don't have to leave right away, it might be difficult to ignore the pull, but we can watch him grow, Flower. We can stay with him until he is a man, until he is ready to rule in my place."

Blossom looked up at his husband, meeting his eyes. "We would have to tell him beforehand, that we will leave eventually," he said, the words passing to Asher without the need to speak them aloud. "You're right in that I already love him like a son. I love all of my children; I'm not going to keep them in the dark."

The corners of Asher's mouth curled up in an indulgent smile. "The blessed are our children, aren't they? It's no wonder you've always cared for them."

"What about the unblessed?" Blossom asked, sitting upright. "If we are meant to maintain Balance then the unblessed are our children as well." He stared at the dark red brick of the balance headquarters. "They are like siblings that have quarreled to the point where they no longer speak. The blessed and the unblessed. This divide is hurting all of our children, my love. We need to have them make up, we need them to understand all they have in common and not just how they differ. We need them to realise that they are family."

"So it's agreed then, we won't bond until we are satisfied that our children are well taken care of and happy," Asher took hold of Blossom's hand and pulled him to his feet. "Once our family are reunited, then we can truly bond and return to our home."

"Our home," Blossom whispered, looking over his shoulder at the veil of shadow enshrouding that home. He let out a hum of agreement, turning his back on the island and walking with determined steps back into the headquarters of the Balance.

∞

A last-minute war meeting was convened the next morning, and Blossom and Asher entered the Elders war room to find them all crowded around an unfamiliar machine.

"Is that...?"

"That's the weapon that hit Edwin," Asher answered Blossom's unfinished question. "Or at least it looks a lot like it."

"You are correct, Your Majesty," Elder Hasham said, lifting a large sphere of metal and holding it out to him. "This is what it fires, the shards the healers have managed to extract from Protector Edwin were made of the same material. It is heavy but brittle, once it comes in contact with something it shatters and the items inside shoot out."

Asher shook the metal ball, which produced an unsettling ringing sound as whatever it contained battered against its enclosure.

"Has anyone opened one of these things? Would it be safe to do so?" Blossom asked, placing a hand over Asher's to halt his continued shaking.

"Queen Lila sent us very specific instructions on how to do so," A Balance member that Blossom couldn't remember meeting before said, gesturing for him to join her by another table. On the table were a series of what looked like the wind-up dolls that Blossom remembered Lila inventing. Except that the limbs had been replaced with lethal looking spikes. "The springs are so tightly wound that it only takes a slight disturbance for them to release," the woman explained, reaching for one of them.

"Wait!" Blossom grabbed her wrist before she could touch anything. "If that's the case then surely they should be left alone."

The woman smiled at him. "I have released some of the tension, Master Blossom. They are no longer a threat. They're more liable to simply fall apart now. I trained with the queen when we were both young members, I know what I'm doing."

"Sorry," Blossom's smile was sheepish as he released her wrist. "I didn't mean to doubt you. Would you mind if I asked your name?"

"Of course not, my name is Askara, Master Blossom. It is a pleasure to formally meet you," Askara bowed her head slightly, before turning back to the assembled Elders when Elder Leena cleared her throat.

"Please continue your explanation, Askara," Elder Leena gestured to the large weapon again.

"Of course," Askara returned to the main table. "This is how it operates..." She paused in her explanation, seeming to weigh the metal ball she'd retrieved from Asher in her hand. "Actually, would it be better to give a physical demonstration?"

"You're not thinking of hitting someone with it!" Blossom screeched.

"No, no, no. I was thinking, we should take it out to the fields beyond the training grounds and aim it at an empty piece of land. No one would get hurt, I promise."

Blossom still wasn't overly happy with the idea but was instantly outvoted so the whole group trooped out to the before mentioned spot.

"Stop glaring at me, Flower," Asher said with a grin, like he found Blossom's pout comical. "This is the best way to see what it does. Or would you rather we wait for the next time the Blossomites point one at us?"

Blossom huffed but didn't argue, and despite his continued reservations he found himself drifting towards the group of excited onlookers so that he could better hear Askara's explanation.

"Now, it sits on the ground like so. Although it wouldn't be hard to mount it on wheels which would make it more useful in battle," Askara explained, gesturing to the tripod of sturdy wood that the main cylindrical shape was resting on. "The sphere goes in this end." She let the metal ball roll into the cylinder through a large opening at one end. "And then these allow you to aim it." Askara fiddled with the two levers on either side of the cylinder, causing the end with the opening to move up and down. Once she was satisfied with its position Askara then gestured to the Fire blessed next to her. "Phyrro here has the ignition stick."

Phyrro held up a long piece of metal, pointing to a wad of cotton stuffed in one end.

"This substance is something that was discovered by the Balance many years ago," Askara held up a small black, cloth bag before sticking her hand into it and retrieving a handful of what Blossom could only describe as coarse, black sand.

"Blasting powder," Elder Hasham said with a gasp, looking from the weapon to the bag. "They're using blasting powder to operate this thing? It's a wonder the whole contraption doesn't explode."

The rest of the group took a collective step back, but Askara didn't seem perturbed in the slightest.

"You are correct, Elder Hasham. However, the Blossomites don't use blasting power as we know it." Askara tucked the black bag back into her deep pockets and retrieved a red one instead. "They use this," She took out another handful, this one a lighter grey than before. "They have refined and diluted traditional blasting power into something more manageable. Less powerful, but with enough of a kick to work." With that she poured the handful of powder into a small opening at the bottom of the weapon.

"I would recommend everyone take a few more steps back. It's not going to explode, but this will be loud." Askara made a shooing motion with her hands before beckoning Phyrro over to her. "On the count of three," she said, taking a single step back. "One."

On the count of one, Phyrro used Fire's blessing to ignite the wad of cotton at the end of his stick.

"Two."

He lowered the stick so that the flame was only a few inches away from the powder.

"Three."

Blossom barely heard the call, as the next thing he knew the metal ball exploded from the weapon with an ear splitting 'BANG'. He clapped his hands over his ears, watching in increasing horror as the ground a dozen feet ahead of them erupted with a force that he could feel in his very bones.

There was a silence once the demonstration was over, made even more pronounced by the shrill whistle sounding in Blossom's head. Everyone stared at the crater that had been formed in the previously lush grassland, and whilst he couldn't speak for everyone there Blossom knew in his soul that this weapon could never be allowed in a just and kind world.

"They must be stopped," he said, unsure how loud he was speaking as his ears continued to ring. "This is a machine of death, and death only. This is an affront to Nature itself."

27

Chapter 27

After weeks of training, and countless days that ended with Asher and Blossom both falling into their bed with sore bodies and exhausted minds, a plan was formed. Asher and Kara had decided that a full-frontal assault on Evelyn and her forces was the best course of action. The Balance needed the element of surprise, and whilst Blossom hated the idea of so much bloodshed, he understood the logic behind a quick siege. Hopefully, if the Balance was able to take back Vaten with one, large show of force there would be fewer lives lost.

If their intel was correct, the Balance now boasted an army that rivalled the Blossomites in size. It was impossible to tell who would come out on top from numbers alone. Hopefully, if they struck whilst the Blossomites were caught unawares, they could get the upper hand. It also reduced the chances of the Blossomites being able to ready too many of those explosive weapons. The thought of those things being used against any living creature made Blossom feel cold to his very core.

It was with a heavy stone in his stomach that Blossom mounted his horse on the morning of the siege. He was supposed to be heading the blessed regiment of the Balance's army, but he was still unsure whether he'd actually be able to do anything when the battle started. He was fairly certain he wouldn't be able to kill anyone.

Asher trotted up next to him, sitting regal and proud in his saddle. "Today is the day," he said, reaching across and squeezing reassuringly at Blossom's hand when he simply nodded. "You don't have to do this Flower. You don't have to kill; you can stay here."

Blossom shook his head. "I have to be here. How can I expect people to go to war in our name if I'm not willing to join them?"

Asher smiled at him, a clear, sharp flow of pride hitting Blossom in the chest. Asher let go of his hand and turned his horse, facing the contingent of soldiers, knights, and normal Balance members who had never once seen battle.

"Today we will make history," he cried, his words carrying over the crowd easily. "Today we will remove the tyrant that has caused such harm to all our people. We will restore the balance that has been destroyed through these decades of unrest. We will bring blessed and unblessed together as one!"

There was a cheer from the gathered crowd, followed by the thudding of spears and swords against shields.

"Some of you have trained for moments such as this for years, others of you heeded the call and are facing your first battle. All of you will be lauded and remembered for years to come." Asher raised his sword. "Today we ride to victory!"

Blossom didn't join in with the responding cheer this time. He was feeling short of breath, a confusing mixture of dread and excitement swirling in his gut. Asher was stunning, so confident and strong in his conviction that it practically shone out of him. Blossom was surprised by just how attractive he found it.

Asher didn't seem to be however as he returned to Blossom's side with a coy grin. "I forget that you have never seen me head an army before," he said, his lips unmoving as he used their rapidly strengthening mental bond.

Blossom huffed and looked away. "I should not be attracted to the knowledge that you are going into battle."

"But you are though," Asher replied, his grin smug. "That's nothing to be ashamed of Flower. In fact, it is something to revel in..." He leant across the small gap between them and whispered in Blossom's ear. "Later."

∞

Asher decided to let his husband simmer in his attraction and returned his attention to what they were about to do. He knew that Blossom could feel his own nerves, knew that the blesser understood that Asher wasn't excited about the idea of war, but he couldn't help but want to reassure his husband. There was no joy in taking the life of another, but he did feel a certain pride in the knowledge that he was going to have a hand in restoring balance to the world.

They waited until the world warmed, the sun high enough in the sky that everybody in the army was well and truly awake before setting off. Every able-bodied, adult member of the Balance was with them, and so Asher wasn't surprised when, about 6 hours after they started their march towards Vaten, one of the scouts came running back with an urgent message.

He dismounted his horse, joining Kara and the Masters in an impromptu war meeting. "What news?" He asked, reaching behind him to take Blossom's hand when the blesser walked up to them.

"Evelyn knows that we're coming," Kara replied. "It's not that surprising really, we're not exactly inconspicuous like this." She gestured at the mass of people milling around. "We have reports that the Blossomites have amassed their own army and marched out of Kilan an hour ago."

Asher nodded; brows furrowed as he contemplated the map in front of him. "If we assume that they are marching at the same rate as us, we should meet them here around dawn." He pointed to a swath of green on the map. After Kara nodded, he looked back down again and gave a snort.

"What?" Blossom asked, clearly sensing his exasperated amusement.

"Do you remember when my father took us to the southern villages?" Asher asked.

"Of course, it was my first time out of the palace," Blossom replied, realisation hitting him as Asher smiled. "No."

Asher nodded, tapping at the map. "We're more than likely going to be making our attack in the very area where we stopped for that feast." He heard Blossom's returning thought as clearly as if he had said it aloud. "I agree," he whispered, "let us hope that the villagers don't come out to see us this time."

· ∞

They decided to march until the sun set and then set up camp. This way the army would be well rested when they met with Evelyn's forces.

Blossom was fairly certain that he wouldn't be able to fall asleep though, despite the way his body ached from a day of riding. He wandered through the camp in an attempt to tire himself more, stopping to speak with various Balance members when they waved him over.

"Master Blossom," Skyla called from where she was sat with a handful of other young, blessed soldiers.

"Good evening, Skyla. Your armor suits you," Blossom said when he made his way over to her.

Skyla looked down almost bashfully, brushing her knuckles over the metal on her chest plate, tracing the double triangle symbol of the Balance. "Thank you, Master Blossom," she said, before standing and taking a deep breath. "Do you have a moment?"

"Of course, what troubles you?" Blossom asked, his head tilted to the side in curiosity. Skyla had always been so steady and sure of herself, but now she looked almost scared, and Blossom was suddenly reminded of how young she really was. "Is it the thought of going into battle tomorrow?"

Skyla shook her head. "No, I mean, partly. I'm not excited to fight but I'm ready to. I know that I'm ready." Blossom could see the way she straightened, pride causing her to puff out her chest. "I just...I need to show you something."

"Okay." Blossom glanced up as he felt Asher's presence, watching as his husband walked over to them. "Is it something you can show Asher as well?"

"I think it best that you both see," Skyla said, gesturing for them to follow her. She took them to one of the soldiers large sleeping tents and ducked inside.

Asher and Blossom shared a look before joining her in the tent. "Skyla what...Aelius?" Blossom asked, incredulity colouring his voice as a familiar head of golden hair peaked up from a pile of packs in the corner.

Aelius shot Skyla a glare before climbing out of his hiding spot. "You said you wouldn't tell them," he groused, pouting at her as he crossed his arms.

"I lied," Skyla replied with a shrug. "It was for the best. You're only a baby Aelius, you shouldn't be on the battlefield."

"I'm not a baby!" Aelius shouted, stomping his foot in anger.

Blossom hid his smile behind his hand at the tantrum, trying to school his features before he spoke. "I agree Aelius, you are not a baby. However, you are still a young child, far too young to fight. We've already discussed this; you were supposed to stay back at the Balance headquarters."

"But I'm strong," Aelius whined, "I want to help."

Blossom opened his mouth to reply but paused when Asher placed a hand on his arm.

"Maybe we should tell him our plan," Asher whispered, his grin widening when the little Sun blessed perked up considerably. "Perhaps he would be less willing to do something so reckless if he knew."

"I doubt it, but you're right," Blossom sighed, holding out his hand. "Come with us Aelius, Asher and I have something we would like to ask you."

Aelius looked between them suspiciously, but after a moment took Blossom's hand and followed him out of the tent. "You're not going to send me back, are you?" He asked as they walked towards Blossom and Asher's tent.

"We should," Blossom mused, smiling over at Asher when Aelius whined, "but right now we can't spare the people it would take to get you back safely. So instead, you're going to be staying back here with the Elders."

Aelius let out another childish noise and tried to tug himself free of Blossom's hold, stopping only when Asher crouched in front of him and looked him in the eye.

"Aelius. We have something very important to ask of you, so we need you to be a big boy right now."

It took a moment, but Aelius finally sniffed and nodded. He sat down on one of the plump cushions inside the tent, crossing his arms with a huff.

Blossom tried to school his features again, which was being made increasingly difficult as he could also feel Asher's mirth coursing through him. "Aelius, remember what we spoke about before we left the Balance? When we were having our picnic by the lake."

Aelius nodded, chewing on his bottom lip. "You said I could come and live with you in the palace," he said, his voice suddenly quiet and hesitant. "A-are you going to tell me that I can't...because I was bad?"

"No Aelius, that's not what we're saying," Blossom soothed, kneeling down and squeezing at the child's shoulder. "In fact, what we were going to ask is this. When you come to live with us in the palace, would you like to do so as our son?"

There was a tense beat of silence whilst Aelius stared at them before he whispered, "you mean it?"

"We do. We want you to be our son. We would like for you to become Prince Aelius."

The little Sun blessed's eyes filled with tears and the next thing Blossom knew Aelius had launched himself into his arms. "Yes, yes please," he cried, the tears that followed causing the shoulder of Blossom's robe to become damp.

Blossom hugged him back, his smile so wide that it was hurting his face. He felt Asher join them, his husband's strong arms wrapping around them both. They knelt there on the tent floor for longer than Blossom cared to count, wrapped around each other. A small, content family. If only for a moment.

28

Chapter 28

Early the next morning, before the sun had risen, Asher mounted his horse and headed up to the front of the assembling troops. He glanced over to where Blossom was, smiling at the sight of little Aelius, their soon to be son, sitting in front of his husband in the saddle.

They'd had an emergency war meeting with the Elders after finding Aelius, after Asher had felt how much Blossom didn't want to be taking part in this battle. This was why Blossom, Aelius, Skyla, Emma, and a few other blessed soldiers were now loitering on the sidelines of the army.

Asher knew that he needed to be part of this. He needed to lead his troops to victory, but his gentle blesser didn't. Instead, Blossom was to take the small group and split off from the marching army. With Evelyn hopefully focusing the main brunt of her forces on the advancing threat, Blossom should be able to sneak back into the palace to face her head on.

Hopefully, if they managed to take her out then the rest of the Blossomites would give in. As long as she was the main thing holding them together.

Without Edwin's expertise they were really working on guesses, but it was the best plan they had.

"Okay troops, head out," Asher shouted, raising his sword in front of him. He looked over his shoulder one last time and returned Blossom's worried smile with one of his own. Blossom nodded before turning his horse, and the small group galloped away.

"You ready for this, Your Majesty?" Kara asked, trotting next to him as they moved away.

"This isn't my first battle Lieutenant," Asher replied, no heat to his tone.

"No, but it is our first battle against an enemy that might not fight fair," Kara said, "I would be surprised if we don't see those monstrous contraptions that hit Edwin out on the field today."

∞

Blossom watched over his shoulder until the mass of bodies that made up the Balance army shrank to nothing but a dot on the horizon. With a sigh he returned his full attention to possibly one of the most daunting tasks of his life; getting to the palace and facing the woman who had stolen him from his home, and his other half.

"You ready for this, Petal?" Emma asked, her voice wobbly and scared.

"As I'll ever be," Blossom replied, digging his heels into his horse's flanks.

The small band of insurgents only managed to get two hours away from the army before the pain started. It was almost instantaneous, and completely overwhelming. Blossom let out a gasp, clutching at his chest as he felt his breath leaving him as though he had been punched.

"Master Blossom?" Aelius asked, turning in the saddle and looking up at him. "Master Blossom, what's wrong?"

"I don't...I don't know," Blossom replied, massaging his chest. The pain was receding slowly, but he couldn't help but feel like the stabbing sensation had merely been the beginning of something much worse. A warning shot of a kind. "Something's wrong."

"Master Blossom?" Skyla turned her horse around and trotted over to him, Blossom hadn't even realised that they'd stopped. "Do you need to rest?"

"N-no, I'm fine. We just... we just need to be careful," he said, shaking his head in an attempt to dispel the fog that was slowly encroaching into his mind. "Let's keep going."

They continued, slower now as Emma, Skyla, and the other soldiers that had joined them watched over him. Aelius kept up a constant stream of chatter in an apparent attempt to distract Blossom from whatever was wrong, but he wasn't listening to it.

The fog was growing denser, his sense of time slipping away, replaced by a confusion that frightened him.

"Wait," Blossom said half an hour later, pulling his horse to a stop and looking around. "What...where are we?"

"We're near the border now, Petal," Emma said, pointing towards something in the distance. "That's the cottage that we stopped at during the pilgrimage."

"Pilgrimage?" Blossom asked, unsure what this woman was referring to. "Cottage?" He nudged his horse into a walk, following the line of the woman's arm. "Are we visiting someone?"

"Master Blossom, what are you talking about?" The little boy sitting in front of him looked up at him in confusion. Confusion which was matched by Blossom himself. "Are you okay?"

"Of course I am, little one," Blossom smiled. For some reason he was having trouble remembering the child's name, or anything about him. He did know one thing though. The child was his, and he didn't want this little boy to feel any fear if he could help it. He ruffled the child's hair, his smile widening when the boy laughed. "We're nearly there. We'll be home soon."

"Oh no."

Blossom turned to look at the woman who had spoken, brows furrowed at the concern in her voice. She looked familiar but for the life of him he couldn't remember her name, or how he knew her.

"Blossom," she said, pulling her horse close to him and taking hold of his hand. "Do you remember where we're going?"

"Home," Blossom said simply. He wasn't sure it was the right answer, but it was the only answer he could give right now.

The woman looked over her shoulder to the other members of their little group. "You need to go and get Prince Asher. We'll wait for you in the cottage, but I think this is happening because they're so far apart."

∞

The ground in front of Asher exploded again, debris and pieces of meat that had once been his soldiers flying in every direction. He leapt back, Shadow's blessing briefly surrounding him in a ball of black smoke before disappearing back into his skin. He had lost his horse a while ago, he wasn't sure when, during battle time often seemed to escape him, moving alternately too fast and too slow.

He rolled to the side as he landed, using the maneuver that Kara had taught him to soften the blow, but then as he stood, a sharp pain shot through his chest. He placed a hand over his heart, feeling the chest plate of his armor for any shrapnel or damage, but there was nothing. Shaking his head, Asher stood again, something wasn't right.

"Wh-where..." He dropped his sword, looking around in a daze at the carnage surrounding him. "What's happening?"

"Your Majesty!" Kara shouted, dragging Asher out of the path of a Blossomite's blade. "What's wrong with you? Where's your sword?"

"What?" He asked, staring at Kara uncomprehendingly. "Where am I?" He looked around, wondering why everyone was fighting, why the smell of blood was so thick in the air.

Kara stared back at him, completely aghast. "Something's wrong." She said, taking Asher's hand and hauling him away from the battlefield. "Your Majesty, did you get hit?"

"Hit?" Asher asked, looking over Kara's shoulder and frowning in confusion. He could see two mounted riders galloping towards them from the opposite direction of the battle. "Who's that?"

Before Kara could respond one of the riders leapt from her horse and ran over to them. "King Asher, you need to come with us."

"What's happening Skyla?" Kara demanded.

"Blossom's lost his memory. He doesn't remember that we were going to the palace, we have him in the cottage that we passed during the pilgrimage. I think it has something to do with how far away Master Blossom and the king are from each other. It started a few hours ago. Emma and Aelius are with him, but he doesn't know them."

Kara nodded, taking Asher's hand again and guiding him towards the horses. "Skyla, you mount with Terra, I'll take your horse and ride with Asher. We'll head straight to the cottage and once these two are back to normal we'll continue with our original mission."

Skyla nodded silently and followed Kara's order, climbing onto the already mounted horse in front of the other Earth blessed. "Follow us."

The small group moved off as fast as their laden horses could carry them, hoping that all of the Blossomite soldiers were too distracted by the battle to notice them trying to sneak away.

"Behind you!" Terra cried, raising her fist and creating a wall of earth, just in time to intercept the explosive ball that had been fired their way. "Skyla, help me."

"Take the reigns, I've got this," Skyla replied, wrapping a hand in Terra's tunic and swinging around in the saddle. Once she was situated again she clenched her hands into fists, before thrusting them upwards. Another wall of earth erupted from the ground, and as Skyla pushed her hands away from her body the wall began to move, slamming into the Blossomites that had begun to run after them.

As they moved further away from the battle, fewer and fewer Blossomites attempted to pursue them, returning their attention to the carnage behind, and with one final push Skyla slumped against Terra's chest, completely spent.

"Where are we going?" Asher asked, about an hour into the journey. They were moving at a slower pace than Blossom had, not wanting to tire the horses too much, and were still a few hours away from the cottage.

"We're bringing you back to your husband, Your Majesty," Kara explained.

"My husband," Asher replied with a wistful smile. "I have a husband."

"Yes you do, and I'm hoping that he can fix you because this is getting weird."

The longer they rode the weaker Asher became, which seemed odd because they should be getting closer to where Blossom was. Asher was nodding off, making it harder and harder to ride as he kept slumping to the side and nearly toppling from the saddle.

"We need a break," Kara called, pulling her horse to a halt.

"We're nearly there," Terra replied, gesturing to a hill in the middle distance. "It's just over that ridge, surely we should push on as fast as possible."

"Asher is liable to slip and smack his head on the ground if we don't rest. So is Skyla, I'm surprised she hasn't already," Kara insisted, letting out a sudden shout when Asher did just that. However, before he hit the ground a plume of shadow surrounded him, cushioning his fall. "Okay, here's what we're going to do," Kara said, climbing down from the horse and gathering the unconscious prince in her arms. "You're going to help me strap him to the horse and I'll lead her on foot."

Terra complied wordlessly, letting out a quiet shushing sound to Skyla when she dismounted. Skyla was slowly returning to consciousness, enough that she could sit in the saddle without Terra's support, but she was still weak. So, Terra chose to lead her horse the same way Kara was, pausing briefly to give the other Earth blessed some of her well of blessing energy.

∞

Blossom was beginning to feel really unwell. He couldn't focus on anything, the wooden beams above him rippling through his vision like he was underwater. The little boy that had been with him all afternoon had stepped outside for a moment, leaving him alone in the oddly familiar cottage. The familiarity of his surroundings was causing an uncomfortable itch at the back of his brain, an alarm of some kind, so Blossom called out, "son. Please come inside, it isn't safe."

The boy returned, confusion marring his smooth features. "What do you mean it isn't safe papa? Have you seen something?"

Blossom shook his head and held out his hand, sighing in relief when the boy took it and sat on the stool next to his bed. "I just don't like not knowing where you are," He whispered, eyes drooping closed.

"The king should be here soon, he'll be able to make things better," his son replied.

Why couldn't he remember his son's name?

"The king," Blossom muttered, feeling the darkness of sleep slowly covering him. "My king."

29

Chapter 29

Kara, Skyla, Terra, and the still unconscious Asher arrived at the cottage just as the sun began to set. Their journey had been slow and arduous, the horses were both lame now and worry was causing all of them to act waspish and short with one another.

"Emma," Skyla called as they made their way through the hillside meadow, smiling with relief when Emma and Aelius emerged from the cottage and ran to meet them.

"Blossom isn't waking up," Aelius explained in a panic, "and he kept calling me his son."

"Asher fell asleep a little while ago as well. Help me here Terra, he's heavier than he looks," Kara said as she untied the ropes that secured Asher to the saddle. "I'm sure they'll awaken once they're reunited."

They carried the king down the hill and into the cottage, settling him in the bed next to Blossom. Both of the Blessers instantly rolled towards each other, resting their foreheads together, their hands finding one another and tangling together even as they continued to sleep.

"Okay, that's something at least," Kara sighed, scrubbing a hand down her face. "We need to keep an eye on them, let's take it in shifts.

The rest of us need to sleep as much as we can before we attempt to infiltrate the palace."

"What's happening to them?" Terra asked, her voice quiet and soft, a far departure from her usual rough, and slightly intimidating presence.

There was an odd glow emanating from the bed, soft pink threaded through with tendrils of black, which grew to envelop both bodies in a sort of cocoon.

Kara took a step back; she wasn't sure why, but she suddenly felt as though they were intruding on something private. "I think... I think they're bonding," she said, lifting an arm to shield her eyes as the light grew brighter and brighter. "I also think we need to leave, right now." She grabbed Aelius by the hand and ran outside, closely followed by the rest of the group.

They made it to the edge of the meadow just in time, falling to the ground as the windows of the cottage shattered and the roof blew clean off. A column of light shot into the air, a myriad of every colour imaginable, just like when Blossom released his mixed blessings at the end of the long day celebration.

"What...what was that?" Skyla asked, her breaths coming in rapid succession.

"Like I said, they're bonding. They were going to wait until after we managed to restore balance, but I wonder if being separated caused it to happen automatically. Like a survival mechanism or something."

The group climbed to their feet and cautiously began making their way back down the hill towards the husk that used to be the cottage.

"What do you mean bonding? What are you talking about?" Skyla pressed.

Kara didn't answer, her focus on the two men emerging from the splintered doorway. It was definitely still Blossom and Asher, but they had changed.

Blossom's hair was streaked with black, multicoloured light dancing beneath his skin as though his veins were glowing, and despite still being a head or so shorter than her, Kara felt as though the Blesser was towering over her.

Asher was much the same, his skin crawling with constantly moving shadows. One of his pitch-black eyes was now a pale pink, and his shoulder length hair moved about his head as though tugged by a non-existent wind.

"Master Blossom, King Asher," Kara said, dropping to one knee. It didn't matter that she had helped to raise both of these men, right then she could sense that they had changed. They weren't human anymore, at least not entirely. They were returning to their purely blessed state.

∞

Blossom and Asher looked at one another in unison. Blossom tilted his head to the side, a small smile tugging at his lips. He wasn't sure how he knew but he realised that he didn't even need to consciously think in order to communicate with Asher now, their thoughts and emotions were so entwined that understanding passed between them instantly.

"We thank you for bringing us back together Kara," he said, surprising himself at how echoey his voice sounded, like it was booming from somewhere deep inside of him. "But we are not yet fully bonded."

"We can't truly become one until we are on the island again. This is as close as we can get right now," Asher finished, taking hold of Blossom's hand, his Shadow twining up Blossom's arm, mixing with the light of the other blessings.

"We are nearly at our full power; it is now that we should return to the palace," Blossom said, his smile growing gentle as he noticed the mixture of awe and fear on the humans' faces. "Don't be afraid of us, we are still as you remember...only more."

"Aelius." Asher held out his hand for the little Sun blessed, kneeling to his height when Aelius hesitated. "Please son."

Aelius swallowed and nodded, sliding his small hand into Asher's own and gasping as the shadows touched him. He held his other hand out to Blossom who mimicked his husband's stance so that they were both crouched in front of him.

"You did such a good job of looking after Blossom whilst I was away," Asher said, directing his gaze briefly towards Blossom. "We have something to give you."

Blossom reached into the pocket of his robe and pulled out the rabbit toy. He kissed it gently on the head before handing it to Aelius. "She is imbued with some of our power, she will keep you safe whilst you grow. Just like she looked after me." He looked up at Emma, mirroring her smile. "She is your connection to us once we are gone."

"Are you... are you leaving?" Aelius' voice was small as he twisted one of Miss Flops long ears around his finger.

Blossom shared a look with his other half, nodding almost imperceptibly, a sad tilt to his lips. "I'm afraid so, my son. I promise you that Asher and I had planned on staying with you once this war was over. We were so excited to watch you grow, to see the man that you became... but now..." He looked down at the way blessing power was still dancing over his skin, feeling the pull towards the island and towards Asher almost like a dagger to the heart.

"We have been changed," Asher continued for him. "Bonding as we have now means that it would be impossible. We are not of this world, not really, and we are not meant to be in separate bodies. We cannot sustain ourselves as we are, and if we were to stay with you... it would be dangerous."

Aelius' large golden eyes were swimming with tears as he nodded. "Can... can I still call you papa?" He asked, hugging the stuffed toy close to his chest.

"Of course you can," Blossom said, ruffling Aelius' hair, causing sparks of Nature's blessing to rain down around him like rain. "You are still our son, and we still love you as one. We will always love you Aelius, even if we are not near you." He bopped the rabbit toy lightly on its nose. "That is what she symbolises."

The Blessers stood again, still hand in hand. "Now, we must go to the palace," Asher said, and before anyone else could respond, the world around them shifted and the group found themselves in the throne room of the Vaten palace.

Asher and Blossom turned in unison, locking gazes with the woman sitting atop the throne that had once belonged to Silas.

"So, your power grows," Evelyn said, a manic glint in her eye as she smiled. "As I knew it would. The more we suffer the stronger we become. The world is breaking apart and the dawn of a new era is beginning." She gestured around herself at the throne room. What once had been opulent to the point of overwhelm was now dark and damaged. Tables were upended, glass and pots lay shattered on the floor, and the unblessed people filling the throne room looked gaunt and grim.

It was almost as though their life force were being drained from them, every good thing slowly seeping from their pores.

"You're wrong," Blossom replied calmly, glancing around the room, spying the blessed gathered there. He could see their power radiating from them, like they were glowing with the colour associated with their deity. The unblessed were also glowing. Their light was dimmer, it was true, but there was definitely something emanating from every person in that room. He was somehow certain that there was something wrong with the glow, it was almost sickly. Blossom wasn't sure why, but deep down he knew that the colours should be more vibrant.

The light should be almost blinding.

He looked over at Kara and Emma and there it was again. Theirs was stronger than the rest, and Blossom couldn't tell if it was simply because they hadn't been in that room as long as the others, or if Evelyn was actually doing something to siphon the Blossomites under her care. The colour of Kara and Emma's light was almost pink, like his own power, with threads of the other blessings coursing through it. He could also see where their light intermingled with each other, small threads of their life force reaching towards one another. He looked down at his hand, where it was entwined with Asher.

It was just the same.

There were threads connecting them all, some weaker than others. The pink tendril emanating from him that combined with Skyla's green one was dimmer than his connection with Emma, but it was still there.

"You're wrong," he said again. "Suffering is not what makes us strong. Connection is. Asher and I have unlocked our power through bonding, by connecting our souls so closely that they can no longer be separated."

Blossom tilted his head to the side, his mouth turning down in a frown when he noticed that Evelyn's light was a lot dimmer than everyone else's, and what was more, it didn't seem to spread out to anyone, not even him. If she was taking the power that dwelled in the other Blossomites, she wasn't using it for herself.

"I see," he said quietly when Evelyn didn't reply, simply glared at him from her throne. He took a step forward, Asher matching him perfectly. "I understand why that concept might be foreign to you. Despite being born as one of three, you have never felt or nurtured connection, have you?"

Evelyn sniffed, turning her glare on her sister. "Connection, family, caring. It only serves to weaken you. You can never reach your full potential if you are always worrying about other people."

"Well, that's where you're wrong again," Blossom said, smiling as Asher chuckled next to him.

"Enough." Evelyn sat forward, gripping the arms of the throne. "I had hoped you would be returning to me having already learnt the truth. I had hoped you would already be tearing this world down to make way for the new order, but it seems my sister has undone all of my hard work," she hissed, standing now and slicing the air with her arm. "So, we'll see if I can't finally get through to you. How strong do you think you'll be against all of the blessed in this room, hmm?"

Blossom looked around, nodding as Asher silently spoke to him, pointing out the people who had been members of his school. "If they were to attempt to harm us or those we love, then it would be a struggle, especially as we have no desire to fight," he conceded, "but that's not going to happen."

Evelyn's responding laugh sent goose bumps shooting up his arms, he'd never heard someone sound so wrong before. It almost didn't sound natural. "Isn't it?" She asked, before pointing at them both. "I have had almost one full year to bless them with all the suffering they could desire, and now, they'll do whatever I order them to do. So, Blossom, prepare to be blessed."

30

Chapter 30

Afew of the blessed in the room stepped forward, hands glowing dully with the power of their respective blessings. However, the vast majority remained in the shadows, shuffling their feet as they looked at each other.

"We have no quarrel with you. In fact, we believe most of you to be our friends," Asher said, squeezing Blossom's hand. "We do not wish to fight."

Blossom nodded in agreement. "Leave now or stand beside us, and we will not raise a finger to you."

Evelyn laughed again, but the sound cut off quickly as the blessed that hadn't come to her side began to move. They walked behind Blossom and Asher silently, and though most of them moved as though their bodies hurt, their faces were set with determination. "You cowards. Your loyalty can shift that fast?" She screeched, her eyes wide and crazed.

"We were never loyal to you," Master Hotem said, their fist clenching at their side. "You threatened our children, our families. You tortured us when we dared to question you. Why would we follow you when the one who always showed us kindness has returned?" Master Hotem looked over to Blossom. "I'm sorry your grace, the Blossomites took so many of the children, we couldn't leave them."

"You did the right thing," Blossom replied, placing a hand on their arm. "We're afraid that it isn't over yet though. Where are the children now?"

Master Hotem shook their head. "In the dungeons. The ones that refused to cooperate or the ones too young to fight were taken down there. The rest are here." They gestured around themself, and Blossom realised that almost the entirety of his school was there. He wasn't sure how he could have missed them before.

Blossom nodded. "Send them outside. Emma, please take the children."

"No, Master Blossom we want to help." Firenze, a little Fire blessed, said holding himself as tall as he could.

Blossom opened his mouth to respond but Evelyn beat him to it.

"You think it will be that easy?" She asked, stepping down from the raised dais that the throne sat upon. "You may have gathered the cowards to your side, but I still have the strongest blessed with me." She gestured behind her to the handful of Blossomites that weren't still lingering in the shadows. "The ones who could withstand every gift of suffering they were blessed with; you think you can break them?"

Blossom and Asher shared a look before Blossom sighed. "Very well. Then let's make this as quick and painless as possible." He held up one hand, a mixture of all of Nature's blessings spreading from his fingertips, curling towards Evelyn.

Asher moved at the same time, plunging the throne room into darkness, the thuds of close to a hundred bodies hitting the floor were loud in the suddenly silent room.

Evelyn's smile dropped briefly, before growing and she stepped towards the blessing now tangling around her. "See, you preach kindness but at the end of the day you are ruthless. Just as you should be."

"They're not dead Evelyn," Asher said, head tilted to the side with a bemused look on his face. "Only unconscious. We do not break those we love."

"We see now that you are too far gone," Blossom said with a heartbroken sigh, tears beginning to track down his cheeks. "We had hoped that it wouldn't come to this, but you are the last piece. The last thing keeping this world unbalanced." He turned to Asher, using the lasso of blessing power that now ensnared Evelyn to pull her closer. "Now my love. Make it quick and make it painless."

Asher nodded, turning his attention back to Evelyn. He threaded his own blessing through Blossom's, tightening the hold on Evelyn and making her gasp. "Blessing be with you," he whispered, clenching his fist.

"I'm sorry," Blossom added, his voice hitching on the last word.

Shadow's blessing enveloped Evelyn in an instant, covering her body the way it had with Silas all those months ago. And just like with Silas, the effect was almost instantaneous. Evelyn never felt a thing. Asher released his hold slowly, letting the now lifeless form of the Blossomite leader lay gently on the ground.

Colour and light returned to the room, revealing its inhabitants as they began to stir from their enforced slumber.

"What?" Emma asked, the word slurring out of her like she'd been asleep for hours. Her eyes travelled over to Evelyn's body and a pained squeak escaped her lips as she clamped a hand over her mouth.

"We're sorry," Blossom said, reaching for his mother and helping her to her feet. "There was no other way."

"I... I know. Deep down I knew it would end like this," Emma replied, hiding her face in Blossom's shoulder, dampening his robe with her tears. "But she was still my sister."

Blossom held Emma close and allowed her to weep as the rest of the hall began to stand, murmuring amongst themselves as they drifted around Asher and Blossom.

"Flower," Asher said, resting his hand on Blossom's back. "We need to speak with them."

Blossom nodded, pulling away from Emma with one final hug and making his way over to the raised dais. He turned to face the crowd, squeezing Asher's hand when the king grasped him. "People," he said, his voice booming out of him in the way it had since he and Asher had bonded. "This conflict ends today. This split between the blessed and unblessed that you have created is over. Neither one is lesser than the other, and it is the imbalance created through small mindedness that has caused such suffering."

There were murmurings through the crowd, the myriad colours of each person's blessing merging and growing brighter as everyone in the throne room stepped towards them.

Blossom opened his mouth to speak again, but before he could the whole of the congregation dropped to their knees, heads bowed in reverence.

"Master Blossom." A man that Blossom had never seen before said, his voice low. "We accept you as our new leader, just as Evelyn foretold. It is different to how we had always imagined it, but you are the destined ruler of this world, we will do as you bid."

Blossom shook his head. "No," he replied simply, smiling when the man looked up at him in surprise. "Asher and I are not of this world. We were brought here to put an end to the division and restore balance. We know that there is more to be done, and we shall do so, but we are not your rulers." His eyes travelled over to where Aelius stood, looking so small between Emma and Kara. "We will appoint someone to take the throne of Vaten, and we will speak with the other rulers before we leave, but it is up to you, all of you now, to work together and make a better world."

31

Chapter 31

"Kara," Asher said quietly, hoping not to startle his mentor with his new, echoing voice. He should have known that the lieutenant wouldn't be so easily caught off guard and smiled when she simply turned to him with a raised eyebrow.

"Yes, Your Majesty?" She asked, waving off another ex-Blossomite as she stepped forward to beg her pardon.

"Have you sent someone to convey the news to the troops? A cease-fire needs to be called," he said, pulling her away from the gathered blessed who had begun milling around whilst they decided what to do with them.

"What do you take me for?" Kara replied, hands on her hips. "I thought you would have had a little more faith in me than that. I sent Skyla over an hour ago."

Asher nodded, a bashful grin on his face. "Thank you." He paused as a thought occurred to him. "Blossom and I were going to go to Shotsen to collect my mother and Edwin. To tell them the good news. But it will take Skyla at least two more hours to reach the battlefield and too many lives will be lost in that time. We will take a detour and make the announcement ourselves; enough blood has been spilled today."

"I don't think you'll need to tell them anything, the queen and Edwin I mean," Kara said, placing a hand on Asher's back and guiding him towards the window. "When you and Blossom killed that woman, something changed in the air. It's been changing since you two bonded, like everything is getting brighter somehow, but that seemed to be the final push."

Asher tilted his head as he contemplated her words, glancing back over his shoulder to where Blossom was stood, speaking with Aelius and Emma. Blossom looked up at him, a rush of love surging through their bond so strongly that Asher could feel himself tearing up. "We need to reveal the location of the island," he said, surprising himself with the statement.

"What? Have you lost your mind?" Kara shouted. "After everything that Silas did in order to find it? After everything that the Balance sacrificed in order to keep it safe?"

"Exactly," Asher replied, holding out his hand as Blossom joined them. "We appreciate everything the Balance did to protect the island but keeping it a secret was a mistake. No human can gain access to its shores without our approval, so the island itself will remain safe. However, it is a sacred place and should serve as a reminder of how things should be."

"It should be a place of pilgrimage. Not just for those in the Balance, but for all who wish to seek it," Blossom continued, "and it should be the location of our gathering."

"Gathering?" Kara asked, she still didn't look convinced but there was a curiosity in her voice as well now.

"Yes. We need to bring all of the kingdoms together. We have a message for all the rulers of this world, one that they need to convey to their people. What better place to do it than the spot where all the kingdoms converge?" Blossom's smile was serene and confident, and he turned to Asher, taking both of his hands in his. "Let us go my love. I believe I now have enough strength to cure Edwin, and we should re-unite Vaten with its lost queen."

"Let us end this war first," he said, waiting until Blossom nodded before moving.

Asher still wasn't sure how he and Blossom now had the power to warp space to their will, but it was as easy and natural as breathing, so he didn't dwell on it too much. He simply stepped forward and they found themselves in the battlefield.

The once lush green field was now pockmarked with craters, bodies scattered about the blood-soaked ground. The size of both armies had dwindled dramatically, and Asher felt Blossom's grief at the sight just as keenly as his own.

"Children," he boomed, releasing the full power of his enhanced voice. That one word was enough to stop everyone on the field in their tracks, and they turned, almost in unison, to look at the two Blessers.

"Stop this now," Blossom continued for him. "Evelyn is dead, the Blossomites are no more, and this destruction must stop." He held up a hand, slowly closing his fist. "Lay down your arms."

Most of the soldiers did so immediately, either too stunned by the sight of Asher and Blossom, or too tired to disagree. Those that didn't soon found themselves dropping their weapons anyway, the handles of their swords glowing red hot, the shafts of their spears splintering in their hands.

"Tend to your fallen, bury your dead. This is a time of peace and mourning," Blossom said, eyes landing on one of the explosive weapons that had caused so much destruction in such a short time. "These are no longer required."

The people closest to the weapons stumbled back as each one began to melt, and soon enough the only evidence left of their existence was a scorched ring of earth.

"Sir Petyr," Asher gestured the Fire blessed over to them.

"Your Majesty," Petyr said with a bow.

"We have trained and fought together for many years; I trust that you will be able to lead the remaining troops back to Vaten. Just as I trust your judgement in the pardon of those who fought against you."

"Of course, Your Majesty," Petyr gave another bow, his brows drawn in what appeared to be worry. "But may I ask, will you not be joining us on our march?"

"We have so much to do," Blossom explained. "We will see you again in Vaten."

Asher nodded in agreement, his hold on Blossom's hand tightening. The lure of the island was getting stronger, he could almost feel himself being dragged towards it. "We don't have much time left," he whispered, sharing a glance with Blossom before they transported themselves again.

The difference between the grim starkness of the battlefield and the warm glow of the Shotsen palace was so striking that Asher felt briefly short of breath. He leant towards Blossom, seeking his husband's comfort. Comfort which was instantly given in the form of Blossom's arm encircling his waist.

"Soon, my love. We will be united soon," Blossom murmured against his hair.

"Oh," Princess Cassandra gasped once she spotted them, covering her mouth with her hand. "What... something has changed."

"Indeed it has, Princess," Asher answered, holding one hand up in a calming gesture. "Don't be afraid. Blossom and I are simply one step closer to becoming our true selves again."

"Or true self, should that be?" Blossom asked with a giggle, and Asher wasn't entirely sure if he'd said it aloud or not, but his responding laugh echoed around the vast room. "We are convening a council of all the rulers of this world. You are to meet us at the shores of the blessing island in one week, all will be explained there. For now, we would like to see Edwin and Queen Lila." Blossom let a ripple of blessing power travel over his hand. "Unless you have managed to cure him in our absence?"

Princess Cassandra stared at them in shock for a few more seconds before coming back to her senses. She shook her head and stood, a tentative smile on her face. "Of course, please come with me." She guided them down a few, airy corridors, sending furtive, worried glances their way every few moments. "Our Moon blessed have been doing the best they can, and he is improving. Just yesterday he regained consciousness for over an hour, but he is still in pain."

"We thank you for all you have done," Asher said, "we know you've done everything within your power. However, such an unnatural wound requires something greater than a singular blessing to heal."

Cassandra showed them into a light, comfortable room. Edwin lay on the rounded bed in the center. He was asleep, but just like the princess had said, he did look better than when they had last seen him. His coppery Castillan skin had regained some of its old glow, and his brow was smooth and relaxed, as though the pain had lessened.

"Your Majesty," Cassandra whispered, tugging on Asher's sleeve briefly as Blossom made his way over to the bed and placed a hand on Edwin's bared chest. "What happened? You both seem... so different."

"We are," Asher agreed, smile widening as he felt Blossom's mirth mix with his own. "So, the Balance hasn't sent word of what we are to their members yet?"

"What are you talking about?"

"Blossom and I..."

"Darling heart," Blossom interrupted, the glow from his hands fading as Edwin's chest knitted itself back together. He stood up after checking that Edwin was still asleep, his hands cupped together as he made his way over to them. "Should we not explain this to everyone at once? We will need to tell the other rulers as well."

"And let Cassandra worry for another week? Best to put her out of her misery now."

Blossom hummed but Asher knew that he'd already conceded. "Very well, tell her. Also..." He opened his hands, showing Asher and Cassandra the metal shards that he had pulled from Edwin's chest. "I know it need not be said really, but those weapons that the Blossomites created must be destroyed, every one of them. Nothing that causes this much pain and destruction should be allowed to exist."

"Agreed, I'll tell Kara to send out troops to collect them, we don't know how many of those things they made," Asher said before returning his attention to the princess. "You might want to sit down for this."

∞

Princess Cassandra accepted their story surprisingly easily, or perhaps not too surprising considering the power that now radiated from Blossom and Asher at all times. Blossom hadn't really considered it before, since he and Asher had bonded it had simply felt natural, like they were closer to their true selves. But their changes were visible for everyone to see, and he could feel the wariness with which everyone approached them.

He knew they couldn't really be considered human anymore.

Even still, Queen Lila greeted them the same way she always had, as though he and Asher were still small children under her care.

"My, my. I always knew you boys had a connection, something deeper than simple compatibility. To think that my own son is one of the great Blessers," Lila said, cupping Asher's cheek with a loving smile. "My special boys."

Blossom crouched next to her chair, placing a tentative hand on her arm. "We have unlocked a lot of our power now. We might be able to heal you."

"Possibly, for a short time," Lila replied, "but this is part of my make up, you know this little flower. The difficulties are a part of me."

"Are you saying you do not wish us to try?" Blossom asked, tilting his head to the side.

"I didn't say that. I would very much like to be able to stand and walk with you to the edge of the lake. I would like to say my goodbyes eye to eye."

∞

They travelled back to the Balance headquarters a few days later in a convoy similar to the one that had taken them there in the first place. However, this time the wagons were uncovered, and any who spoke to them on the journey were invited to join. Blossom and Asher arrived with a gaggle of nearly 500 people, an even mix of blessed and unblessed from Shotsen, Castilla and Vaten.

They convened on the shore of the lake, the rulers of each kingdom, as well as the Elders of the Balance, standing in a semi-circle facing Blossom and Asher, waiting to hear what the Blessers had to say.

"Thank you very much for joining us today," Blossom began, placing his hand over his chest as he smiled. "I am sure you are all aware of the battle that was waged only a few days ago, of the loss of life and the destruction of the Blossomites."

There was a general sound of murmuring from the crowd, but Blossom continued on before it could get louder. He explained all that he and Asher had learnt about themselves, about the history of the Balance, the false beliefs of the Blossomites. He couldn't tell how many of the gathered people believed him, but it didn't really matter, once he and Asher made their departure the proof would be unmistakable.

"Needless to say, this violence and clamour for power are what has caused such unbalance in this world, and what brought us to you in the first place. So, we have invited you all here to create a pact."

Asher stepped forward, pulling a large scroll out of his pocket, which he unfurled and laid on a table set up in front of them. He placed an empty inkwell down next to it, calling Shadow's blessing forth and pouring the dark matter into the glass receptacle.

"We ask that you, as representatives of your kingdoms and organisations, make a formal declaration of peace. This pact here will work as a binding contract, signed using the blessing of protection. Your signature will guarantee that those under your banner will forever fall under our protection," Asher said, placing a raven feather quill into the inkwell. "As long as you adhere to your promise."

"So, what are the terms?" Elder Hasham asked, the glow that Blossom could now see from every living being turning a pale green. Over the last week or so Blossom had discovered that the colour of a person's internal glow correlated to their emotions just as much as it did their blessing. Now Blossom was able to read the humans around him simply by looking at the strings that connected them. Right now, Elder Hasham was both curious and hesitant.

"The terms are fairly simple. We have three requests of all of you," Blossom said, making sure to make eye contact with each person in the semi-circle in turn. He smiled gently when his eyes landed on Aelius, standing proudly next to Queen Lila's chair, his small crown sitting lopsidedly on his golden locks. "Number one, the blessed and unblessed shall be treated equally in all things. Number two, disagreements between kingdoms shall be resolved through the use of political discussion and not war. Number three, the use of weapons that result in injuries that cannot be healed through Moon's blessing are banned."

There was another, louder murmur through the crowd as everyone discussed the terms.

"We will give you until sundown to make your decision," Asher said, taking Blossom's hand. "Once the moon has risen, Blossom and I will be returning to the Blesser's temple. But know this, though we may no longer have physical forms in this world, we will be watching over you."

"And what will you do if we break any of these new rules?" Hasham asked.

"We are nature itself; we are the source of all blessings in this world. If you sign this declaration and then break the promises stated within, we shall revoke our blessing from your land," Blossom said as plainly as he could. "Now, who shall be the first to sign?"

As he'd suspected, Queen Lila and Prince Aelius were the first to come forward, signing in turn before returning to their place in the circle. The king and queen of Shotsen followed after, along with Princess Cassandra, signing their names and promising the names of their descendants as well. The other kingdoms representatives took longer to sign and there were many lively debates. But sure enough, by the time the sun began to set the Pledge of Nature contained signatures from all present.

"Thank you all," Blossom said, rolling the declaration up and sealing it with a blast of Nature's blessing. "This will be housed in the Balance archives and protected by the Elders. However, the headquarters and this shore will remain as an open place of pilgrimage for all those who wish to seek us." He handed the scroll to Elder Leena. "Now, in celebration a feast is being held in the great hall, please make your way into the headquarters and eat your fill."

The crowd dispersed slowly, leaving Blossom, Asher, Lila, Emma, Kara, Aelius, and Edwin standing on the shoreline.

"So," Blossom said, smiling at his family. "This is goodbye."

Aelius was the first to come to them, hugging Blossom and Asher as hard as his little arms could manage. "I know you've only been my fathers for a little bit, but I'm going to miss you."

Blossom knelt down, gesturing to the bunny held in Asher's hand. "We will still be your fathers Aelius, we will always be with you. Remember that."

Aelius nodded, sniffing as he returned to the queen. Kara and Edwin came next, hugging both of the Blessers in turn.

"You've become so much more than I could ever have imagined, I'm so proud of you," Kara whispered, knocking lightly against Asher's chin with her fist. Her eyes glistening with rare tears which she hid with another hug.

"I'm sorry I wasn't more helpful, your grace," Edwin said, bowing slightly and glancing up when Blossom tutted.

"None of that, you were a tremendous help, uncle," Blossom said with a shake of his head. "I hope we can trust you to keep the records for all that transpired here."

Edwin's eyes widened and he nodded emphatically. "I will make it my life's work," he promised, stepping aside to let Emma through.

Emma stepped forward, tears streaming down her cheeks even as she smiled. "My lovely, gentle, boys. It has been an honor, and such a joy to watch you two grow. I'm going to miss you both, so much," she said, her voice hitching on her sobs as she pulled Blossom and Asher into a tight hug. "I love you."

"We will miss you too, thank you for being my mother," Blossom said, hugging her back. "Just remember that we will never be that far away."

Emma gazed up at him, cupping his cheek in her hand. "When it is time for me to die, will you come to take me to whatever comes next?"

"Of course, but that is many years off yet." Blossom pressed a kiss to Emma's forehead, passing some of his blessing to her the way he had with Aelius' bunny toy, before letting her go.

Lila walked over to them next, resting only slightly on her cane. "My sons," she said, kissing them both on the cheek. "I am so glad you found each other, and so glad that I got to see you two become what you were always meant to be."

Asher squeezed Blossom's hand as his mother returned to where Emma was standing.

"We don't have to go right now, if you're having second thoughts." Blossom made sure to keep the statement between their bond and smiled when Asher responded in kind.

"No, it's the right time. You feel the pull of the island just as much as I do. We would be of no help if we remained here."

Blossom couldn't help but agree, and though he could already feel the grief beginning to build at the thought of never physically seeing the people who had been his family again, he could also imagine the joy of his and Asher's union.

They turned, hand in hand, to face the shadow covered lake. "We should let them see it, just this once," Blossom said quietly as Asher raised his hand, dissipating the protective covering of Shadow's blessing and revealing the glistening island.

There was a collection of gasps behind them, but Blossom didn't look back, instead he stepped forward, in perfect unison with Asher and they made their way over the water. It wasn't until they set foot on the lush grass that Blossom allowed himself one final glance at the humans. He raised his hand in a silent farewell, tears streaming down his cheeks as everyone returned the gesture.

And then they were alone.

The shadow returned, shielding them from the outside world, but Blossom found that he could still see through it, almost as if it wasn't there.

"We should raise it, for a few moments on this day each year, don't you think?" Blossom asked, no longer bothering to verbalize his thoughts.

"I think you're right. We remained separate for too long last time, that may have had a hand in allowing such unrest to spawn. People forgot that we existed, at least in a physical sense. A yearly reminder should go a long way in helping to maintain peace," Asher replied, looking up at the temple. "Now, shall we go?"

"Yes, my love."

As they entered the temple Blossom was sure that the air was vibrating, their excitement manifesting into something almost physical.

Standing in the middle of the temple Blossom and Asher faced one another.

"I'll miss this body I think," Blossom thought, reaching up and cupping his husband's cheek. "I'll miss the warmth that you gave me."

"Can I confess something, Flower?" Asher asked, the question clearly rhetorical as Blossom could already feel what he was about to say, but he nodded his consent anyway. "I'm scared."

"Me too." Blossom smiled at him, taking a step closer. "But all big changes are a little scary, aren't they?"

Instead of replying with words, Asher leant forward and kissed him, wrapping his arms around Blossom's waist as they began to meld into one.

Blossom had his eyes closed as they kissed, but he could feel the glow of their power as it exploded out of them. As their bodies melted away, he couldn't help but let out a laugh of happiness, because he was soaring, free and light in a way he had only ever dreamt of before.

"Asher," He cried, reaching with a hand that no longer existed as his consciousness spread to every corner of the world.

He could see everything, everyone under their protection. Their lives playing out before him.

"I'm here Flower, I'm still here," Asher replied, sounding just as jubilant as Blossom felt.

"Are you witnessing this?"

"I see everything you see. Feel everything you feel."

"We are one. We did it."

"We did."

32

Epilogue

"Are you sure you don't wish for me to wait with you?" King Aelius asked, kicking down the break on the wheeled chair to ensure that his surrogate mother didn't roll into the water.

Emma smiled up at him, her heavily lined face creasing with the action. "No, my darling boy. Thank you, but I would like to embark on this next journey alone."

"You won't be alone," Aelius replied, pressing a kiss to Emma's grey hair. "Papa promised that he would collect you when the time came."

Emma took a deep breath, shifting in her seat. "That he did, and Petal was never one to break his word."

"He hasn't yet. In all these years since they left us, they've never missed the greeting day, even if we haven't physically seen them. I just wish you'd hold on until the next one."

That pulled a laugh from Emma, followed by a hacking cough, the same one that had been plaguing her since the previous winter. "I'm afraid I don't have control over that, Sunflower." She held out a hand, squeezing Aelius' fingers when he took hold of it. "All I know is that it's time for me to go... I feel it in my bones."

Aelius heaved a sigh. "I know, but I will miss you. Sometimes, I feel as though all of my family are destined to leave me."

"Now Sunflower, this is just Nature's way. It's natural for your parents to be the first to go, but I'm sorry that you have had to witness so many loses over your short life. Try to look to the future, focus on Phola, on your children. Phola will be going into labour any day now, they should be your focus, not an old lady like me."

Aelius finally smiled, leaning down to press one more kiss to Emma's cheek. "You're right, though I feel as though thirty isn't that short an amount of time. I will raise a glass to you tonight and leave a flower for you next to Blossom and Asher's. I love you, and I'll miss you."

"I love you too," Emma said, watching as Aelius made his way back up the slight hill to the Balance headquarters. Once he was out of sight, she turned back towards the lake. Taking a deep breath, she closed her eyes. "Okay, I'm ready. I'm ready to leave this world."

"Then let us go."

Emma opened her eyes again. The shadow that enshrouded the Blesser's island was gone, and before her stood Blossom and Asher, looking exactly as they had when she had last seen them.

Blossom smiled, holding out a semi-translucent hand. "Hello mother, it's good to see you again."

"Petal," Emma breathed, taking the hand and standing. The fact that she hadn't been able to walk for the past year suddenly didn't seem to matter, and when she looked back at the chair Emma realised why. "Oh, it was as easy as that," she said, unsure how to feel about the sight of her lifeless body, slumped down in her chair as though she had just fallen asleep.

"It is," Asher said, taking her other hand, "and the walk is just as easy."

"Come, there are quite a few people who have been waiting for you." Blossom inclined his head towards the island and as they began to walk Emma could see that the usually empty beach now contained three figures.

"Kara," Emma cried, falling into her wife's arms once she reached her.

"My darling dove, how I've missed you," Kara replied, cupping Emma's face in her hands. "You really held on there didn't you? We were almost certain that you'd never join us."

Edwin and Lila joined in with the hug as Emma laughed, enveloping her on all sides.

Emma wasn't sure how long she spent in the arms of her family, but she found she didn't care. She glanced back at the Blessers when she pulled away. "Is... is my sister here?"

Blossom gestured towards the temple at the top of the island. "Once you pass through, you'll see her again. We only have the power to bring those with the strongest bond to you back through."

Edwin took hold of her hand. "It's a work in progress but she is coming back to me," he said, a joyful smile crossing his face. "And hey, we've got eternity, she'll come round."

Emma began to follow the small group up the hill, feeling lighter than she had in years. She paused when she realised that Blossom and Asher weren't with her, turning back to see them lingering on the beach. "You're not really here, are you?"

Blossom beamed at her, suddenly by her side. "Of course we are, we're always with you." He stroked through her hair in a mirror of how Emma used to soothe him. "But we cannot follow you to the other side, you must go through the door without us."

"At least I got to see you one last time," Emma said, hugging Blossom close, feeling the warmth of him that was still so familiar. Even after all these years. "I love you, Petal."

"I love you too, Emma. Rest now, you've earnt it."

The End

Acknowledgements

Thank you to everyone who joined me in the world of the blessed. Thank you to my amazing beta readers, my cheer readers and all of my friends and family who have supported me along the way. Thank you to those who have loved Blossom and Asher as much as I have. Those who see their love for what it is, pure, unconditional, and the source of their strength. Thank you to everyone who has encouraged me to keep writing even when imposter syndrome reared its ugly head.